THE LIGHTNING FLASHED!

In its bright light I thought I saw a human form standing on the pier. I used the oars to slow my approach and felt the boat touch the side of a piling.

Then, with a violent splat, a sharp flash of lightning split the water a few feet from me. I screamed, and the oars flew from my grasp and slipped into the black water. I managed to move to the prow of the boat to pick up the worn rope on the iron ring so that I could attach the boat to the piling. . .

Suddenly, a bony hand came down and *pushed the boat away from the pier!*

I lost my balance and pitched headlong into the water. The tall grass entangled me, but somehow I fought my way to the surface and caught onto a piling. I looked up into a face only inches from mine, and in the eyes hatred burned.

"Go away!" the man shouted. "Private island."

"It's my island," I screamed back, "I'm Aldis Greyfield."

Warner Paperback Library Books
By Dorothy Daniels

Island of Bitter Memories
The Apollo Fountain
Image of a Ghost
Jade Green
Hills of Fire
The Caldwell Shadow
Prisoner of Malville Hall
The Possession of Tracy Corbin
The Silent Halls of Ashenden
The Duncan Dynasty
The Stone House
The Larrabee Heiress
Dark Island
The Maya Temple
The Lanier Riddle
Shadows From the Past
The House on Circus Hill
Castle Morvant
The House of Broken Dolls
Conover's Folly
Witch's Castle
Diablo Manor
The Tormented
The Bell
The Beaumont Tradition
Voice on the Wind
The Dark Stage
Emerald Hill
The Man From Yesterday
The House of Many Doors
The Carson Inheritance
Darkhaven
Lady of the Shadows
The Lily Pond
Marriott Hall
Shadows of Tomorrow
Island Nurse
House of False Faces
Mystic Manor
Shadow Glen
Cruise Ship Nurse
World's Fair Nurse

The *STRANGE PARADISE* Series

Dorothy Daniels

Island of Bitter Memories

WARNER
PAPERBACK
LIBRARY

A Warner Communications Company

WARNER PAPERBACK LIBRARY EDITION
First Printing: February, 1974

Cover Illustration by Vic Prezio

Warner Paperback Library
is a division of Warner Books, Inc.,
75 Rockefeller Plaza,
New York, N.Y. 10019.

A Warner Communications Company

ONE

I'd been driving for more than three hours, going faster than I should, so I was grateful for the increasingly frequent shafts of lightning which lit up the darkness on either side. It helped to guide me along the narrow, winding, pothole-filled road. But the resounding claps of thunder, now plainly evident above the sound of the motor, further jarred my already jagged nerves. I wanted to reach my destination before the storm broke. I had a hunch that if I didn't, I'd more than likely get mired in mud. If that happened, I'd have to remain here until someone came along to pull me out. Since the road was private and led to the pier, also private, goodness knows when that would be.

I'd seen the weather-beaten sign which identified the road as Greyfield Lane. Below it hung a smaller legend, just as weather-beaten, saying

PRIVATE
KEEP OUT

At the end of the road was Greyfield Pier. From there, one took a boat to Greyfield Island. All this I knew, though I'd never come here before. I'd never had any desire to. But now I was running away, pursued only by the storm.

Each flash of lightning, coming almost steadily now, seemed to seek me out and mock me, and the ever-nearing crashes of thunder screamed *Coward! Coward! Coward!*

I couldn't deny it. It's exactly what I was. Cowards run. Only the brave have the courage to stay and face up to their mistakes. I had played the fool. Falling in love with a man merely because he had plied me with attention while on a voyage back from Europe. Believing he loved me for myself.

Tomorrow, May 1, 1917, would be my twentieth birthday. I'd also selected it to be my wedding day. Until an hour ago, I'd believed it would be. But the mere ring of the telephone had shattered my entire world.

A few drops of rain spattered the windshield, a warning that the storm was now overhead. I pressed my foot harder on the accelerator. The car jumped forward, then hit a pothole, stalling the motor. I tried unsuccessfully to get it started, pushing the throttle in and out and only succeeding in flooding the motor.

I was too nervous to remain here, and I figured it couldn't be much farther to the dock. If there wasn't a boat there, I hoped there'd be a shelter of sorts until daylight. I got out, reached for the small overnight bag I'd tossed on the back seat, and started the trek that should lead me to Greyfield Pier.

I was grateful to Laurie Cummings for having thought of it. I never would have. To my knowledge I'd never even been there. Nor had I had the slightest desire to investigate the place. But I had two aunts living there. As they said, they'd done their duty in raising me, and now they were entitled to live out their lives as they wished. They'd wished to do so on Greyfield Island and had bade me farewell once my engagement was announced, though assuring me they would return for the wedding. It was to have been held in the large house in Savannah where they'd raised me, following the death of my parents in a boating accident.

Fortunately, I was wearing a sensible pair of shoes, making walking reasonably safe. Even so, I kept slipping into ruts and potholes. If I remained here for any time, I'd certainly have the road repaired. It was a menace as it was, though I imagined my aunts preferred it that way, knowing it would discourage visitors who had no business using it anyway.

A sharp crackle of lightning almost overhead signaled the approach of the storm. It was followed by an endless rolling of thunderclaps, and now the rain began to fall steadily, though fortunately not yet a downpour. Though unnerving, the almost constant play of lightning worked in my favor, for it lit up the road and enabled me to see the small pier straight ahead. In darkness, I could have walked directly off it into the water, for it was narrow and certainly not very long. I hoped Greyfield Island had more to offer.

The lightning again worked in my favor, enabling me to see a small rowboat tied to one of the pilings. I wondered if that was the only means of transportation to the island. I couldn't imagine my aunts venturing forth in such a flimsy craft. As for me, if I wished to reach the island, this seemed my only means of doing so. I had no desire to linger in the hope someone would come along. My thin silk dress was already sodden and clinging to me.

I sat on the pier, gripped a post that protruded above it, and cautiously lowered myself. My feet touched the bottom of the boat, which immediately moved away from me, almost pitching me off balance. Keeping my feet firmly anchored on the bottom, I pulled myself and the boat back to the pier. Carefully standing on tiptoe and stretching myself full-length, I loosened one hand and reached up for my overnight bag. I couldn't stretch far enough to get a grip on the handle, but I maneuvered it with my fingers over to the edge and then eased it onto my shoulder. I started to slide it down along my body in an attempt to get a more secure grip on it.

For the first time since I'd made my furtive departure from the house, I felt pleased. At least I could do something right. But my triumph was shortlived, for the wet leather and my wet hand were the perfect combination to allow it to slip from my grasp and splash into the marshy water alongside the boat. The lightning revealed it falling beneath the water. At least, I had more sense than to try to retrieve it. I'd only upset the boat. I could manage until tomorrow when Laurie Cummings would come with my clothes. Tonight I had only one desire—to escape Savannah and the wagging tongues. I felt disgraced and humiliated by what had happened.

The rain was coming down harder now, and I had no

time to waste on self-pity. Laurie had told me it was no more than five minutes from the pier to the island. I'd assumed that meant in a launch. Since there wasn't one in sight, I now hoped she'd meant in a rowboat. Not that she'd been here, either—all she knew about it was what my cousin Keith had told her.

Fortunately, I knew how to row, and I started out in a course directly opposite from the pier. That, too, Laurie had informed me I should do. Of course, she'd also pleaded with me to wait until daylight, but I wanted escape.

I stopped thinking and devoted my attention to guiding the boat. The lightning was a help, though the thunder still unnerved me, and the rain, though steady, was still not torrential, for which I was grateful. I couldn't both bail out the water and row. Also, I saw nothing in the boat with which to bail.

Probably no more than ten minutes had passed when the pier loomed up before me. In a brief flash of lightning I thought I saw a human form standing motionless on the pier, though I wasn't certain. I used the oars to slow my approach and felt the boat touch the side of a piling.

There was a tremendous electrical explosion caused by a sharp flash of lightning that hit the water with a smack a few feet from me. I cried out in fear and let go of the oars. They promptly slipped into the water.

Then it seemed as if the skies lit up, perhaps the whole world, as streaks of lightning chased each other back and forth across the sky. But I was not so unnerved I couldn't check the pier.

I was right. A man was standing above me. His lips moved, but his words were lost in a succession of ear-deafening claps of thunder. I moved cautiously to the prow of the boat and picked up the worn rope which was tied to an iron ring. I needed only to shift my position slightly to encircle a piling with it when a bony hand, with incredibly long fingers, came down and pushed the boat away from the pier.

I lost my balance and fell headlong into the water. I got tangled in the tall grass that grew in the water, but fought my way to the surface. I caught onto a piling and looked up, still too startled to be angry. The face was only inches from mine, and I saw a burning hatred revealed. Or was it fear? No. I was the frightened one. He was angry.

"Go away!" he shouted.

He had to shout because it seemed as if the heavens had let loose.

"I own this island," I shouted back. "I'll have you arrested."

He was squatted on his haunches, regarding my struggles as I held onto the piling, but making no attempt to rescue me.

"Private island," he shouted. "Go away."

"It's *my* island. I'm Aldis Greyfield."

I don't know whether he heard me, or whether the continuous play of lightning revealed to him my fear and the fact that I was a young woman, who certainly was no threat to him. *He* was probably on the island illegally. Anyway, his long arms reached down and grasped my wrists. He raised me gently until I could get a grip on the pier. Then his hands moved to my armpits and he pulled me free of the water. He had surprising strength; he was also gentle.

Once I was on my feet, my legs buckled. He eased me onto the pier. I lay on my back, using my arm to protect my face from the rain, which now pounded down.

Once my breathing was back to normal, I sat up and regarded the man standing before me. He was skeleton-thin and enormously tall—well over six feet. He seemed to know I was ready to get up, for he bent and gripped my waist, lifting me without the slightest effort.

I had no idea who this man was, but I'd seen enough of him during the prolonged flash of lightning to know he was aged. Over six feet tall, he stood straight and proud. His skin was brown; his hair, though now darkened by the rain, was gray, with a tight curl and cut close to his head. He seemed enormously strong despite his age, and he was oblivious to the storm all around us, plus the torrent of rain that forced me to raise my voice.

"Who are you?" I asked.

"I live here."

I nodded acceptance of the idea. "A servant of my aunts."

"No." His reply was disdainful. "A servant of Mademoiselle Eulalie Laboulaye."

Mad, I thought. "Which way to Greyfield Manor?"

He pointed a long bony finger. "Stay on path."

"Where is it?"

I thought he hadn't heard, for he made no answer. Just kept staring at me in the now intermittent lightning. Finally, he nodded.

"I think first she come back. You look like her."

"Who?"

"You want big house?"

"Yes." Whoever he was, I could talk with him later. Just now, I wanted to get out of my sodden clothes.

He motioned for me to follow. Apparently I didn't move swiftly enough, for he reached down, grasped my wrist, and pulled me after him. I went willingly, knowing now that something about me had frightened him. He'd frightened me, too, but now I felt better, knowing I was no longer alone, though I was also aware I could scarcely consider my escort a friend.

We'd only gone a few steps when we reached what seemed to be a forest area. The lightning revealed enormous live oaks so heavily branched that when we moved along the path, the rain seemed almost nonexistent. Not that it wasn't dripping down from the trees, but we weren't buffeted by it.

I was glad my guide had chosen to lead me, for I'd never have found the house in darkness. I'd been rash in coming here tonight, but I feared that with daylight, I'd be inundated with reporters asking for a statement regarding my canceled wedding.

It seemed like an endless walk, though it couldn't have been long. Just weariness made it seem so. Then we left the protection of the forest and moved along a walk of ground seashells. The lightning was less frequent, but still sufficient to enable me to see the house, which was on a rise.

He said, "Steps," and pointed down.

I ascended them.

He said, "Walk."

I obeyed and when he again said, "Steps," I was alerted for them.

Finally, he paused, released my wrist, and pointed to the door.

He said, "Go in. Not locked."

"What's your name?" I asked. "Who are you?"

But he was already retreating. Even if he'd heard, I doubt whether he'd have answered. He'd brought me here, and now he was going back to wherever he came from. No matter where it was, if he wasn't in my aunts' employ, he had no business on this island. I'd investigate his whereabouts in the morning. Just now, I was concerned only with my well-being.

I moved slowly to the door. It was large and wide, and the knocker gleamed, even in the night. My hand moved for the knob, found it, and prayed the man was right about the door not being locked. I was reluctant to disturb my aunts. I knew they retired early and disliked having their sleep interrupted. I breathed a sigh of gratitude when the door opened. I stepped inside, closed it, and shut out the storm.

The quiet seemed blessed and for a minute I leaned against the door, eyes closed, reveling in the stillness broken only by the dripping of rain from my clothes onto the marble floor. I was in my stockinged feet, having lost my shoes when I toppled from the boat.

The lightning slipped through the fan windows above the door, and I saw wall sconces on either side of the small entranceway. My fingers explored the wall and found a switch. I pressed it and was rewarded with light. I was grateful that there was electricity here. Apparently a generator hummed somewhere in the house. Probably at the rear.

Before me was a wide stairway. The reception hall was ample, but I was interested only in getting out of my wet clothes and washing the marshy water from my hair. After that, sleep. It would be the only thing to shut out the agony of my disgrace. I pressed the switch again and made my ascent in darkness.

I inspected several rooms upstairs, using the light switches, finally selecting one that caught my fancy. It was old-fashioned, perhaps pre-Civil War, but immaculately kept up. It had a deep mahogany four-poster bed, with dresser and highboy of the same wood. The rug, even in the artificial light, reflected beautiful shades of blue. A writing table caught my eye. It was barren of any decoration, but the surface was heavily inlaid with mother of pearl. I raised the cover, which was mirrored beneath. Even that sparkled with cleanliness.

A sterling silver comb and brush set rested on a tray. Otherwise, the interior was empty. The sides and bottom were covered with pink satin that gave off the faint scent of lavender.

I took out the comb and brush and lowered the cover. A large wardrobe with two glass doors flanking the mirrored center occupied a large section of one wall. The doors were curtained. Each had a lock with a key in it and opened easily. Again, the faintest whiff of lavender touched my nostrils. I moved aside a filmy curtain and saw some nightgowns and negligees. I selected a gown that was high-necked, beribboned, and ruffled. Certainly of another era, but it would do nicely. I brought it into the bathroom and noted a complete absence of towels.

I went into the hall and opened doors until I found a linen closet. I found towels and also took some bed linen in case there was just a bare mattress beneath the lace spread. There was also a supply of soap to which I helped myself.

Back in my suite, I bathed and shampooed my hair. I removed the bedspread and made up the bed. Once in it, I was lulled by the steady rain. The lightning and thunder had waned, and the heavy downpour had lessened. It was as well I'd gone through what I had to get here. It had left me exhausted. It almost seemed as if I were someone else. I felt that by donning this nightgown, I'd slipped back into the past—a past that had none of the heartache and misery I'd been subjected to. I put out the lights, got into bed, and closed my eyes, letting sleep claim me. Sleep and blessed forgetfulness.

TWO

I'd neglected to lower the shades or draw the draperies, and so I awoke to a world full of sunshine so bright it brought a smile to my lips . . . until I remembered it was to have been my wedding day. That sobered me quickly. So did another thought. I had nothing to wear. I touched the ruffled neck of the nightgown I was wearing, and my eyes strayed to the wardrobe. There were soft silk, lace-trimmed negligees there that still yielded faint traces of lavender.

I splashed my face with cold water, opened a drawer, and moved aside a cloth that covered the contents. Neatly arranged were ribbons of different colors, veils dotted with tiny stones that seemed happy to come alive at the touch of daylight, and various hair ornaments. I selected a pink ribbon and tied back my tawny hair. I wondered if the closet contained dresses worn by an ancestor who'd occupied this room. If not, I'd have to wear this outfit until Laurie arrived. I wondered how she'd get here. I'd taken the only boat and lost it. No need to worry. She was resourceful and would manage.

I paused at the window. It was sparkling clean. Not even the rain had marked it. I had an excellent view of what I believed must be the side and one end of the island. I must be on the east, because I could see the mainland beyond the marshes and water. Directly facing me, the island stretched to the end where there was a goodly expanse of water and then another island.

One stretch of land was covered with wild plum trees covered with silvery blossoms. Beyond them was another stretch of shrubbery covered with pale pink blossoms. The path I'd traversed last night was nowhere visible, so heavy was the growth of live oak and pine. Even in daylight, it looked formidable. The beach gleamed golden in the sun. Something that moved caught my eye. A horse had stepped from the forest and galloped onto the sand. It was followed by another. They frolicked, circling each other, one clockwise, the other counter. Then, as suddenly, they stopped, cocked their heads in a listening attitude and took off at an amazing speed, evidence that they were wild and unapproachable.

I left the suite, descended the marble staircase, and moved across the vast expanse of hall. My bare feet made light smacking sounds on the cool marble, which was spotless and glistened with care. Somehow, it made me feel guilty. This was my responsibility, yet I'd never once thought of its existence, much less wondered about the care of it. I knew of Greyfield Island, but it was vague in my mind, and I'd never given any thought to it.

The odor of freshly brewed coffee and fried bacon lured me to the proper room. Both my aunts were sitting at a Duncan Phyfe table, sipping coffee and talking in muted tones. I wondered just what they did with their time here. Granted, the island was beautiful. It was also isolated, and certainly no one else lived here. Then I remembered the poacher who had tried to drown me last night until I identified myself. I didn't think he'd be here today. He knew he'd made a grave error in upsetting my boat and had tried to atone for it by guiding me to the house.

Aunt Hannah almost choked on her coffee when I appeared in the arched doorway. "Jayne!" she exclaimed, her tone one of disbelief.

Aunt Mabel had her back to me. She set down her cup and looked over her shoulder. A cry of dismay escaped her.

"Oh, dear God, no!" she said.

I smiled, despite myself. "Who's Jayne?"

Aunt Hannah set down her cup, took a deep breath to regain her composure, and smacked her lips in a gesture of disapproval. "It's Aldis. What are you doing here on your wedding day?"

"There'll be no wedding."

"No wedding?" They exclaimed in unison.

Then Aunt Hannah became the spokesman. "Keith was coming in the launch this morning to take us to your wedding."

I said, "He'll come, no doubt. But with Laurie Cummings. She's bringing me some clothes."

"I should hope so," Aunt Hannah said. "You look preposterous in those."

"They're all I have. I was knocked in the water last night by a black man. Probably a poacher, living here illegally."

I was already at the sideboard, helping myself to bacon, eggs, hot rolls, butter, and steaming coffee. But the mirror before me revealed my aunts exchanging glances.

"What happened, Aldis?" Aunt Hannah was the more formidable of the two, being a strict disciplinarian. She'd seen to it I'd had the proper rearing. The right schools, trips to Europe to acquire culture, a coming-out party which I'd not wanted, though my mere mention of disapproval had brought a shocked glance and a stern reprimand. The shocked glances were again in evidence. The reprimand, I was certain, would come, once Aunt Hannah learned the story. Aunt Mabel would follow her lead. She'd not dare do otherwise.

I sat down, arranged a napkin on my lap, and took a sip of water from a glass Aunt Mabel had filled and set before me. I buttered a roll, savored its sweetness, and nodded approval.

"Aldis," Aunt Hannah spoke in her usual stern manner, "we're waiting for an explanation."

"Please let me finish the roll. I'm famished."

I did so, washed it down with coffee, regarded my plate longingly, but knew better than to start on it. I wondered how I could even eat. I should have been crying my eyes out. The thought made me smile.

"What's so amusing?" Aunt Mabel's thin features tensed with apprehension.

I voiced the thought passing through my mind, adding,

"My heart is broken, and yet here I am looking at my filled plate, with an eye to devouring all of it. It doesn't make sense."

"Your being here doesn't, either." Aunt Hannah's plump features and triple chin seemed to quiver in disapproval. "Will you please enlighten us?"

"I'm sorry. I know you're both shocked because what I've done will cause talk. But marriage to me is a very serious business. I thought Jim Canby loved me. Instead, it's my money he found so fascinating."

"What a dreadful thing to say!" Aunt Hannah exclaimed. "He comes of an excellent family. Generations of Southern stock."

"I know all about it, aunties. I also know he hasn't a dime."

"You said that didn't matter," Aunt Mabel said quietly.

"It didn't. But I'm not going to buy a husband. Apparently he was making a supreme sacrifice by bestowing on me the hallowed name of Canby."

"You needn't be so sarcastic," Aunt Hannah said. "What did he do—or say—that made you think he was marrying you for reasons other than love?"

"He was arrested last night after he engaged in an argument with another gentleman concerning a girl the other man was with."

"Unfortunate, I'll grant," Aunt Hannah said, "but certainly it doesn't necessitate calling off a wedding. Perhaps it was a situation that called for his interference."

"It was not," I said. "He intruded. Obviously, he felt the other gentleman had no business with the girl. He said in the restaurant that she preferred his company to that of her escort. He was asked to leave. When he refused, the management had no recourse other than to call the police. When they arrived, Jim threatened to have their badges, stating he was marrying into the Greyfield family, who carried great influence in Savannah."

Both aunts gave gentle shudders. Any public display was distasteful to them. Now that they'd learned the reason for my appearance on the island, I was certain they'd give full approval for my course of action. Thus assured, I picked up my fork and attacked my bacon. It was crisp and tender. The eggs were delicate and done to my liking.

"I don't know who the cook is, but she's good," I said.

"She's from the village on the mainland," Aunt Hannah informed. "We've had her come whenever we rested here."

"Rested?"

"This is our favorite resting place. When you were at school or abroad, we came here frequently. Now we wish to live out our lives here. We enjoy the tranquillity of it. At least, it *was* tranquil."

The verb was faintly accented. "What do you mean?"

"We believe you made a mistake," Aunt Hannah said.

I set down my fork, scarcely believing my ears. "Both of you?" My glance switched to Aunt Mabel. Her features registered the same coolness as those of her sister. I wondered if Papa had been like them. I couldn't believe it. And Mama. Had they been as cold and unrelenting with her as they had with me? I hoped not. Or, if so, I hoped she'd had spirit enough to fight back. That was exactly what I'd have to do now, and I was going to.

Aunt Mabel said, "I'm sure the incident was distasteful to you. But young gentlemen do get into scrapes. One expects it."

"The humiliation I could endure," I said. "If Jim really loved me. But I don't believe he did. And while I'm no beauty, I'm not repulsive. And certainly, I'll not wed a man whose sole interest in me is the Greyfield fortune, which, I believe, is considerable."

"You are the sole custodian of that wealth now," Aunt Hannah said, her manner softening ever so slightly. "You may order us out of this house if you wish."

"Such a thought never occurred to me," I said. "I only hope you have no objection to my living here."

"Certainly not," they exclaimed simultaneously. Though not relenting completely, they were obviously relieved.

I nodded approval of their attitude. "In that case, we'll

not discuss the matter further. Laurie Cummings will arrive sometime today with a wardrobe for me."

"Can't you even pack a bag for yourself?" Aunt Mabel said.

Aunt Hannah sighed. "Does that girl have to come here?"

"I left in a rush, otherwise I'd have done my packing. As for Laurie, she'll be here as my guest. Just as she was in Savannah."

"So long as you don't object to her," Aunt Mabel said.

"Don't you like her?" I asked.

"Of course we do," came the solemn reply. "Only we think you've grown to depend on her too much. Besides," Aunt Hannah added, "it's time she got out on her own."

"There's no need for her to do that," I said. "I'm wealthy. I pay her a salary to act as my secretary. Otherwise, she wouldn't stay."

"How was she able to afford Miss Alexander's school?" Aunt Mabel asked. "Not only was the tuition exorbitant, but the room and board." Her eyes went heavenward.

I smiled. "Laurie was orphaned when she was three. Her aunt made all kinds of sacrifices so she could attend that school."

"In the hope she would meet a gentleman of means, I suppose," Aunt Hannah said.

I laughed. "Probably. That's why most of us go to those places, isn't it? So we'll know the right things to do when we entertain in our mansions. Or meet a gentleman who stands to inherit a mansion."

"Must you be rude?" Aunt Hannah's mouth tightened in disapproval.

"I'm sorry, Aunt Hannah," I said. "But I abhor snobbery, and it seems as if I've been surrounded by it all my life. Even Jim, without a sou to his name, is snobbish."

"It didn't seem to bother you," Aunt Hannah said remindfully.

"I wasn't aware of it before. I suppose because he didn't have anything, it made him more appealing in my eyes."

"What a ridiculous way to think."

"Perhaps. But that must have been in the back of my

mind. I think I was even glad he didn't have money. I was sort of breaking the code. You know—money begets money."

"You're being vulgar, Aldis," Aunt Mabel said.

"I wish we didn't have to argue like this. I'm really not such a bad sort—if you'd only try to know me."

"We have tried—all though the years," she said. "But you were always defiant. You've a lot of your father in you—*and* your mother."

"Were they so dreadful?" I asked.

Aunt Hannah's eyes expressed disapproval. "They were rebels."

"What do you mean?"

Aunt Hannah gave a shrug of despair. "I prefer not to talk about it."

"I wish you would," I urged. "I know so little of them."

"Some other time," she replied.

"Every time I've asked you about my parents, that's been your stock answer."

Aunt Hannah arose, her plump body moving so swiftly to the side, she almost took the linen cloth with her. I held on to it while she freed her satin negligee. "I'm too upset by your rash act to talk now."

"I'm upset, too, Aunt Hannah. But not so much I can't say this. Should Jim Canby come to Greyfield Manor, I'll not see him. Not under any circumstances."

"I will obey your wishes," she said primly.

"Thank you." I stood up also, no longer interested in finishing my breakfast. I started from the room, then turned. Aunt Hannah's eyes were glued on me.

I said, "I met an elderly black man at the dock last night. He upset my boat. I fell into the water. I think he'd have let me drown if I hadn't identified myself. If you see him, let me know. I'll not have anyone here who doesn't belong here."

"He belongs here." Aunt Hannah's smile was triumphant.

Aunt Mabel had risen and moved to stand beside her sister, as if to protect her against any further verbal attacks I might make.

"You mean—he works for you?" I recalled his look of disdain when I mentioned such a thing last night.

"He does not. He lives in a house at the far end of the island. What suite did you take?"

"I don't know whom it belonged to, but I got these garments from a wardrobe in the bedroom."

"It was Jayne Greyfield's, your great-grandaunt."

"When you walked in the room, Aldis," Aunt Mabel said, the merest trace of a smile touching her thin, pale lips, "you really gave us a start. You looked the image of Jayne. There's a portrait of her hanging over the mantel in the library."

I looked down at the old-fashioned negligee. "So that's why you called me Jayne."

They nodded simultaneously.

"I'm sorry I startled you. About this man. He seems ancient."

"He's very old, but very proud. As is his mistress."

"Who's she?"

"His sister. He serves as butler to her. His name is Setley. Hers is Eulalie Laboulaye."

"What a beautiful name."

"She was a beautiful woman, and your great-grandaunt granted her the use of a house, the land on which it stood, and all the furnishings for as long as she lived."

"Why?"

Aunt Hannah sighed. "You ask so many questions. I suggest you forget Setley and his sister. They never come here, and we never go there."

"How do they live?"

"There is a sum in the bank set aside for them. It will more than provide for them while they are on this earth. Your great-grandaunt saw to that also."

"This is the first you ever spoke of her."

"And it will be the last." Aunt Hannah's tone was one of disapproval. "She was no asset to the family."

They each eyed me meaningfully. "What you're saying is that I apparently have some of her traits."

"God forbid!" Aunt Mabel exclaimed.

They both looked so frightened and shocked, I didn't pursue the subject.

I went into the hall and paused, looking around me. I wanted to examine my aunt's portrait, but to seek out the drawing room now would only serve to irritate them further. They'd been subjected to enough. I really didn't want to hurt them. They had raised me as best they knew how. It hadn't been easy for two maiden ladies to have a three-year-old placed in their laps. I could well imagine it had upset their well-ordered lives.

I'd not known they considered Greyfield their retreat. No wonder it had been kept up so beautifully. They wanted peace, and I had brought them more turmoil. I'd do my best to keep out of their way—and be gracious and warm while with them. Though that wasn't easy. They seemed to have been born without the gift of love.

I breathed a silent prayer of gratitude I hadn't and headed for the door. I needed a breath of fresh air and the warmth of the sun to lift my spirits.

I went down the stairs and turned to observe the house. It was four stories high and constructed of tabby, a concrete-like mixture of limestone and oyster shells. From where I stood, four chimneys were evident. Perhaps more were visible from the rear. I wondered how many rooms it contained. I wouldn't even venture a guess. Now that I was here, many questions came to my mind. Yet I knew better than to ask them of my aunts. At least, not immediately. My canceled marriage had upset them.

I now realized why they'd never spoken of the island to me. It was their sanctuary. An escape from the responsibility of rearing me. The thought had never occurred to me that I'd been a burden to them. Now that it did, it didn't even hurt. Perhaps because there was no room in my heart for more of that. But I wondered if Greyfield was the right place for me. I'd hoped for both sympathy and understanding from my aunts. I'd received neither.

I hoped Laurie would arrive soon. Keith would probably bring her. He was my first cousin, our respective fathers having been brothers. Other than my aunts, he was my only living relative. He was four years my senior and a carefree bachelor. It was he who had told Laurie of the island owned by the family. She, in turn, had spoken of it to me and was surprised that I'd never been here.

I was grateful it had been she who'd answered the telephone when the reporter called last night to inform me of the fact that Jim Canby had been arrested by the Savannah police for creating a disturbance at an exclusive restaurant. She'd informed the reporter I was not at home, adding that she doubted I'd have any statement to make.

Nor would I. After the initial shock of learning what Jim had done, I wanted only to get away from the city. Laurie suggested the island, knowing my aunts were here. It was an excellent suggestion. She then called Keith, informed him of what had happened, and got directions on how to get here. He supplied them and I packed an overnight bag and left immediately.

I turned and looked at the path leading into the forest. I'd been through it last night. Even in the sun, the darkness caused by the tremendous live oaks gave it an ominous look. But there was nothing to fear except wild horses. I imagined there were probably deer, too. They'd be as startled as I, were we to meet face to face.

I wondered if Setley or his sister would be about. Eulalie Laboulaye. What a beautiful name. I wondered what she was like. Probably very old and wizened. My mind conjured up a not very flattering picture.

Completely forgetful of my unconventional attire, I moved into the forest. The path was narrow, but adequate, with a carpeting of pine needles. I supposed I'd missed seeing the cottage where Setley and his sister lived. In the storm it wasn't surprising. I'd only entered the forest and gone a few feet when I noticed there was another path branching off. On a hunch I took that. It seemed to circle one side of the house and then proceed in a straight line to the opposite end of the island. Not even a bird's song broke the quiet of morning. The road was perfectly straight and I started to move more briskly, until a form stepped from behind a tree trunk and blocked my path.

It was a lady, her skin a beautiful bronze in color, her

eyes a startling blue. She was oval-featured, the flesh stretched tightly across her high cheekbones. Her hair, a silver sheen, was drawn back tightly to form a topknot that was entwined with pearls.

What impressed me most was her posture. She was as tall as I—over five feet eight inches—and stood erect, with shoulders back, head high. Her manner was one of great pride, but her eyes studied me keenly.

"You look like her." She was soft-spoken, though her words were clearly enunciated.

"Your brother said I did." It had to be Eulalie Laboulaye.

Her eyes traveled the length of my figure. "You're wearing her clothes."

"It's all I have. Mine were ruined when your brother tried to drown me last night."

My statement didn't surprise her. I gathered she'd not have cared if he had.

"I'm Aldis Greyfield. I own this island, and I don't want your brother ever to do to anyone who comes to this island what he did to me last night."

Her diction was precise, her manner cold. "Your aunts don't want strangers on this island."

"Perhaps I don't, either. I'm not sure, since this is the first time I've set foot on it."

She refuted that. "Your parents brought you here when you were a baby. They drowned when their sailboat capsized."

"Then you knew my parents."

She nodded.

"And you know my aunts."

"They stay to themselves. I do the same."

"I'll not bother you. Just tell your brother, since I own the island, I'll determine whether anyone is unwelcome."

"There is no need for you to come further. Once you come to the clearing, you are on my property. It is as private as yours. So long as I live, you do not own the entire island. Remember that."

I was still too hurt to feel anger at her rudeness. I smiled, though I felt little like it. "I'll not set up the same restriction for the area of the island which is mine. You may feel free to traverse it whenever you wish."

"I'll not wish."

She stood motionless, elegant in her silken gown, whose folds concealed her slender form. At least, I assumed she was slender. It wasn't easy to tell with the high neck and copious sleeves which hung almost to the ground and in which her hands were concealed.

She said no more, but neither did she move from the path. I was, in so many words, ordered to return to my part of the island.

"I'm sorry you dislike me," I said. "I had hoped we might be friends."

"I have no wish to be a friend to a Greyfield."

"After my aunt's generous gesture to you and your brother?"

"Your aunt is dead. So far as I am concerned, so are you. So are all Greyfields. Your aunts leave me alone. You must learn to do the same."

She had finally succeeded in angering me. "Be assured I will. And should we meet again, there will be no need for you even to speak to me."

For the first time, a smile touched her lips. She knew she had triumphed. I turned and moved briskly along the path. But I had to slow my step, for I slipped on the pine needles and almost lost my balance.

I wondered why my great-grandaunt had deeded the house and land to Eulalie Laboulaye. I also wondered about the age of the woman. To my eyes, she seemed ageless. At least, in the dim light of the forest. Bright sunlight might not be so kind. Nor was I, thinking in this fashion.

I reached the path that led to the house and lost no time returning. If Laurie didn't come by noontime, I'd appropriate a garment from Jayne Greyfield's wardrobe. I imagined the two closets contained something of hers. The sight of me so garbed would upset my aunts, I knew, but I couldn't move about in negligees. Nor could I go back to the house in Savannah, even if I had a desire to. My dress was ruined, and without that I couldn't very well return to the mainland. I wondered if Setley had salvaged the boat

I'd come in. I doubted it. Or if he had, it would be with the idea that I'd use it to leave the island. Certainly, his sister wasn't pleased by my presence. Nor were my aunts.

I, the owner of Greyfield, was *persona non grata.* The very thought made me determined to stay. I'd had no idea I was so unpopular. At least, I had a friend in Laurie. If only she would come. I couldn't wait to tell her about Eulalie—and Setley, who had tried to drown me last night.

"Well, that's it." Laurie snapped the locks shut on the last piece of my luggage. She'd done a miraculous job of packing so much so beautifully in the brief time she'd allotted herself.

There were two closets in the bedroom. One was filled with my aunt's clothes carefully covered with muslins. The other was devoid of everything but hangers. I used that one.

I said, "I know you must be famished."

"I'm not," she said. "Keith and I ate on the launch. I should never have let you leave last night. Fortunately, Keith was still in town, though he'd expected to be at Greyfield, since he was bringing your aunts here tomorrow. So he brought me here on the launch."

"Nothing could have kept me in Savannah," I said. "Did the reporters call this morning?"

"Yes. Keith called again last night, after you left. He bailed Jim out immediately and checked him into a small hotel on the outskirts of town, with the warning that he was to remain there until he sobered up."

"Frankly, I don't care what he does. It's over."

Laurie eyed me carefully. "Are you sure?"

"Absolutely."

I gave myself a final appraising glance in the standing mirror. I'd already changed to a soft voile dress and brushed my hair up into a soft knot, coiling the excess and fastening it with amber pins. I felt myself again.

We went into the sitting room. Laurie stretched out on the chaise with a sigh. I didn't blame her. All I'd done was flee. She'd remained behind, covering my retreat. I curled up in the window seat and regarded the only friend I had on this earth.

Laurie Cummings was a sophisticated beauty. She was also intelligent. She had jet-black hair and green eyes that turned up slightly at the corners. She was more slender than I and not as tall, which I considered a blessing. She described herself as independent, proud, and church-mouse poor.

She'd been my roommate all through the last four years at Miss Alexander's School for Girls. It was exclusive, expensive, and, so far as Laurie was concerned, a waste of her years. As it happened, she was right. Her aunt had made every sacrifice to keep her there. She'd died of a heart attack the day before commencement. Shortly after, Laurie had learned she was destitute and, with her private-school education, ill-equipped to cope in a business world.

I insisted she come home with me. She did so because she had nowhere else to go. She learned that her aunt, during her last years, had lived in a one-room apartment. She'd insisted Laurie accept every invitation extended to her while a student, the object being for her to meet an eligible male who would lose his heart to her. It hadn't worked out that way. Laurie was Laurie. Still independent. She'd never marry merely to attain security.

She'd continued to live with me—over two years, now—and we'd become close friends. I valued her loyalty, and she had a sharp sense of fashion. I'd never cared too much for shopping, and Laurie was God-sent. She also insisted on attending to my social calendar, with the result that she had taken on responsibilities which were mine and which I was quite capable of doing, but knew if I insisted, she'd pack and go her way. As she said on several occasions, if she couldn't earn her keep, she'd leave. I didn't want that. So I insisted on paying her a fee. She accepted, designating herself as my social secretary.

Now I was glad I'd let her have her own way. I was still smarting under the humiliation of Jim Canby's statement to a newspaper reporter. But at least he knew things were not as he'd thought. There'd be no wedding. The announcement of the cancellation would be in the papers this morning. Tongues all over the city would be wagging. Aldis Greyfield has jilted Jim Canby. Or was it the other way around? No matter. I was away from it, and certainly Laurie wouldn't relay to me any of the cruel gossip.

"Penny for your thoughts," she said. Her warm smile revealed beautiful teeth.

"He's not worth it," I said.

"What if he comes here?" she asked.

"He wouldn't have the nerve."

"You don't know him," she said.

I countered that with, "What do you know about him?"

"Only what Keith told me. He wanted me to relay the gossip to you before this happened, but I wouldn't."

"What gossip?"

Her slender hands gestured helplessly. "Oh—that he was a woman-chaser. That he drank too much."

"He never did with me. I'll give him credit for that."

"Apparently he was on his best behavior. I suppose I should have told you, but you were so happy and so in love. Besides, I didn't know if it was true. And Keith didn't really know. He said there was talk at the club." She gave me a knowing look. "What else do they have to do there, except sip cocktails and destroy characters with their idle gossip?"

I nodded agreement. "It's just as well you didn't tell me. I'd probably have resented it."

"Exactly what I told Keith. Lord knows, I didn't want you hurt, but I've always felt that things have a way of working out. I'm just sorry you had to learn in the manner you did."

"What did the girls say?" For the first time I remembered I had left the house in the middle of a dinner I was giving for four of our classmates. Laurie was not at the table when the phone rang, and she had taken the call. She'd returned to the table and asked the girls to excuse me for a minute or two. She's not said a word until we were in the privacy of my bedroom. Once there, she'd closed the door and suggested I sit down. I refused, but from her somber manner, I sensed something was wrong.

"It's about Jim," I said.

She nodded.

"Was he in an accident." He loved automobiles, and his fast driving had unnerved me on more than one occasion.

"No. He'd been drinking and created a disturbance in a restaurant. He refused to leave and the police were called."

"You mean he was intoxicated?" I still couldn't believe it. I'd never known him to drink excessively.

She nodded. "I hate to be the one to have to tell you this. But you have to know it."

"Who called?" I exclaimed impatiently.

"A newspaper reporter. He related what had happened and asked to speak to you. I sensed something might be wrong and said you were out. I told him I was your secretary and would deliver a message to you. He asked if it was true you and James Canby were to be married tomorrow. I replied it was. Then he described what had happened in the restaurant. Jim Canby, in a drunken state, had approached a table where a lady and gentleman were dining and demanded she leave her escort and come with him. When she refused, he pulled the other gentleman from his seat and struck him with his fist. The other gentleman fell. Jim became more violent and had to be restrained. The police were called. He threatened to have them dismissed from the force, stating the Greyfield fortune was all-powered in Savannah. He was brought to the station anyway."

I was standing at the foot of my bed, and as Laurie related the story, I gripped one of the bed posts. The room spun madly, and her words seemed to come from a great distance. I thought I was going to faint. I didn't, but Laurie quickly came to my side and eased me onto the bed. She talked comfortingly to me, but I didn't hear a single word she said. All I wanted to do was to get away. To escape the ugly publicity. I knew I never wished to see Jim

Canby again. I remembered removing my engagement ring and placing it in Laurie's hand, requesting that she send it back to him.

I asked her where I could go. At first she urged me to stay and brazen it out, but the idea was repugnant to me. Then she suggested Greyfield Island. The very name was alien to me, though I knew there was such a place off the mainland and it was owned by the family. It was one of a group of islands, though I never recalled being there. Nor had I ever given a thought to the place. Even then, I hadn't the slightest idea of how to get there.

Laurie took care of that. She'd never been there, either, but she called Keith, who gave her directions for reaching it. She told me he'd told her about it. He had taken my aunts there and was well acquainted with the place. Once I agreed to go, Laurie packed an overnight bag, stating she'd come the following day with a wardrobe that would last until I made other plans. Five minutes later, I'd left the house through the kitchen.

Laurie brought me back to the present. "They thought it was some kind of a joke at first when I told them there would be no wedding. I gave them the honest story, knowing there would be enough false ones making the rounds in the next twenty-four hours. Sue Bittner and Misty Addison were stunned and wanted to go to the bedroom and console you. I told them you preferred to be by yourself. They understood. Alice Campion stood up and delivered a speech on the inhumanity of the opposite sex."

I had to smile. "Alice can't make a simple statement."

"Or if she does, it ends up in a speech always directed against the male. She's the most dedicated suffragette I know. If woman is ever to get the vote, she'll be the instrument through which they get it."

"And Nora Lange?" Nora had theatrical aspirations and had come down from New York just for the dinner.

"She quoted some lines from *Macbeth,* then added she'd seen Jim Canby in New York with a dancer in a Broadway show. They were cutting capers in a roof-garden restaurant. But it was over a year ago."

"What did she mean by cutting capers?"

"I asked the same question. She said they had drunk too much champagne and were making a spectacle of themselves on the dance floor. She said you're well rid of him."

"I shouldn't have run off like that, though. It was cowardly."

"Coming here in that storm wasn't cowardly. I was terrified you might not make it. Not that you aren't a good driver. It was the trip to the island that concerned me."

"Me, too." Setley came to mind. "Especially when I was almost murdered by drowning."

"You must be joking!" But she knew I wasn't, and sat up, sober-faced.

"No. There are a brother and sister living on this island. My great-grandaunt deeded both the land and the house to the sister for as long as she lives. Her name is Eulalie Laboulaye. Her brother's name is Setley. He pushed the boat away from the pier, upsetting it and spilling me into the water. Of course, he didn't know me, and once I identified myself, he pulled me out and set me on the dock."

"Why would he do that?"

"I guess he and his sister like their privacy just like my aunts." I'd already revealed to Laurie the dubious welcome I'd got from them.

"Why did your great-grandaunt do that?"

"I don't know. But I'm going to find out."

Her features flushed. "Who am I to ask such a question after what you've done for me? I really must get out on my own. I know I'd make a good social secretary."

"I'm paying you a salary to be mine. And don't talk about leaving me. Not at this particular time. If ever I needed someone, it's now. I don't know what I'd have done last night if it hadn't been for you."

"You'd have done whatever was necessary."

"No," I countered. "You've spoiled me and the worst of it is, I not only like it, I'm grateful. I didn't know until this morning that my aunts found raising me distasteful."

"You're exaggerating. They love you in their own way."

"No, Laurie," I said, "I've been blind. But I'll not hurt

them. After all, they did assume the responsibility for my upbringing."

"And they've been kind to me," Laurie said. "They always made me feel welcome."

I said, "I imagine they were delighted to have you at the house during the holidays. It meant they didn't have to worry about keeping me amused."

"We weren't there much," Laruie mused.

"No. We did a lot of partying. We really had fun."

"And we'll still have it. You'll get over Jim."

"I hope so. It's strange. I can't even cry. Last night when I was driving here, I thought about that. I had a terrible hurt inside. And an empty sort of feeling. But I didn't shed a tear."

"Not even after you got here?"

"Not even then."

"You were still probably in a state of shock. I hope the tears don't come—ever. He was a fool. A selfish, self-centered, ignoble fool."

"I was the fool. I wonder how I could ever have been so naïve."

"You believe in the goodness of people. Even Jim has some goodness in him, or he couldn't have fooled you as he did."

"I hope so. He made me feel so important."

"You *are* important. You're a Greyfield."

"I didn't mean it that way."

"I know you didn't. Nonetheless, people sit up and take notice whenever the name of the Greyfield heiress is mentioned. Your endless wealth."

"It's proved one thing. It can't buy happiness."

Laurie stood up. "Let's forget Jim Canby and go on a tour of the house. It looks fascinating."

"First I'd like to see my great-grandaunt's picture."

"So would I. Then I'd like to meet Eulalie Laboulaye and Setley."

"She's beautiful," I said, remembering my encounter with her in the forest.

"Anyone bearing that name would have to be. And

yet," Laurie frowned thoughtfully, "she must be quite old."

"I'll say no more. I want you to meet her, though that may not be so easy. She let me know I'm not welcome on her property. She assured me she'd not set foot on the part of the island that's mine."

"She must be a character."

"She knows her mind. Far better than I know mine."

"She has a few more years than you," Laurie pointed out.

"And you," I replied. "But you're far more competent than I."

"Perhaps it's as well." Laurie's hand rested lightly on my shoulder. "You'd have no need for me if you were the practical-minded woman I am."

"You won't be with me always," I said. "And I'm going to have to learn to depend on myself. I'm beginning to feel very ashamed of myself for having run from that dinner last night. I should have faced the girls. It would have been a beginning for me."

Laurie comforted me with, "All you could think of was that your world had crashed around you. And it had."

I nodded my thanks. I knew she had made another excuse for me. And I guess it was what I wanted. I needed Laurie. She knew it, and she wouldn't let me down.

THREE

Keith met us at the head of the stairs. He had come from my aunts' suite, which was in the opposite wing. He waved a sheet of paper on which was some kind of list.

"Groceries," he said and thrust it into his coat pocket.

He came directly to me and embraced me lightly. "I'm sorry, Aldis," he said. "I felt like beating the tar out of Jim."

The thought filled me with dismay. "I'm glad you didn't. It would only have given my disgrace further publicity."

"Don't think of it as a disgrace. Better you found out what he was like now than after the marriage."

"Yes," I agreed.

"I wanted you to know about him." He gave Laurie a chiding glance.

I said, "Laurie was right in dissuading you from telling me. I'd never have believed you. Or I'd have believed he'd changed once he'd met me."

"His kind never do," Keith said wisely. "It's sort of a sickness with them."

"Well, I'm safe from wagging tongues here."

"And don't let our aunts persuade you to go elsewhere until you've got over the shock."

"I won't," I assured him, "though I think they'd be much happier with me elsewhere."

"Never mind what they think." His glance switched to Laurie. "Take care of her."

"I will," she assured him.

"What are you going to do with yourself?" he asked.

"At the moment, we were on our way to the library to see great-grandaunt Jayne."

"A rare beauty," he said. "Come along. I never tire of looking at her. She was way ahead of her time, though."

"What do you mean?"

His boyish smile made itself evident. "Oh, they still tell tales about her in Savannah. It was never dull around her. Cousin, we have an ancestor whose skeleton still rattles in the closet."

I frowned. "Strange I don't remember ever having been to this island."

"Our aunts planned it that way. They feared you might have a recollection of the time your parents' bodies were washed ashore. Men were searching for the bodies, but quite a way out. You were walking along the shore with your nurse. Your parents' bodies were washed ashore almost at your feet. She screamed and ran to the house, leaving you there. When help came, you were seated beside both of them. You never shed a tear. But you didn't say a word for a week afterward."

"So that's why they never mentioned Greyfield Island," I said.

He nodded. "They're incapable of showing emotion, but I'm sure, in their way, they love you—and me."

"I know they're fond of you, Keith," I said. "And they should be. You take them everywhere. I'm pleased you do."

"What else have I to do, since you and Laurie outgrew me? I used to take both of you around, remember?"

Laurie and I exchanged smiles. She said, "We had the handsomest escort in Savannah."

His eyes scolded her. "And that's still all you think of me as—an escort."

"I value my independence," she said. "But I'll say this, I've not met anyone yet I like as well as I do you."

"Then I'll continue to hope," he said. "Now let's go see great-grandaunt Jayne."

Our heels made clacking sounds on the Georgia marble floors. So far, it seemed that all the floors were of marble.

Even the stairway was a beautiful shade of pink marble, intricately veined. The family fortune had been made from Georgia marble—a quarry of such length, width, and depth it would go on forever.

I matched my long strides to Keith's. He was taller than I and athletically inclined. I wished Laurie would fall in love with him.

He was fun to be with and had been a sort of guardian to me, young as he was, during my growing years. When Laurie came home to spend the holidays and vacations with me, he was our escort. Besides being handsome, with his dark wavy hair and matinee-idol features, he was soft-spoken with a shy, boyish smile. Yet he had poise and, for all his manly beauty, he was singularly modest.

The library was partially carpeted with Persian rugs that glowed with color. Three walls were shelved from ceiling to floor and were well-filled with books. At intervals there were cabinets with ornately carved doors. I opened one at random. It contained candlesticks, some of glass, others of silver. They, too, were sparklingly clean. Certainly, my aunts saw to it that the place was immaculate.

I suddenly became aware of both Keith and Laurie regarding me with amusement.

He said, "I thought you wanted to see our great-grandaunt Jayne's portrait."

"I do. It's just that I got carried away by the books and cabinets. It seems like a very special sort of room."

"I think a library is always impressive," Laurie said wisely. "All the minds and the thinking that have gone into putting those words on paper."

Keith nodded approval of her statement. "Well said. But Aunt Jayne is beginning to look a little pained, being ignored by her look-alike. There she is, between those two long windows."

I turned and walked as far as the velvet-covered bench surrounding the fireplace. Jayne's portrait hung above it. Midday sun flooded the room, giving more than sufficient light to view the painting.

"Good heavens!" Laurie exclaimed. "It *is* almost like looking at Aldis."

"Yes," Keith agreed. "I noticed that as Aldis matured. But I'd say the resemblance stops there."

"Great-grandaunt Jayne must have been quite a character," Laurie mused.

"Perhaps it could be best stated by saying she was born too soon. Today, her antics would be ignored. In those days, they were not, and she was ostracized."

"Antics?" I questioned.

"As you can see from her portrait," Keith said, "her eyes hold a hint of devilment, as does that touch of smile at the corners of her lips. I can't help thinking about it each time I look at that portrait. It's as if she was even scheming mischief while her portrait was being painted."

"How do you mean?" I asked.

He shrugged. "Who knows? Anyway, I have to take the launch across to the little town on the mainland. I assume your car is there, Aldis."

"It is—along that private road somewhere. The motor stalled on me last night. My fault, I guess."

"I'll get it started. There's a shed to one side of the dock where it can be garaged. How about you girls coming with me?"

"After last night, I've had enough of boats," I said. "Besides, this library fascinates me. I'd like to stay here awhile."

Keith turned to Laurie. "Would you care to come?"

"Absolutely not. Aldis mustn't be alone."

"Please go," I urged. "You've been wonderful, Laurie. But I really would like to be by myself."

"If that's what you want." She still looked doubtful.

"It's what I want," I said.

"Have you eaten?" Her tone was solicitous.

"No, but I'll ring for something." I went over to the bell pull beside the fireplace and gave it a tug. I knew Laurie wouldn't go until she was convinced in her mind that I really wanted to be alone. "Run along, you two. I'm going to get acquainted with great-grandaunt Jayne."

"Good luck," Keith said.

"I could use some," I said.

He sobered as he regarded the portrait. "Then don't emulate her."

"I know nothing about her," I said. "But perhaps if I stare at her likeness long enough, I'll learn something."

"Forget her." A sternness crept into his voice. "Live in the present."

A maid entered the room in answer to my ring. She was dark-skinned, young, with large brown eyes and a polite smile. She looked prim and neat in her gray uniform and small apron.

Keith said, "This is Cora. She's both the upstairs and downstairs maid. Her mother's name is Esther, and she's the cook. They oversee any other help necessary to keep this place up. Cora, this is Miss Aldis, your employer."

Cora bowed her head and murmured my name almost in a whisper, but I could see puzzlement on her features.

"Please bring me a sandwich and some iced tea, Cora," I said.

"Yes, Miss Aldis," she replied quietly and went as quietly as she had come.

Laurie again asked for reassurance that I would be all right. I gave it, and she and Keith left. Their voices drifted back to me as they moved through the reception hall.

Then the door closed softly and all was silent—an almost tomb-like silence. It didn't seem possible my aunts were upstairs. I supposed they were napping. It was early afternoon. I opened the windows and let the mild breeze drift in. The room soon filled with the salty tang of sea air. It was invigorating and relieved the closeness of the room.

I moved about, idly inspecting the books that lined the shelves. There were historical tomes, classics, and novels. My aunt must have been a linguist, for there were complete courses in languages.

I was intrigued by the heavily carved cabinets that interspersed the bookshelves and was about to investigate them when Cora returned. She brought with her a tablecloth and napkin and proceeded to cover a small tea table alongside a chair, after first removing the ornaments that graced it. Then she took from the tray what appeared to be a chicken sandwich, iced tea, and a generous serving of cream cake.

"It looks delicious, Cora. You still look surprised at seeing me."

"I am, Miss Aldis. Mama and me live in the village on the mainland and come here only when your aunts are in residence. I thought your aunts owned Greyfield. I never even knew about you."

"How strange."

"Yes, Miss Aldis," she said agreeably. "Then again, it ain't so strange. Your aunts are very proper. They don't talk to us unless they give us orders. And Mr. Keith. He's nice. He jokes with Mama and me—but not when your aunts are around."

"Don't you bother Miss Aldis." The stern voice came from the doorway. A buxom woman of middle years, dressed in a white uniform, eyed Cora with disapproval.

I said, "You must be Esther."

"Yes, Miss Aldis," she replied, though not venturing into the room.

"Didn't you know about me, either?" I asked.

She gave her daughter a reproving look. "No, Miss Aldis. But it ain't our business to know any more than we're told."

I made light of it. "I suppose my aunts never told you about me because I only came into my inheritance on my twentieth birthday." I didn't add it was today.

She nodded agreement. "That's about it, Miss. Come along, Cora. Let Miss Aldis eat her lunch."

I walked with Cora to the door. "Before you go, Esther, I want to say that I really am the mistress of Greyfield."

"Yes, Miss. But don't trouble yourself. Your aunts told me this morning things would be run just as they were before. And your aunts do a really good job of it, if I do say so."

"Yes," I agreed. "The place is spotless. I'm grateful."

"I don't let no shiftless good-for-nothings come here to do the extra cleaning. Your aunts pay well, and I sees to it they gets their money's worth."

"I'm sure you do," I said. "I'll put the tray outside the door when I've finished with it."

"Thank you, Miss." Cora nodded and flashed me a brief smile, and the two women moved across the hall in the direction of the dining room.

I closed the door and moved my chair so that I faced the portrait as I ate. There was a definite resemblance between my great-grandaunt Jayne and me. She had the same shade of tawny hair as I, only hers was dressed high in front, with curls dropping down the back, some of which rested on one shoulder. Pearls were intertwined in her hair and her coral off-the-shoulder gown made her fair skin seem fairer. She didn't seem tall, but her figure was voluptuous in the close-fitting satin gown. The toe of a satin slipper, matching the color of the gown perfectly, was barely visible at the edge of the hem.

Her eyes were hazel, just as mine were. Her face was youthful. She was, perhaps, younger than my twenty years. They married as young as fourteen then. I wished I knew more about her. Had she married, and had she had children? There were family pictures of ancestors in the town house at Savannah, yet not one of Jayne. Her name had never been mentioned by my aunts. I wondered why. Or did I wonder? Keith had given a hint when he spoke of her, saying she'd been born before her time. Did he mean there was a scandal involving her?

I regarded the portrait with fresh interest. Her eyes did hold a hint of devilment, and her smile—was it mischievous or mysterious? I was becoming more and more curious about my great-grandaunt. I wondered what she'd have done if what had happened to me had happened to her. I was certain she'd not have run away. She seemed too poised for that. I wished I had such self-assurance. Laurie did. She had neither money nor social standing, but no one would have guessed it from her competent manner.

I finished my sandwich and tea and took a few bites of my cake. It was delicious, but I was too impatient to explore this room to finish it. Perhaps there would be a diary of some sort. In those days, all girls kept them. I was glad I hadn't. I'd not like having to enter the fact that I'd fallen in love with a ne'er-do-well who had ingratiated himself into my affections to acquire wealth.

I put the dishes back on the tray and set it outside the door, again closing it after me. I wanted privacy, and this room with its large, leather-covered chairs, and oversized divan seemed made for it. I examined the books hastily, looking for Jayne Greyfield's diary. If she'd kept one, it wasn't among the books I scanned. My attention was again drawn to the small cabinets with ornately carved doors. I'd already looked into one, which had contained only candlesticks. I checked others. Most were empty. One had old ledgers that pertained to the business of the marble quarry. Others recorded expenses concerning the island. One contained a list of her gowns and other garments and the cost of having them made. My sympathies went out to the seamstress whose eyes must have suffered from having to sew the seed pearls on one ivory satin gown.

Ivory satin gown! Could it have been a wedding gown? I had one hanging in the closet back in Savannah. I was to have worn it today. I didn't dwell on that; instead, I completed my inspection of the cabinets. None of them contained anything resembling a diary. I went back to the first one I'd opened. The candlesticks were true objects of beauty, both the sterling ones and those of crystal. I picked up one of the latter and held it toward the window. Iridescent shafts of light shot around the room as the sun's rays caught the glass prisms. No matter what else they might have said about her, my great-grandaunt loved beautiful things.

I set the candlestick back on the shelf, but still stood there, admiring the beauty of each of them. My hands lightly gripped the top frame of the cubicle, my fingers resting on the inside. Something seemed to give. Not paying too much attention, I increased the pressure. My eyes widened as I saw the back, with shelves attached, recede about six inches. Only then did I notice this cabinet was more shallow than the others.

When I released the pressure, the back came forward. I increased the pressure again and watched the back move away from me. When it had gone back as far as possible, it stopped, and I looked down in an aperture. I saw something gold gleam, and my hands reached down to grasp it. Immediately the back started to come forward. The pressure had to be maintained. I used my left hand to press on the hidden frame, and the back receded again.

I reached down and my fingers closed around a soft leather book. I brought it into the light. It was scarcely dusty, the niche was so airtight. I broke out in goose pimples, and my excitement knew no bounds when I read the title in gold script. *My Diary.*

I released my hold on the frame, for I needed my other hand to open the book. My hopes soared when I saw the name written in flourishing script.

Jayne Greyfield

So she *had* kept a diary! I flashed a smile at the portrait and almost seemed to be rewarded with one in return. Foolish me! Her likeness smiled anyway. But no matter. The aperture had closed, and I shut the cabinet doors. I went over to a leather chair that was close enough to the open window to give me light. I hoped Laurie and Keith would delay their return. I didn't want to set this book down until I had completed every page.

JAYNE

"Mama, isn't my wedding gown beautiful?" I posed before the standing mirror and smiled at Mama's reflection. She was standing behind me.

"Yes, honey," she replied soberly. "It's beautiful, and so are you. I only wish you weren't so vain and so reckless."

I laughed at her somber look, and my eyes mocked her. "I'm not reckless, Mama. And what if I am vain? Haven't I been called the most beautiful belle of Savannah?"

"Every word you speak is the truth," Mama admitted. "But you know it's bad luck for the groom to see you in your wedding gown before the wedding."

"Who says he saw me?" The mirror revealed the deepening color of my face.

"I'm saying it, and so are the servants. They're frightened half to death because you made Mecca bring Scott Morton to your suite by way of the back stairs. It's not seemly, Jayne. I'm deeply hurt and shocked my daughter would do such a thing."

"Oh, Mama, I did nothing wrong. I wanted Scott to see me in my wedding gown. I'm not superstitious. He'll see me tomorrow, anyway. What's the difference? And he wasn't here more than five minutes. Only long enough to compliment me and give me a fervent embrace. Which, I may add, I returned."

Mama's head moved sadly from side to side. "You've always been rash and over-venturesome. You're only seventeen, you know. Still a child."

I stamped my foot. "I'm a woman, Mama. I know my

mind. And I saw nothing wrong with Scott Morton seeing me in my wedding gown. Nor did he."

But Mama was still dubious. "He's much older than you, but perhaps you'll mature as his wife. I hope so."

I turned and went to her. My movements were slow, not only because of the long train of the gown, plus that of the wedding veil, but the gown was weighted by millions of seed pearls. I embraced her.

"Smile for me, Mama. You'd think I was going to my funeral, rather than my wedding."

"Don't talk that way, honey." Mama's voice was almost a plea. "And please take off that gown. You've worn it steadily for two days."

"And why not?" I teased. "After tomorrow, I'll never put it on again."

She managed a smile. "Thank heaven, the wedding is tomorrow. From then on, you'll be Scott's worry. Not mine."

I turned back to the mirror. "I can hardly wait. I'll not sleep a wink all night."

"Nor will I," she said, "wondering if you're downstairs promenading in your gown."

"I'm glad the wedding is going to be in the reception hall. I wish Scott would consent to live here at Greyfield Manor. But he says it has to be Savannah or there'll be no wedding."

Mama nodded approval. "I'm amazed you abided by his decision."

"If I want him for a husband, I must. And I want him."

Mama frowned. "Are you sure, my dear? You know he's much older."

"He's mature. I hate young men. They're silly and fickle."

"But he's a man of the world."

"No matter. He's what I want. I must have him, Mama. That's all you need to think about."

"I've given it a great deal of thought. Somehow, I've a feeling he doesn't love you the way you do him."

"What a thing to say!" I exclaimed impatiently. "Just because he doesn't look at me with cow eyes. As you said,

he's a man of the world. I'm so proud just to be with him, I think I'm about to burst."

Mama nodded. "I know. And since you're the one who's marrying him, I'll say no more."

"Good. Send Mecca in. I want her to help me out of my gown."

Mama's face brightened. "Indeed I will. And please put it away until tomorrow."

I laughed again. "I'll tell Mecca to hide it so I won't be tempted."

"Even if you did and you asked her to bring it to you, she would. She worships you."

But I didn't remove the gown. I couldn't bear to. Mecca, the same age as I, and just as excited about the wedding, exclaimed anew at the picture I made.

"Never mind that," I said. "Go to the library and get my diary."

"It's in your writing table, Missy," she said. "I couldn't put it back. Too many guests in the house, and the gentlemen were having spirits there."

"Of course. I'd forgotten. Then you may run along. I want to write in it."

"Perhaps I can put it away tonight after everyone's asleep."

"Just so no one sees you. Remember," I raised a cautioning finger, "you must never reveal the hiding place of my diary."

"I won't, Missy," she said. "I'd die first."

"And after today you must call me Miss Jayne."

She nodded agreement and moved quickly from the room. I could depend on Mecca. We'd grown up together, and she was completely loyal to me, though she'd been assigned to me as my personal maid only a year ago.

I sat at my writing table, raised the lid, and retrieved the diary hidden beneath pages of stationery. This would be the last entry I'd make. Tomorrow I'd begin a new diary. Tomorrow I'd begin a new life.

I still couldn't believe it. I glanced at the standing mirror and turned away quickly. My eyes were swollen from crying. I stood up so abruptly, the delicate chair on which I was seated fell backward. It made a terrible clatter in what was now an empty house. Mama had sent everyone back to the mainland; all the servants, including Mecca, who had begged to be allowed to remain with me, were gone.

Mama was right. I should be alone. My heart was bleeding from the shocking news. I'd thought Scott Morton was as wealthy as I. I'd believed he loved me for myself, that my money held no meaning or importance to him. I stood before the standing mirror. I was wearing a negligee over my undergarments. My wedding gown lay across the bed. It seemed to mock me. Mama was right. I had flouted the Fates. It was bad luck to let anyone see you in your wedding gown before your marriage. Or was it just the gentleman to whom you had pledged your troth who shouldn't see you? No matter. It was ended.

Scott Morton loved my money, not me. Mama must have sensed it—or had heard rumors. She'd tried, in her gentle way, to warn me. But I'd been too sure of myself.

I'd be the laughing stock of Savannah. Girls far less attractive than I would whisper the gossip about the wedding that never took place and the awful reason why. That Scott Morton had wanted to marry Jayne Greyfield only for her money. He was broke, deeply in debt, and had held off his creditors with the promise that he would fulfill all his financial obligations once he married into the Greyfield family. And he would have. My pride wouldn't have allowed me to do otherwise.

A light tapping penetrated my consciousness. I thought it was Mama. "Go away," I called out. "Let me alone, Mama. Please let me alone."

"Jayne, darling." The voice was a caress.

The door closed as quickly as it had opened. For a few moments the room spun, and I thought my heart would burst. It was Scott.

Apparently he'd come up the back stairway. It had been easy for him to gain entrance to the house. The doors were never locked. The island was private, and no one lived here other than Mama and me.

I went to him, but when his arms sought to enclose me, I stepped back.

"How dare you come here?" I demanded.

"Why shouldn't I? I love you."

His deeply masculine voice and resonant tone had always stirred me. He'd been educated at Harvard, his mother having come from Boston, so he had the broad tone of a Bostonian. He was handsome, too, with warm brown eyes, a dimple in one cheek that gave him a rakish air, and a smile that reached straight to my heart. He was so tall that I came no higher than the region of his heart. I remember him saying that was as it should be, for then I could hear it pounding madly for me.

Oh yes, he was worldly and I, in my girlish innocence, had fallen under his spell. But my eyes were open now, and I found myself wondering if there was someone else he loved. If so, he was a consummate actor.

His arms again moved to embrace me, but I stepped just beyond his reach.

"If we had been married today, as it had been planned, you would have a right to be in this room," I said primly. "As it is, your behavior is most unseemly."

"To hell with my behavior," he said, moving up to me. "I want you. I love you. All right, I am in debt over my head. I have extravagant tastes, but so do you, and you have the money to indulge yourself. What made you think I had money? I never said I did."

"I can't imagine you having the nerve to court me if you were penniless."

He smiled the smile that had made me go all soft inside. Once again, he moved toward me.

And again, I stepped back, but the heel of my shoe caught in the trailing hem of my negligee, and I'd have fallen backward if he'd not scooped me up in his arms. He rained kisses on my face and murmured endearments that had always left me breathless. Tonight was no exception. When his lips covered mine, I was helpless to resist.

"You love me," he exclaimed. "You love me, Jayne. Never mind the silly big wedding. We'll elope and go

north. I'll work to support you. I'll dig ditches, hammer nails, do anything, if only you'll come with me."

We both heard the sound of a door closing. Scott released me and looked around for a place to conceal himself. I pointed to a tall screen. He slipped behind it only moments before Mama, a wrapper over her nightgown, appeared in the doorway.

"I thought I heard voices," she said worriedly. She'd been in the act of braiding her hair, and she resumed doing so as she regarded me.

I went over to my writing table, picked up the snuffer, and extinguished the three-stemmed candelabrum. I hoped Mama didn't notice my trembling hand. "No, Mama. I was just going to bed."

She looked around the room. "I'm sure I heard voices."

I shrugged. "I may have been talking aloud. Naturally I'm upset."

"Would you like a sleeping draught?"

"No, Mama. I'll sleep. I'll get over this. I'm young, you know."

"Don't be too bitter, darling. It's better that you found out about him before the wedding took place. I was always suspicious of him."

"Why, Mama?" I don't know what devilish impulse caused me to ask the question. I suppose it was my way of getting even with Scott, standing behind the screen.

"Well . . ." She paused as if pondering whether or not she should reveal what she knew. I didn't think she would tell me, for she finished braiding her hair and secured the ends with a narrow strip of ribbon. "He had a reputation as a bon vivant. I mean, of course, with ladies of our social standing, I regret to say."

I dismissed the information with a casual shrug. "I didn't expect an innocent young man. I told you how they bore me. And so long as his—indiscretions—were with ladies, I can be tolerant."

"I wouldn't say they were ladies," Mama replied primly, "even if they were in our social strata."

"Oh, Mama, you're so old-fashioned."

She shook her head. "You're much too modern for me.

I'd never marry a man whose name was bandied about in the manner Scott's was."

"But I love him, Mama," I countered. "And I think gossip is evil. Not to be listened to."

She appeared astounded by the revelation. "Then why did you call off the wedding?"

"I was hurt. I suppose it was one of those foolish ladies who gave her favors lightly who sent that anonymous letter."

"If so, it was a vicious thing to do," Mama said. "I hadn't thought of that, though."

"What did you think of?" I asked.

"I wondered if it might have been someone in your set. A girl of your age."

"One infatuated with Scott?"

"No. One who had formed a dislike for you."

"I hadn't thought of that," I admitted. "Anyway, it was a foolish waste of her time."

"What are you saying?" Sternness crept into Mama's voice.

"That if Scott were to walk into this room this instant and ask me to elope with him, I would."

"Jayne Greyfield!" Mama paled. One hand covered her eyes; the other reached for something to steady her.

"Don't faint, Mama, please." I went to her, placed an arm about her waist, and urged her to the door. "I'm only boasting. When I sent him away today, it was final. He'll not return."

"If he does, I hope your pride will prevent you from doing what you just said you would."

"He won't come back." I spoke with the decorum befitting a girl of seventeen years. "He's probably with some other woman now, making passionate love to her."

"Jayne!" Mama's shocked tones made me smile. "I don't know whom you take after. Certainly not me. And your papa was not a philanderer. Not even before he met me. Not like so many of the swains of my day—or of yours."

I kissed her cheek. "Go to bed, Mama. I'm tired, too."

She cupped my face in her hands. "I'm glad my little

girl had the courage to send Scott packing. He deserved it. I'm also glad you're not bitter. But then, how could you be, when your heart is bleeding?"

"Thank you for being so understanding, Mama. You know I could never hate Scott, don't you?"

"Yes."

"I'll always love him."

"I hope you'll meet someone else who can take his place. And I hope that after a proper amount of time passes, you'll do that."

"I'll try, Mama."

"Promise?"

I nodded. She kissed my brow, expressed the hope I would be able to sleep, and left the room, closing the door behind her. Neither Scott nor I stirred until we heard the muted sound of Mama's door closing.

He stepped out from behind the screen and extended his arms; I went to him. His face lowered to mine, but I held it back with my hands.

"Will you elope with me tonight?" I asked.

"Tonight?" He seemed surprised by my eagerness.

"Isn't that what you had in mind?"

"Yes, but not necessarily tonight."

"I want it to be tonight. And you won't have to go north and dig ditches or hammer nails. I'll pay all your debts."

He looked unbelieving.

"Yes," I insisted. "You mustn't worry about a thing. Leave the house now. Mama may be restless. I'll pack a small bag and meet you at the dock."

"Are you sure you don't want me to wait downstairs to carry your bag?"

"Positive. At the dock. I'll not be long."

He looked hesitant, worried almost. "Are you sure you don't want to wait till another night?"

"It's tonight or not at all."

"Then it's tonight."

"Do be cautious. Mama can't have retired yet."

"I took off my shoes coming up the damn marble staircase. I'll do the same when I leave. One more kiss."

I'd not deny him that, even if he was playing a game.

And if he was, I didn't care. I wanted him. As much tonight as the first night when he'd been introduced to me. I still remembered the wonderment of it. His soft brown eyes had seemed to devour me with a mere glance, and the touch of his lips on my hand seemed to burn through my skin. But when his mouth closed over mine, I knew he was as much my prisoner as I was his.

But I was denied the elopement, for when I got to the pier, there wasn't a sign of him. Only the boat he'd rented on the mainland was there. I waited until dawn, figuring he had become restless and was moving somewhere about the island. I finally returned with the bag I'd packed. It wasn't heavy, but it seemed leaden. And so was my heart.

The next day, my beloved Scott's body was found, tangled in the marsh grass alongside the pier. He had been stabbed in the back. Someone whose presence we weren't aware of had hidden on the island. Had undoubtedly followed him here and waited for his return. Whoever did it must have concealed his body beneath the pier. Certainly I'd seen no sign of it during the lonely hours I sat at the pier awaiting him, believing he had taken a stroll along the beach.

I never told Mama he'd been in the house or that I'd gone to the pier, portmanteau in hand, to elope with him. I knew I'd be the prime suspect, and I was. The tongues wagged viciously, and I took to my bed for two months, my nerves as well as my heart shattered. Physically I healed, but mentally I suffered and will continue to suffer in the knowledge that if I had ignored that anonymous letter, my love would be alive today.

I did ask Mama what had happened to the anonymous letter I'd received only minutes before the wedding had been scheduled to take place. She replied she had gone to her room and burned it immediately after I'd sent Scott from the house.

Though no one knew at the time my reason for canceling the wedding—not even the guests who were awaiting the ceremony—once Scott was murdered, Mama and I revealed the reason. Unfortunately, there was no letter to prove the truth of our statements. Mama also told the authorities that she was positive she'd heard an intruder in the house that night and had made a search, but had uncovered no sign of anyone. The doctor's verdict was that Scott Morton had been murdered by person or persons unknown.

Now, even though I was innocent of any wrongdoing, my name was besmirched. There was nothing I could say that would convince anyone of the all-encompassing love I'd borne Scott. A love so great I'd swallowed my pride and consented not only to elope with him, but to pay his bills.

I wondered anew who the coward was who had mailed that anonymous letter. I made a silent vow not to rest until I found out. I wanted my name cleared so that I could once again walk with head held high, free of suspicion of a crime so hideous it made me ill even to think of it.

I will write no more in this diary. This is the end of my girlhood. But I have set it down just as I lived it. The words written were the words spoken.

FOUR

"Aldis, are you all right?"

I blinked my eyelids a few times to rid myself of sleep. Laurie's concerned features softened as I smiled up at her.

"At least you can sleep," she said. "That's a good sign."

"What time is it?" I looked around the room at the deepening shadows.

"After five."

"Good gracious." I stood up so quickly the book resting in my lap dropped to the floor.

Laurie picked it up. "You must have read yourself to sleep."

I pointed to the book. "That's Jayne Greyfield's diary. At least, one of them."

"You mean there are others?" she asked.

"I don't know. I hope so. Where's Keith?"

"Having a swim. I was concerned about you and came directly back to the house. Especially when Cora told me you didn't want to be disturbed. Your aunts are having their evening meal in their rooms."

"My coming here has really upset them."

"I think the canceled wedding has upset them more. Keith said they're concerned about scandal."

"I certainly did nothing to create a scandal."

"It was all Jim Canby's doing. Keith said he deserved a good trouncing."

"I'm glad Keith didn't lose his head."

"He's too mature for that. He did the right thing in getting Jim out of jail and into a small hotel on the outskirts of town."

"I'm grateful," I said. "I guess I really feel sorry for

Jim. It must have been difficult for him to pretend affection for me when all he wanted was the Greyfield money. It's like history repeating itself."

Laurie looked puzzled. "What do you mean?"

I motioned to the diary. "The same thing happened to Jayne."

"You mean the man she married turned out to be a ne'er-do-well?"

"She didn't marry him. She received an anonymous letter the morning of the wedding, causing her to cancel the festivities. However, her fiancé returned that night and begged her to elope with him. She consented and told him to wait for her at the pier. She packed a small bag and went there, only to learn he wasn't there. The next day his body was found in the marsh grass. He'd been stabbed."

"How horrible." Laurie regarded the diary she held.

"You may read it if you wish," I said. "I'm going upstairs to change for dinner. I hope you and Keith haven't eaten."

"No. But I'm getting ravenous."

She stepped back for me to precede her. I did so, but when I reached the doorway, I turned sideways and lifted my skirts.

Laurie, watching, said, "What was that for?"

I looked down at my hands, still holding the fabric. "I don't know."

Laurie's glance switched to the portrait of my aunt. The dress skirt was voluminous, and it was obvious it was held out by a hoop beneath it.

Laurie regarded the diary she still held. "Perhaps I should burn this. Jayne seems to have had quite an effect on you. I'll grant the hobble skirts we're wearing aren't the easiest thing to walk in, but they don't warrant turning sideways to get through a doorway. A hoop skirt would, though."

I felt myself blushing. "Please don't tell anyone. They'll think I'm daft."

She laughed. "Don't worry, and don't feel embarrassed." She gave a slight shiver. "I think it's this room. The portrait seems to dominate it."

"It does," I admitted. "But I like it. And I think I'd have liked Jayne Greyfield."

"Strange," Laurie mused, "how the same tragic thing happened to you."

"Not quite the same, thank goodness," I said. "Jim Canby is still alive."

"And sobering up in some obscure hotel. At least, I hope he is. And I hope Keith did the right thing in getting him out. He'd be harmless in jail."

"And at the mercy of reporters," I reminded her.

"It's as well you didn't know about this island. *Or* the reporters. They'll never look for you here."

"I hope not. Which means my aunts will have to endure my presence for a while."

We headed for the stairs and our suites. I'd given Laurie the one across the hall from mine.

Laurie let out a little cry of remembrance. "I saw Eulalie Laboulaye and her brother Setley."

"Did you talk with them?"

"No. We passed them on our return. They were also in a launch. Your aunt certainly must have left her well provided for."

"Were you able to see her face?"

"Just barely. She was swathed in a gorgous soft cotton burnoose like those worn in Africa, covering most of her face. But we passed very close. Her brother was piloting the boat, and he and Keith exchanged waves. She made no attempt to speak, but I knew she studied me keenly."

"My aunts aren't the only ones who resent my presence on this island. She does, too."

"Are you certain?"

"Quite."

"I wonder why."

"I have no idea, in view of Jayne Greyfield's generosity toward her. Both she and her brother told me I resemble Jayne."

"Perhaps they're superstitious and your presence frightens them. They may think her ghost has returned."

"Once they hear the story about me—my canceled marriage—they'll probably become more frightened."

"Probably. But I doubt you need fear anything from them."

My smile was dubious. "I wonder. I haven't forgotten Setley upset the boat last night. I was terrified."

"You should report him to the authorities on the mainland."

I rejected that idea. "I think, as you say, he thought I was Jayne's ghost. Once I identified myself to him, he pulled me from the water. I could have drowned, because my feet had become entangled in the marsh grass. I have scratches on my legs to prove it."

"Let's forget Jayne Greyfield and get freshened up and changed for dinner."

"Let's," I agreed. "I'll race you to the landing."

We ran up the stairs, our laughter reverberating through the house and echoing up to the fourth floor. The stairway was open, with galleries around the perimeter of each floor. Our shoes added to the clatter, and I could imagine my aunts' look of strained patience if they heard. I'm sure they hoped I'd become bored and seek sanctuary elsewhere.

I was glad my aunts had chosen to dine upstairs. I'd gone to their suite for a few minutes to pay my respects. It was quite lavish and certainly no hardship for them to have their meals there. Their bedrooms connected with a large, high-ceilinged living room. One wall, which seemed to contain a chimney—and perhaps had at one time—was really a dumb waiter. It was concealed by a portrait that had been swung open and revealed the aperture where foods and dishes could be brought up from the kitchen.

They seemed to have adjusted to my presence, because their manner was more relaxed. Perhaps *resigned* would be a better word. But they were gracious and expressed the hope that I found everything to my liking, adding that they had done all possible to keep up the place. I expressed my pleasure with the house. They looked pleased, then told me what Keith had—that they'd never brought me here or even discussed it in my presence, except when it might have slipped out a few times—because they feared that in the back of my mind I still retained the mental image of my parents' bodies lying on the beach.

When I assured them I had no recollection of it, they looked relieved.

Dinner with Keith and Laurie in the medium-sized dining room was fun. I knew they deliberately made it so. Laurie had scanned the diary and told Keith about it, asking if he would be interested in reading it. He asked to be excused from such a chore, saying that that sort of thing was not of interest to a man. At least, not to him. We agreed, though I added that I felt since Jayne was an ancestor of ours, he should be interested on that score.

"According to our aunts, the less said about her, the better," he replied. "Though frankly, I'd like to have known her. I'm sure life was never dull with her around."

Laurie said, "Some people seem to invite tragedy through no fault of their own."

"I hope I'm not one of them," I said.

She was instantly contrite. "I didn't mean you, Aldis."

"I know you didn't. It's just that the circumstances seem almost parallel."

"Not exactly," Laurie argued. "You didn't receive an anonymous letter."

"True," I agreed. "But Jim didn't love me any more than Scott Morton loved Jayne."

"Again, there's a difference," Keith said. "According to what you and Laurie say, Jayne loved him so much she didn't care about his infidelity and was willing to elope with him. But someone did him in."

Laurie said, "The anonymous letter-writer, I'll bet."

"It would seem so," I said. "And that would be a woman. Too bad Jayne's mother destroyed the letter."

"Why?" Keith asked.

"Someone might have identified the handwriting," I said.

"Did you know," Laurie said, "that they say a person's character can be determined by their script?"

Keith derided that.

Laurie was insistent. "I believe it. I heard there are people who make a living out of reading handwriting."

Cora interrupted our discussion. "There's a gentleman in the hall who wishes to see you, Miss Aldis. He doesn't look presentable, though."

"What do you mean?"

Keith was already on his feet.

"He's all wet. And real mad. Said he got pushed in the water."

Laurie and I followed Keith from the room. A gentleman awaited us in the hall, his features a mixture of puzzlement and anger as he stood there, water dripping from his clothes.

Keith said, "I'm Keith Greyfield. What happened?"

"I got dumped in the water by your servant," the man replied. His soaking hair covered his forehead, and he made vain attempts to brush it back as he spoke.

"An elderly black man?" Keith asked.

"Wearing a butler's uniform that probably goes back to pre-Civil War days," came the indignant reply.

"He's not our servant," Keith's manner was quietly apologetic. "He lives at the south end of the island with his sister. Perhaps you didn't know the island is private."

"I know. That's why I'm here." Though his statement didn't make much sense, he took a card from his vest pocket, started to hand it to Keith, then crumpled it in his hand. It was too sodden to present to anyone.

He managed a smile. "My name is Dennis Curran. I deal in real estate, and I'm here to discuss with you the sale of parcels of this island for development purposes."

"There's been no talk that I know of regarding the selling of any part of this island," Keith said. "Or am I wrong, Aldis?"

"You're right," I said.

Keith said, "Which means you're a trespasser, Mr. Curran."

He managed a smile. "I wouldn't be if I'd known you had a watchman to keep off trespassers. He may be old, but he's determined."

"I'm sorry about that," Keith said. "Come upstairs. I'll give you a change of clothes. They might be a little big, but you can manage until you get back to the mainland."

"I'll appreciate it," he said. "But I'd also like the opportunity to discuss the idea of turning over this island and the one north and south of it for private development. I happen to know it's owned by you. You could make a fortune."

Keith said, "By my cousin. I'm not certain she'd be interested. You'd have to discuss it with her. I'm Keith Greyfield. This is my counsin, Miss Aldis Greyfield. Her friend, Miss Laurie Cummings."

We acknowledged the introductions.

I said, "Before we discuss anything, I think Mr. Curran is entitled to a change of clothing and an apology for Setley's behavior. He's the man who dumped you in the water. He lives at the far end of the island with his sister."

Mr. Curran looked surprised at the news, but he followed Keith's beckoning gesture gratefully. They went upstairs, and Laurie and I retired to the library. Floor lamps with fringed silk shades gave soft electric light. I wondered if Eulalie Laboulaye also had electricity. I also wondered what her home looked like.

I would know tomorrow, for I intended to pay them a visit. I'd had enough of Setley's arrogant behavior. It might be I'd decide to live here. If so, I had no intention of having any invited guests subjected to a ducking. Eulalie had assured me she'd not set foot on my property. I wanted such assurance from her brother, and I would insist on it before I left her house. I said as much to Laurie, who nodded tacit agreement.

The gentlemen returned shortly and joined us. They were followed by Cora with a decanter of brandy and four glasses. Both Laurie and I refused it, so Keith poured the amber liquid into two inhalers. Mr. Curran eagerly accepted a glass. He downed it quickly and Keith poured him another which he took, but held between his hands, letting the spirits warm. I judged his age to be about thirty-five; he was of medium height and going to corpulence.

He said, "I'm from Florida. I've developed several cays there, formerly privately owned. It seems rather selfish to let all this land lie fallow when other humans could be enjoying it."

"I never thought of that," I said. "Perhaps because I wasn't even aware of being the owner of it."

I smiled at his puzzlement.

Keith said, "My cousin never came here. She's only recently come into her fortune, and I'm sure she hasn't the faintest idea of her worth. Though I can assure her it's considerable."

"Then why not make it more so?" Mr. Curran asked. "You know the old saying—money begets money."

"I'm not interested in becoming a Croesus," I said. "But I agree, it isn't fair to keep this island to oneself, though I believe it is a wildlife sanctuary."

"It's so large," Mr. Curran mused, "that part of it could still be set aside as a sanctuary for them."

Laurie said, "Imagine a real-estate developer thinking of such a thing."

"I'm interested in making money, Miss Cummings," he said, "but I also possess some humane qualities. I cannot say the same of the individual who overturned my boat."

"I'm quite familiar with that," I said. "It was done to me last night during a violent electrical storm."

"And you own the island?" Mr. Curran looked incredulous.

"Setley didn't know it, since I'd not been here since I was a child. I don't even recall being here."

"Now that you are, are you interested in seeing the islands developed for the enjoyment of others?"

"I'd like a little time to think about it," I said.

"Fair enough. I've left my card upstairs in your cousin's suite. I'm sure the printing will still be legible, once it's dried out." He stood up. "I'm grateful for being received so graciously, and my thanks for the change of clothing."

Keith said, "I'll see that yours are returned to the address on the card as soon as they've dried."

"I appreciate that. And I hope you'll bring me good news. Good night, Miss Greyfield, Miss Cummings."

Keith said, "I'll take Mr. Curran back to the mainland in the launch. He'll spend the night at the inn in the village and return to Savannah in the morning."

"You may spend the night here, Mr. Curran," I said.

"I appreciate that, Miss Greyfield, but I have an early business appointment and I don't wish to disturb the household. I'm afraid the rowboat I rented went skittering out to sea."

"I'll be glad to oblige," Keith said.

"If you don't mind taking me back to the mainland tonight, I'd prefer that," he replied hopefully.

"Come along," Keith said.

Mr. Curran again expressed his thanks, I repeated my apology regarding Setley, and he and Keith left.

Laurie looked bemused. "Do you suppose Setley has all his mental faculties?"

"He seemed quite normal the night I encountered him. I figured, as you did, that he became frightened when he saw me because of my resemblance to Jayne."

"You couldn't say Mr. Curran resembles her."

"No. And I intend to pay Eulalie Laboulaye a visit the first thing tomorrow. I've had enough of Setley's idiosyncrasies. He's to remain away from that pier."

"What if he doesn't? You can't put him off the island."

"No," I agreed. "But I'll call in the police. What he did to me was one thing. And I'm sure the only reason I put up with it is because I didn't want further publicity. Mr. Curran was most gracious. I must ask Keith to see that he's reimbursed. Certainly the damage to his suit by the salt water is irreparable."

"He was gracious about it," Laurie agreed. "Do you think it might have been in part because he has a lot at stake here?"

"You mean selling the property?"

She nodded. "I couldn't tell from your manner what you thought about it."

"I don't know, myself. I didn't even know I owned it until last night when you suggested it as a place to escape the reporters."

"I don't know what made me think of it," she said. "Keith only told me about it once when he mentioned he was bringing your aunts here."

"All they ever said about it was that they were vacationing on the island," I mused. "I knew it was a place they went to, but I didn't even think about it belonging to the family."

"To you now."

I shuddered. "It almost seems like an island of death."

"What a gruesome thought." Laurie's tone was chiding.

"I mean it. My parents' bodies were washed ashore here. The man my aunt Jayne was going to elope with was murdered here. I fled here to escape publicity, but I doubt that I would have, had I known it had only bitter memories."

"Your bitter memories are of Jim Canby."

I nodded. "I'm going to take a walk before going to bed. Would you care to come?"

"Not unless you're afraid."

"I'm not afraid. Just restless."

"I'm exhausted, Aldis. Keith walked me all over the village this afternoon. And the heat was ghastly."

"He should have known better."

"He got carried away. I enjoyed it, really. But it left me debilitated."

"Run along. I'm only going to take a brief stroll along the beach."

I moved around the house to the ocean side of the island. I could well understand Mr. Curran's interest. The beach was beautiful, and it extended for a great distance. Walking wasn't particularly easy with my shoes, so I removed them and placed them beneath a piece of driftwood. I'd retrieve them in the morning. I also slipped off my stockings. I preferred the sand sticking to my feet to the uncomfortable feeling of it slipping through my hosiery.

For the first time since I arrived, I felt relaxed and carefree. I didn't know whether it was because I was walking on bare feet or whether it was the sound of the surf lapping at the shore. The water was calm and the salty air invigorating.

I turned once, whether on impulse or because I thought someone was behind me, I didn't know. But I had the feeling I wasn't alone. Perhaps I wasn't. I didn't believe Eulalie would deign to spy on me, but Setley was another matter. He resented the presence of strangers on the island. I wondered what his reaction would be were he to learn I intended to turn the island into a summer resort.

The thought, slipping through my mind so easily, surprised even me. I hadn't found it particularly appealing at first, but now it did seem selfish to keep all of this for myself. As for my aunts, I doubted whether they ever ventured on the beach. And as for Eulalie and Setley, certainly I owed them nothing. I wondered why my great-grandaunt had given them title to land and house. More and more, I found my curiosity whetted by Aunt Jayne. As Keith said, her life hadn't been dull.

I resumed my walking, but had gone only a few paces when I heard my name spoken above the lapping of the waves on the shore. I turned, scanned the beach, then shifted my search to the forest edging it.

A figure stepped out—tall, hatless, and minus a coat; his blond head glistened in the half light of the moon. Jim Canby! I turned and started to run. Aimlessly and without a thought as to direction. I wanted only to be free of him. But his long legs proved too much for me. That and the silly hobble skirt—aptly named—which made running impossible.

His hands enclosed my waist, and he spun me around to face him. "Aldis."

"It's over, Jim. Let me go."

"I thought you loved me." His manner was questioning, as if, in spite of his behavior, he couldn't believe I'd suffered a complete change of heart.

"And I thought you loved me," I countered, still struggling to free myself.

"I do." He spoke with such vehemence I wondered how I could doubt him.

"No, Jim. You thought you could use me."

"That isn't true. I'll admit I can't handle alcohol. I never could, but I swear I'll never touch it again."

"Your getting drunk wasn't the reason I called off the wedding. And let me go. Your hands are pressing into my waist so tightly, you're hurting me."

"Aldis, I'd never have made a public spectacle of myself if it hadn't been for an anonymous letter I received. It frightened me. The sender threatened to inform you of an earlier indiscretion of mine."

"Jim, if you don't release your hold on me, I'll scream."

"Will you hear me out if I do?" His eyes pleaded with me.

"Yes. Though it doesn't mean things will change for us."

"I wouldn't expect to be that lucky." He released his hold on me. "Just give me a chance to explain."

"Very well." I took a few paces back, in case he attempted to take me in his arms again.

He read my mind, and as if to reassure me, he thrust his hands into his pockets. "The letter threatened to inform you of the fact that I'd had an alliance with another girl, even naming her. It was in a feminine handwriting, and I believed the girl named was the one who'd sent the letter. I called her home and was told where and with whom she had an engagement. By then, I was tortured with fear she would go to you, and I started to drink. I have little tolerance for alcohol, and by the time I arrived at the restaurant, I was intoxicated. I became obnoxious and ended up in the police station—which was exactly what I deserved. I'm grateful Keith got me out. I'd like to thank him."

"He took a gentleman to the mainland. I don't know when he'll be back."

"And you'll not invite me in to wait for him." Jim's mouth widened in a smile that had always touched my heart. Now I was strangely unaffected by it.

"I'd rather not. I'll tell him, though."

"I didn't finish my story."

"I don't want to hear it, Jim. I suffered last night, too, when the reporters called to tell me of the scene you made in the restaurant and asked for confirmation regarding the wedding today. After I fled from the house, Laurie called the newspapers and canceled the wedding plans."

"I read it in the newspapers." His tone was bitter.

"Didn't Keith tell you?"

"He talked with me, but he was angry. Justifiably so. And I can't remember anything he said."

"I'll say this, Jim. I wish it hadn't happened. I wanted to be your wife. I was so proud that of all the girls in Savannah, you'd chosen me."

"So far as I'm concerned, you're the *only* girl in Savannah. Please, Aldis." He took a step toward me. "Give me another chance. It's true I don't have money. But I've been working on an invention that, if successful, could make me as wealthy as you. You'll never believe it, but it wasn't your money that attracted me to you. It was you. It still is. I know I—at least the police told me—I said I'd have their badges. I hate myself for that. It was drunken talk. I don't even remember saying it."

"Why didn't you tell me about the invention?" His manner was so earnest I found myself believing every word he spoke.

"I have a little more work to do on it. It'll take more time and—money. That's embarrassing to say, but it's the truth."

I couldn't doubt his sincerity. This was the Jim Canby I knew . . . the one who'd been so devoted to me every moment we were together.

"I'll make a bargain with you," I said. "All you need do is prove you're telling the truth regarding the invention. If so, I'll advance you the money to complete it."

He looked unbelieving. "I don't deserve it. Why are you doing it?"

I said, "I'm not sure. But I'm going to do it."

He moved to embrace me, but I stepped back. "Not yet. I was hurt too much by what you did. Of course, I didn't know about the letter." I paused, then asked, "How did you know where to find me?"

"I went back to the police station to see what I was charged with," he said. "I couldn't remember anything that had happened. They told me no one wanted to press a charge so I was free. Then I asked where Keith was. I wanted to express my appreciation for what he'd done. They told me he'd left for Greyfield Island. I drove to the village and rented a boat to come here."

"Wasn't there a man on the pier who tried to prevent you from coming here?"

"No." His surprise was genuine.

"You're lucky." I couldn't repress a smile.

"Is the island guarded?"

"No. Just an elderly brother and sister who live at the far end of it. He thinks no one should set foot on it. When I came here last night, he overturned my boat and dumped me into the water."

Jim said, "I'm sorry I made such a mess of things."

"I'm beginning to think I'll survive." I wondered how I could make light of it. Only twenty-four hours ago, I thought my world had come to an end. Now my concern was all for Jim. I wondered who could get such sadistic pleasure out of wrecking two lives. Or trying to. I also wondered whether I still loved him. At present, the numbness that had filled me at the news of what he'd done was still present. Perhaps now it would leave me and my faith in him would be restored.

I said, "I'll have Keith bring me back to Savannah tomorrow. I'll make immediate arrangements with my bank to forward a loan to you."

"I have a laboratory of sorts, if you'll come and see what I'm doing. It's a new kind of starter for an automobile. I've never talked of it to anyone. I just wanted to prove I was something other than a social snob."

"You were never a snob," I said.

"I was never in love until I met you," he said. "I did fritter a lot of time away with women—and alcohol. I'll never touch it again. I swear."

"I believe you, Jim."

His features brightened. "May I walk you back to the house? It's quite impressive."

"It's beautiful inside. You'll see it one of these days, but not tonight. Now that things aren't as bad as I thought, I'd just like a little time alone to adjust."

"Does that mean I have a chance?"

"I wish I could say yes, but I don't know."

He gave a nod of understanding. "Thanks for not hating me. And thanks for your offer of help."

"I'll telephone you as soon as I reach Savannah."

"I don't deserve it, Aldis."

"Perhaps I acted too hastily," I said. "I need a little time to think about us. In the meantime, I'll lend you any financial help you might need to perfect whatever you're working on."

He reached for my hand, squeezed it gently, then released it. In the moonlight, I could see his eyes regard me hopefully. I managed a smile, but that was all the encouragement I gave him. I was still smarting inwardly from the humiliation he'd caused me.

He released my hand and stood there a moment, waiting for me to make the next gesture. When I didn't, he turned and headed back for the pier at the end of the island. My arms raised and my mouth opened to speak his name, but I couldn't. My foolish pride, I suppose. I turned abruptly and walked in the opposite direction. I was sorry I couldn't tell him we could start anew. Yet I was devoid of any feeling toward him. Had my hurt been so great I would never again feel love? The very thought terrified me. I wanted to love and to be loved. Perhaps I'd been too impatient for it. Was loneliness the reason I'd let Jim Canby sweep me off my feet? I knew he was popular and much sought after at social affairs in Savannah. Yet he'd chosen me. Already doubts were clouding my mind. Was he honest with me tonight? He seemed so. Questions I couldn't answer kept prodding my mind all the way back to the house.

I thought of going to the pier to await Keith's return and ask him to take me to Savannah tomorrow. I'd not tell him why, for I had a feeling he'd discourage me. And he'd probably be right in doing so. But I believed Jim deserved another chance. Not only to have financial backing to complete his invention, but if he applied himself diligently, perhaps my faith in him would be restored—even if the invention wasn't all he believed it would be.

But when I neared the house, exhaustion claimed me.

Inside, I wrote a note and propped it on the silver tray on a table in the reception hall. Keith would see it. If he didn't, I'd rouse him in the morning, if he wasn't about when I came downstairs. I hoped Laurie would come with me. More and more, I was coming to depend on her. I was glad she'd consented to live with me, though I knew one day she'd tire of it and strike out on her own.

Upstairs, I lost no time getting ready for bed. A lot had happened today—my twentieth birthday. I was thinking of Jim, not of poor Mr. Curran. I couldn't repress a grin, though, thinking of his chagrin when Setley overturned his boat. I made a mental note to pay Eulalie Laboulaye a visit tomorrow also. She had to impress on her brother that he was to remain away from the pier and was not to harass anyone who came to the island.

I came awake slowly, with the uncomfortable feeling that I wasn't alone in the room. I kept my eyes closed, but my senses were instantly alert, though I was careful not to move, except to turn my head. Something seemed to be annoying me. Then a hand touched my hair. Lightly, exploringly. I slitted my eyes. I saw the hand feel the ends of my hair, which was fanned out on the pillow. The gesture seemed foolish, yet it unnerved me. There was a light of sorts. It was a flashlight, but covered by a hand, which muted the light but enabled the intruder to find his way about. No—it was a she.

The scent I detected was that of jasmine. Not unusual in these parts, but Laurie didn't use a scent of any kind. Who, then? Eulalie Laboulaye!

In a lightning-like gesture, I gripped the hand holding the flashlight. Despite her age, she was strong and quick in her movements and freed herself, striking my wrist with the flashlight, now extinguished. I cried out in pain and again tried to get a grip on her. My hand caught hers, but it was still smarting with pain, and she shrugged it off easily, scraping my palm with the metal of the flash.

Her soft feet padded swiftly across the room. I felt moisture on my hand and knew the scratch had drawn blood. I slipped from bed and ran into the hall. There was a switch at the head of the stairs which lit the chandelier in the hall. I found it and pressed the button, and the electric light softly illuminated the area below. Just as it did, the front door closed softly.

Eulalie had made good her escape. What did she want? Why had she come here? And why did she touch my hair? I didn't attempt to pursue her. She knew the island far better than I and could elude me with ease.

I put out the light and returned to my room. I was tempted to waken Laurie, but decided against it. It would serve no purpose. Eulalie wasn't interested in Laurie, only in me. But for what purpose?

I glanced over at the chaise, which stood before a window. I'd spread my dress over it when I returned. Now it was thrown in a heap on the floor. I regarded it with growing puzzlement. What was that woman after? Why had she invaded my suite? Even my undergarments had been picked from the chair and thrown in a heap on the fl or. My shoes, which had been on the floor, were thrown on the chaise. I'd retrieved them before I returned to the house. Sand clung to the soles, but I'd been careful to keep away from the water, so the white leather tops were not water-stained.

I carried the dress to the closet, noting that the skirt near the hem had been pressed together so tightly, the fabric had wrinkled badly. The same with my petticoat. It didn't make sense. I wondered if Laurie's clothes had been mishandled in this fashion. Or if she'd been studied by someone holding a flash whose light had been muted by a human hand. Laurie's hair had been cut short in the style made recently popular by Irene Castle of the famous dancing team of Vernon and Irene Castle.

I went back to bed, but lay sleepless, impatient for daylight. I refused to allow myself to become frightened, yet I sensed I was a less-than-welcome occupant of the island, even if I did own it.

Perhaps I should dispose of my share of it, plus the two islands adjacent to it. I'd give it serious thought. I could make a provision that this house would belong to my aunts until their death, at which time it would be disposed of. The more I thought of it, the more determined I was to go through with the idea. With that problem disposed of, I lay quietly, waiting for daylight.

FIVE

Laurie and I had to drive to Savannah, for my aunts had asked Keith to take them for a sail. Once we reached the city, we drove directly to my home in Savannah and I immediately went to the telephone to call Jim.

I'd given his number to the operator several times and I'd heard her ring over and over, but there was still no answer.

Laurie said, "Do you suppose he was serious about an invention?"

"I'm as certain of it as I am that he was sorry for his behavior in that restaurant."

"Did he show you the letter he said he got?"

"No," I admitted. "But I'm sure he wasn't making it up."

The operator broke in with, "I'm sorry, Miss, but there is still no answer."

I thanked her and once again put the receiver back on the hook.

Laurie still looked perplexed. "We've been here over two hours, and you've called at least twenty times."

I nodded. "I wonder if something could have happened to him."

She gave me a knowing look. "I hope not. You've been through enough."

"I don't mean his drinking. He swore he'd never touch liquor again, and I believe he was serious."

"You told me he also said he'd be home when you called."

"Let's go to his house."

"I think we'd better—and quickly. We have a long drive back."

"I'm sorry, Laurie, I shouldn't have asked you to come with me."

She quickly reassured me. "You don't think I'd have let you come alone, do you?"

She picked up our purses, which we'd left on the hall table, handed me mine, and we left the house after a brief appraisal of our appearances in the mirror-paneled hall. We'd chosen crisp organdie dresses and large, soft-brimmed picture hats. Despite the intense heat of day, they made us look cool. They were practical as well as feminine, for they kept the sun off us.

When Keith took us to the mainland in the launch, he pointed out the shed where he garaged the car I'd come in. As he said, it was useful to have it there. It made shopping for groceries much easier. But it now meant we had the long drive to Savannah and back.

Jim Canby's home was in an old section of town. The houses needed care, but the yards were well kept up, and the tree-lined street was quiet and in mid-afternoon devoid of pedestrians or traffic of any sort.

I parked the car in front of his residence and we moved up the short walk to the door. The house was charming, built of red brick and ivy-covered. I pressed the doorbell and when there was no answer, I used the knocker. It reverberated through the house. I listened for approaching footsteps, but only silence prevailed.

Laurie and I exchanged glances. I said, "Let's go around to the back. Perhaps he's outside. There's a screened gazebo that's completely shaded by trees."

We followed the flagstone path to the rear of the house. The gazebo looked invitingly cool. Wicker furniture, with chintz cushions and pillows, added to its charm. But there was no sign of Jim.

The sliding door of the barn which he'd converted into a garage was closed, but opened under my urging. We stepped inside. Two automobiles occupied the interior, one of which was partially dismantled. On a long work table were several batteries with wires extending to a large, flat board on which more mechanism was attached. It looked mysterious and puzzling, and to Laurie and me it was.

"He told you the truth about working on an invention," she said, studying the maze of wires.

"I never doubted him," I said. "I just wish I knew where he is."

"Are you sure he said he'd be here?"

"He said he'd not stir from the phone until he got my call."

"Do you suppose there might be something wrong with his phone?"

"I heard the operator ring him. But let's see if the place is unlocked. If we can get in, I'll ask the operator to ring the number."

She brightened at the thought. "A brilliant idea."

"I think it's desperation that made me think of it. I have a feeling something's very wrong."

I was already on my way to the back door. I wasn't surprised that it opened. Even though Jim lived alone, he wouldn't think of locking it. He'd even made a joke of it, saying there was nothing in the house worth stealing. But that wasn't true. There were some beautiful pieces of furniture worth a small fortune, and he knew it. But he had a lot of family pride and couldn't bear to dispose of them. I knew now, more than ever, he'd been honest with me. At least, most of the time. And I reasoned that perhaps he did think that the Greyfield fortune could help him to perfect and market his invention. In truth, there was nothing wrong with that.

I moved through the kitchen, with Laurie following. The place was clean, for he had a cleaning woman in twice a week. We passed through the small butler's pantry and crossed the dining room to the reception hall where the telephone was.

I picked it up and was immediately rewarded by the operator's voice asking me what number I wished. I explained I wanted to reassure myself that the telephone was in working order and when I hung up, I would like her to ring it. She agreed, and I placed the receiver on the hook.

Immediately the phone rang. Laurie and I exchanged glances before I picked up the receiver and answered. It was the operator. I thanked her, assured her the phone was in working order, and hung up.

Laurie and I left the house the way we'd entered it, in thoughtful silence. I broke it only after we were on our way.

"I'm going to go back to my house before we set out. Perhaps Jim had an errand of some kind and being late, figured it would be better to come by my place."

Laurie nodded agreement, then asked the question I knew had been on her mind. "Are you sure he was—sober when he came to the island last night?"

"Positive," I said. "Why do you doubt it?"

"It isn't that I doubt it," she replied soberly. "But if he wasn't, he might have overturned in the boat he'd rented."

"We could certainly check that, couldn't we?"

"Yes. Whoever rented him the boat would certainly know if and when he returned it."

"All we have to do is find out who that person was."

"It shouldn't be too difficult," Laurie said. "I don't think the population of the village is more than six hundred people."

I said, "Do you suppose he might have gone back to the island?"

"The best way to find out is to get back there as quickly as possible."

"I'll bet that's it." Excitement tinged my voice.

"You could be right," Laurie said. "I hope so. You're as upset as you were two nights ago."

"I can't help it," I said. "Something happened last night I didn't tell you about. At the time, it frightened me."

"What happened last night?"

I told her quietly and briefly.

"That *is* strange," she said. "Why would Eulalie Laboulaye want to examine your clothes and feel your hair?"

"I don't know. Of course, I couldn't identify her, but there was the heavy scent of jasmine in the room. I also have proof I didn't dream it."

"What do you mean?"

I took my hand from the wheel long enough to let Laurie observe the long scratch on the palm of my hand. "I got that from a ring when I tried to keep whoever it was from running away. I also have a bruise just above my wrist where I was struck with a flashlight."

I was again holding the wheel with both hands. Laurie leaned over to observe the bruise on my left wrist.

"That must have hurt."

"What hurt most was my pride. But I wanted you to know about it."

"You mean forewarned is forearmed?"

"Yes."

"That woman and her brother bear watching."

"I know her brother does, but now I'm wary of her."

"And with good cause. Are you afraid of her?"

"No. How could I be? She must be very old."

"Yes. But didn't you get a good look at her?"

I gave a negative shake of my head. "It was dark in the forest the day we met. But I'm going to get a good look at her. I'm going to call on her. Or send a message inviting her to pay me a visit."

"Do you think she'll come?"

"I have no idea. But if she doesn't, I'll go to her."

Laurie made no reply, and I took my eyes from the road momentarily to see her regarding me with admiration.

"Either you're acquiring spirit or you've always kept it well hidden."

"I hope I'm acquiring it." We reached the dirt road that turned off the highway and led to the pier. "I also hope Keith is there to meet us. It's been a hot, sticky drive."

"We could both use a bath and change of clothing," Laurie agreed.

We made the ride over the dirt road in good time, and I drove the car into the protection of the shed. Shrubbery hid the shed from view and it also, by the same token, concealed the pier. Our shoes sank into the soft dirt, sending up small clouds of dust around our ankles which we ignored. It concerned us even less when we rounded the shrubbery and came face to face with a gentleman who tipped his hat and identified himself as Deputy Sheriff Tim Eckles. He was about forty, but looked older, for his face was deeply lined from exposure to sunlight. His hair was still dark, his features lean as was his face. Before we could recover from surprise, he asked us to identify ourselves.

I said, "I'm Aldis Greyfield. This is my friend and companion, Miss Laurie Cummings."

Sheriff Eckles addressed me. "Your cousin said you and your friend drove to Savannah this morning. That he brought you as far as the pier."

"He did," I said. "Is there something wrong?"

"I'm afraid so, Miss Greyfield." He motioned to a small launch. "I'll take you both to the island. Mr. Greyfield is with the two ladies. Your aunts and his, I believe."

"Yes," I said. "But what's wrong?"

"I'd rather not say until I get you to the house."

"Why not?" I demanded. "The island is private, and I assume you wouldn't be there unless you had a right to be."

"I have a right to be, Miss Greyfield. There's been a murder."

"Jim Canby."

My reply startled him for a moment. Then he said, "I understand you and he were to be married, but you . . ."

His voice trailed off. I completed the sentence for him. "I asked Miss Cummings to issue a statement to the newspaper that there would be no wedding."

"Had you quarreled?"

"No. But Mr. Canby made a public scene which I felt was demeaning to me."

"Had you seen him since?"

"Last night. I met him on the beach."

"A prearranged meeting?" Sheriff Eckles' tone was quiet, almost fatherly, but his keen eyes never left my face.

"No. I was surprised to see him."

"Did you quarrel?"

"Our parting was amiable. I went to Savannah today to meet him. I don't care to discuss this further until you tell me how you know Jim Canby was murdered."

"One of your aunts was out for a stroll and came upon

his body. Her screams brought a man who lives on the island with his sister. Mr. Canby's body was lying in the swamp, face down. He'd been stabbed. A knife protruded from his back."

Everything started to spin, and I'm sure I'd have fallen had not Laurie got a firm grip on me. When I awakened, I was being carried to the house by Sheriff Eckles. Awareness quickly returned, and I groaned.

I felt completely responsible for Jim Canby's murder. I should never have sent him away.

Sheriff Eckles looked down at me. "Sorry the news gave you such a start, Miss Greyfield."

"You may let me down, Sheriff. I'm sure I can walk."

He did so. I held on to him a few moments until I steadied myself. When he offered his arm, I accepted it gratefully. Laurie walked on the other side of me, but I had no need of additional support.

"How is my aunt?" I asked.

"Miss Mabel—the one who discovered the body—is in her room. The medical examiner, Dr. Lind, is with her."

"What a dreadful shock it must have been to her," I said. "Do you have any clues to the murderer?"

"No. A search of the area has already been made," Sheriff Eckles said. "When Mr. Canby left you, did he go directly to the pier?"

"I have no idea," I said. "Though I got the impression that's where he was headed. Wasn't the boat he rented at our pier?"

"No, ma'am. Was it there when you left this morning?"

"I didn't notice. Did you, Laurie?"

"I don't recall seeing one, though I paid no attention. Even if I had, I'd not think anything of it."

"We found no trace of one," Sheriff Eckles said. "I understand no one knew he was on the island last night except you."

I said, "He came unannounced. We had a friendly talk. In fact, I was to see him today. Miss Cummings and I went to Savannah for just that purpose. I had an appointment with him."

"Does that mean you had changed your mind about not marrying him?" Sheriff Eckles asked.

"No. Though I was no longer angry with him. And . . . well, I may as well tell you the entire story."

I did so. Sheriff Eckles listened quietly. When I finished, he said, "He could have been followed here. Perhaps by the person who sent the anonymous letter."

"It has to be something like that," I said. "He was in a happy frame of mind when we parted. I hope you believe that."

"I have no reason to doubt it, Miss Greyfield," he replied.

Not yet, I thought. But you're certainly not going to take just my word for it.

Keith was framed in the open doorway when we left the forest. At sight of us, he ran down the steps. He came directly to me, eyeing me with concern.

"You know." He made it a statement.

I said, "I insisted that Sheriff Eckles explain why he was questioning me."

"I told the Sheriff you saw Jim here last night. Did you, by chance, walk back to the pier with him?"

"I wish I had. Was the boat Jim came in at the pier when you took Mr. Curran to the mainland?"

Keith shook his head. "There wasn't even a sign of the boat Mr. Curran rented."

I said, "Do you suppose Setley could be the guilty one? He resents anyone coming to this island."

Sheriff Eckles addressed Keith. "He's the elderly man who lives at the south tip of the island with his sister."

"Yes," Keith replied.

"Has he given you trouble, Miss Greyfield?" Sheriff Eckles asked.

"He tipped my boat over when I came here the night before last."

"Why?"

"For no reason other than that he resents anyone invading the privacy of the island."

"Does he resent your aunts?" Sheriff Eckles asked.

"Apparently not."

"Or you, Mr. Greyfield?"

"Never, to my knowledge," Keith said. "Of course, he didn't know who Aldis was when she first set foot on the island."

"I hadn't set foot on it," I said indignantly. "Though I was about to and he reached down and deliberately overturned the boat during a raging thunderstorm."

Sheriff Eckles said, "Your cousin told me of another guest who came here last night. A Mr. Dennis Curran."

"He was a surprise guest," I said.

Keith said, "I already told Sheriff Eckles about him and the welcome Setley gave him."

"Was Mr. Canby welcomed to the island in the same fashion by Setley?" Sheriff Eckles asked.

I said, "He couldn't have been. His clothes were dry. Mr. Curran had to be given a complete change."

Sheriff Eckles looked thoughtful. "Did Setley know Mr. Canby?"

Keith said, "I have strong doubts, but you'd have to question Setley on that."

I said, "Jim really came to the island to thank Keith for getting him out of jail and placing him in a hotel until he sobered up."

"Then I don't think Setley knew him, but I'll question him all the same. About that *and* the murder." He addressed Keith. "Do you own a hunting knife?"

"No," Keith said. "I couldn't kill any kind of animal. But a hunting knife would come in handy here with the abundance of wild life."

Sheriff Eckles nodded. "I'll see both Setley and his sister before I leave the island. You folks understand your privacy will be disturbed until this murder is resolved. The island must be searched from one end to the other for any clue leading to the murder."

I said, "We understand, Sheriff. And we'll cooperate in any way possible. I feel responsible for what happened to Jim. I should have invited him to be our guest overnight, but I wasn't certain of my present feelings for him, and I wanted more time to think."

"You shouldn't have any guilt feelings, Miss Greyfield,"

Sheriff Eckles said. "You couldn't have foreseen his murder."

"I might have prevented it."

No one replied. How could they? The only answer could be an affirmative one.

I addressed Keith. "How did Aunt Mabel happen to find Jim's body?"

He said, "I could have taken both you girls to Savannah. When I returned from bringing you to the mainland, Aunt Hannah pleaded a headache. Aunt Mabel decided to take a walk in the forest. You know the rest. Except that I had to make a hasty trip to the mainland and walk to the village to report the murder."

I said, "May I be excused? I want to see my aunts."

"Of course, Miss Greyfield."

Sheriff Eckles' tone was kindly, but I knew his eyes followed me as I went up the stairs and entered the house. Small wonder, I thought, since I was the prime suspect. Who but I had reason to wreak vengeance on Jim Canby? He'd humiliated me. But he'd displayed far more courage than I. He'd come here and begged for forgiveness.

I wondered if I'd been hurt as much as my foolish pride. I had only one small consolation. I'd offered Jim financial assistance on his invention. One that would never be completed. I felt a growing anger toward the individual who had plunged a knife into Jim Canby's back.

Aunt Mabel was moaning softly, though Dr. Lind was trying to console her. I stood on the other side of the bed, not certain what to say—not even certain I should speak, except to identify myself to the doctor.

Dr. Lind, a gray-haired man of middle age, said, "I'm going to prepare a sleeping draught for her. The shock of her discovery has been too much. Don't leave her, please. She's been tossing and turning and at times has been irrational."

I moved to the side Dr. Lind had vacated and talked softly to her, but she made no answer.

The doctor busied himself at a table on which was a

small tray, a glass, spoon, and pitcher of water. He poured water into the glass, emptied powdered medication into the liquid, and stirred it vigorously.

He returned to the bedside and gave me the glass to hold while he raised my aunt to a sitting position.

I said, "Drink this, Auntie. It will help you rest."

She opened her eyes and moaned softly when she saw me. "Oh, my dear child. I can't believe it. You must be worried . . ." Her voice trailed off, and she moaned again.

My mouth opened to ask why I should be worried, but the doctor gave a brief negative shake of his head. He took the glass from my hand and brought it to her lips. I feared she might refuse it, but she drank it almost eagerly. He placed the glass on the table and eased her back onto the pillows.

"I'll stay with her until she dozes off," he said. "Please tell Miss Hannah her sister will rest now."

"Thank you, Doctor." I entered the sitting room and moved across it to Aunt Hannah's bedroom. I had a feeling she'd be there, removed from the unpleasantness of what had happened.

I tapped lightly on the partially closed bedroom door.

"Who is it?" came the querulous voice.

"Aldis."

"Come in." The shades were partially drawn against the heat of day, so I couldn't be certain whether the look she directed at me was one of distaste or annoyance.

"I'm sorry it had to be Aunt Mabel who made the gruesome discovery," I said. "I'm even sorrier about what happened to Jim."

"Disgraceful!" Aunt Hannah exclaimed.

"Dr. Lind has given Aunt Mabel a sleeping draught. He wants you to know she'll rest now."

"That poor man." Aunt Hannah said. "I had no idea Jim Canby was on the island last night."

"I told both Keith and Laurie about my meeting with him last night while we were breakfasting. If you'd been present, you'd have heard about it."

"Did you quarrel with Jim last night?"

"I never quarreled with him, Auntie."

"Well," she made an impatient gesture with her hand, "you broke off your wedding."

"I felt at the time I had a good reason for doing so."

"I don't understand that statement."

"Jim told me something last night that shed a different light on his behavior. Oh, he admitted he was intoxicated and his behavior was boorish. But it all happened because of an anonymous letter he had received."

"An anonymous letter?" she asked, eyeing me impatiently.

"Yes. It frightened him. He told me about it last night. We had a pleasant talk—perhaps conciliatory would be a better choice of words. He wasn't a wastrel. Unbeknown to anyone, he was working on a different type of starter for an automobile."

"What are you talking about?"

I explained patiently, knowing she had good reason for being upset. But I was becoming annoyed with her attitude toward me.

"If you'd married him, he'd be alive now."

I couldn't argue that point. "I know."

"Did you quarrel last night?" she asked.

"You already asked me that."

"Are you sure?"

"Do you think I murdered him?" I demanded, unable to hide my growing irritation.

"I hope not." She turned away, as if the very sight of me was distasteful.

"Aunt Hannah, you raised me. Have you ever known of me to display violence toward anyone?"

"No," she admitted. "But you're a very proud person."

"Not *that* proud, I hope."

"I hope not," she said. She sighed wearily and stood up. "I've already talked with Sheriff Eckles. I can add nothing to what I've already told him."

"Just what did you tell him?"

"Only that you were to be married to James Canby and broke off the engagement because of some unfavorable publicity."

"The way you're treating me, I feel as if I was completely in the wrong."

"I didn't say that," she retorted coldly.

"You might as well have."

"I'll not quarrel with you, Aldis," she said. She went to the closet and came out trailing a negligee. "I'm going to lie down and see if I can nap a while. If I'm needed, send Cora to summon me."

"Yes, Auntie." It was clear she wanted no more contact with me than was necessary. She obviously felt I was completely to blame for Jim Canby's murder. It only added to my already guilt-laden mind.

I fought back tears. Not of self-pity, but that a life had been cut off, cruelly and needlessly. I wondered if Sheriff Eckles had seen Setley or his sister. I'd find out immediately. I didn't realize until I was walking along the gallery that I was still wearing my hat. I removed it, tossed it on a long refectory table, and headed for the stairs.

Laurie and Keith had just come in and waited for me in the hall below.

Keith said, "Sheriff Eckles has gone to question Setley. How is Aunt Mabel?"

"Dr. Lind has given her a sedative."

Keith said, "I wish he'd give Aunt Hannah one."

"Why?" I asked.

He made an impatient gesture with his hands. "She's impossible. Blaming you for what happened to Jim."

"Does she really believe I murdered him?" I exclaimed.

He hastened to reassure me. "I'm sure she doesn't. But she's concerned about the publicity that will result."

"I know this sounds selfish, but I wish she'd be concerned about my feelings just once."

"She's concerned about reporters flooding the island," Keith said.

"So am I, now that I think of it. Yes," I acknowledged, "she has reason to be annoyed. I should never have come here. I can see now you can't run away from trouble."

Laurie eyed me with sympathy. "Don't blame yourself for what happened."

"I have to assume some responsibility," I reasoned. "Jim wouldn't have come here if it hadn't been for me."

"He came to thank me," Keith pointed out. "Or have you forgotten the reason he gave you for being here?"

"Yes," I said, "but if I hadn't been so concerned with my own feelings, I'd have stayed in Savannah and given him a chance to explain his behavior."

"You can't undo what's been done," Laurie said wisely. "But from now on, you can tell yourself you'll stop running."

"I've no place to run to."

"You can't leave the island, Aldis," Keith said. "Sheriff Eckles just informed me I was to tell the occupants of the house they're to remain here until further notice. He'll also inform Eulalie and Setley of that."

"I was going to pay them a visit, but I'll wait until Sheriff Eckles leaves."

"Do you think she'll let you in?"

"In view of what has happened, I'm sure she will. On second thought, I'm going to extend an invitation to her to have a quiet dinner with us tonight."

Keith looked thoughtful. "I don't believe she or her brother has ever set foot in this house."

"Then it's time she did," I said. "As my guest. I'll go to the library at once and write the note. Cora can take it."

"Good luck," he said. "There are sherry and glasses in the library. I think a glass of it would do you girls good. I'm going to see Aunt Hannah."

Laurie said, "I could use a glass. So could you, Aldis. Come along."

A slight musty smell still lingered in the room, yet it wasn't unpleasant, for it mingled with the tangy scent of sea air. Laurie had opened the windows wide. Our chairs faced Jayne's portrait. She seemed to be observing us both with approval as we sat sipping the sherry.

Laurie looked at me curiously. "A penny for your thoughts."

"They're grim," I said soberly.

"That's understandable." She glanced up at the face

staring down at us. "I thought your mind had slipped back into the past."

"It has. It just occurred to me that tragedy stalked Jayne just as it did me. The similarity is uncanny."

"Yes," Laurie said quietly, "I was hoping you wouldn't think of it."

I looked up at the portrait. "She was a prime suspect in Scott Morton's murder. I will be in Jim Canby's."

"That's not true," Laurie said sternly.

"Don't let Sheriff Eckles's quiet manner fool you. He suspects me. Who else would have a motive?"

"Setley, for one," Laurie replied promptly. "He could be quite mad, you know."

"If he is, I hope Sheriff Eckles realizes it and puts him where he can do no harm."

"No further harm, you mean," Laurie said.

"We don't know," I reminded her.

"True," she agreed. "But his behavior leaves much to be desired."

"I hope Eulalie Laboulaye will accept my dinner invitation."

"I'm sure she will," Laurie said.

"I'm not. I've met her. Her manner was as hostile to me as her brother's was."

"I wonder why," Laurie said.

"I don't know, but I'm going to find out."

Laurie savored the sherry, swallowed it, then smiled. "You sound angry."

"Perhaps *determined* would be a better word. I'm going to find out why Jim Canby was murdered. I'm going to learn why Eulalie and her brother resent me."

"After what your great-grandaunt did for them, I should think their feeling would be one of deep appreciation."

I disagreed with that. "They owe me nothing. However, I wonder why my aunt deeded them the land and the house."

"Perhaps your aunts know."

It was my turn to smile. "I wouldn't bother Aunt Mabel about it even when she comes out of her drugged sleep. As for Aunt Hannah, it's painful for her to look at me, much less converse with me. Besides, who could tell me more about Jayne Grayfield than Eulalie Laboulaye?"

Laurie struck upon a sudden thought. "I wonder if your aunt kept other diaries."

"She must have."

The thought was so exciting, I almost spilled the wine when I got up. I put the glass on a table and went to the cabinet with the secret compartment. When I opened the doors, Laurie exclaimed aloud, first at the beautiful candlesticks, then at the receding shelf as my hand exerted pressure on the frame above.

I looked down into the interior, but it was so dark I could see nothing. I eased my hand through the narrow space and let my fingers explore the entire base, as well as the walls, to see if there might be a recess somewhere through which the books might have slipped. There was nothing.

"Is there anything there?" Laurie asked impatiently.

"Nothing." I slipped my hand free.

"Let me try." She slipped her arm through as far as the elbow, her fingers engaging in the same search. She gave a little sigh and slipped her arm free.

I loosened my pressure on the frame and the entire back moved into place. I closed the cabinet doors.

"Do you suppose," Laurie asked, "there might be other secret compartments in those cabinets encased among the bookshelves?"

"It's certainly worth investigating."

However, our efforts were of no avail. There were ten cabinets in all, some empty, some containing papers and ledgers dating back to the time of Jayne Greyfield.

"She *must* have kept other diaries," I said.

"It would seem so. The one I read was in such detail. She seemed to like setting everything down on paper. She was daring for her day. Most ladies would never have acknowledged that the gentleman to whom they were betrothed had gained admittance to their bedchamber before marriage."

I glanced up at the portrait. "She was daring, though I'm sure she was a lady."

"A lady with a tragedy that matched yours in almost every detail," Laurie said.

A soft tap at the partially closed door revealed Cora, an envelope in her extended hand.

"For you, Miss Aldis."

"Thank you, Cora." I slit open the envelope and took out the note, scanning it quickly, then passing it on to Laurie. She read it and gasped.

"The nerve of her, refusing an invitation from the mistress of the island," she exclaimed.

"I don't believe she meant to be rude."

I took back the note and read it aloud.

Dear Miss Greyfield:

Thank you for your invitation to dinner. In view of the tragedy of Mr. Canby, I am refusing. I am of the opinion you believe my brother responsible. Or, if not he, then I, and that is the reason for your invitation. To trick me in some way to reveal our guilt. You would be wasting your time. We are innocent of the identity of the murderer.

I can understand your grief since you were to be married to the gentleman, but canceled the ceremony. I learned of this through the newspaper.

Yes, Miss Greyfield, I can read as well as write. And I am as proud as you. However, despite your suspicions of me, I am extending to you an invitation to visit me at any time. I am always here.

Setley will give you no further trouble and I have assured Sheriff Eckles of that.

I extend my sympathies to you in your loss.

Sincerely,
Eulalie Laboulaye

"What beautiful script," I said.

"And what overwhelming pride," Laurie observed. "I wonder if she's really certain of her brother's innocence."

"Why?"

"What was she doing in your bedroom last night?"

"If it was she, though I'm just about certain it was," I exclaimed.

"You said she felt of your hair," Laurie mused.

"And my clothes," I exclaimed in new awareness. "Of course. She wanted to see if my hair was wet or matted from the marsh. Or if the skirts of my clothes were sodden. She must have found Jim's body and wondered if I might have murdered him."

"Or if Setley did," Laurie said.

"What do you mean?"

"If your hair showed evidence of having had contact with the marsh or if your clothes were wet, you could have been the one who plunged a knife into Jim's back. If not, Setley might well have been the murderer. That was what she was afraid of."

I nodded. "It could well be. I'm going to see Miss Laboulaye."

"When?"

"Tonight. After dinner."

"You'll have to go through the forest. I heard Keith give Sheriff Eckles directions. Her house is at the very end of the island."

"I know. I'll approach it from the beach. It's not so direct, but it's open."

"Let Keith and me go with you."

"No."

"Then let me go," she urged. "I don't trust Setley. I don't care how old he is, he still looks as sturdy as an oak."

"I don't doubt that he is," I said. "But I'll be on guard."

"What could you do?" she demanded. "Jim was husky and strong. He could have fought off an attacker."

"If he hadn't been taken by surprise," I said. "I'll be wary."

"Don't go, Aldis," she entreated. "She might be deliberately luring you into that forest so Setley could waylay you."

"It's a chance I'm going to take, and you must promise me you'll not tell Keith."

"I can't make such a promise. Not after what's happened here."

"You must. Otherwise . . ." My voice trailed off.

She smiled. "You can't send me back to the mainland. Sheriff Eckles gave orders no one is to leave here."

"Because of that, I'm certain I'll be safe."

"I wish I could be as certain."

"You haven't given me your promise to remain silent about my visit."

"It's a hard one to give."

I went to her and touched my cheek to hers. "I'm grateful for your loyalty. But I made one mistake—running away. I'll never run again. And I'm not going to run from Eulalie Laboulaye or her brother. I must see her. I want to learn everything I can about her. I want to hear from her lips why my aunt gave her a house and property."

Laurie relented. "I understand. It's just that I have to get used to the change in you."

"I hope it's a change for the better," I said. "I leaned too much on you."

"You had no one," she replied loyally. "Your aunts were dutiful, but not loving. You were lonely and needed companionship. I provided it."

"And I'm grateful. But now I must walk alone. Because there's something else I'm determined to do."

"What's that?" Laurie queried.

"Find out who plunged that knife into Jim Canby's back."

Dinner was a somber affair attended only by Keith, Laurie, and myself. Aunt Mabel was still under the influence of the drug, and Aunt Hannah had sent her regrets through Keith for not coming down to dinner. Dr. Lind had left with a word that he would return the following day, though he felt that by then Miss Mabel would be herself again.

Laurie and Keith went for a stroll on the beach, and I went upstairs to my room to wait until the house had quieted before I went to pay Miss Laboulaye a visit. I sat quietly in the darkness and thought back to my encounter with Jim Canby last night. He had been so eager and—yes, even hopeful. I'd seen it in his eyes. I felt a deep sadness that life had stopped for him. Yet I didn't feel the shock that losing one dear should bring. Was I incapable of such feeling? I hoped not. I knew I felt grief, plus a sense of guilt, but not heartache. Was I like my aunts?

In one way, yes. I ran to avoid unpleasant publicity. I couldn't stand wagging tongues and pointing fingers. I'd have stood them now. I'd have stood anything that would bring Jim Canby back. As for my aunts, they were displeased with me because my running away had brought unfavorable publicity. Jim's murder had added to it and would draw reporters to the island—the one place on earth they considered their refuge, a place where they had come in the past to forget I was their responsibility and burden.

I was grateful for Laurie's friendship. And yet I was aware now I'd leaned on her too much. In doing so, I'd not accepted the responsibilities of womanhood. From this point on, I would do so.

An awareness of my weaknesses—admitting them—was half the battle. Now I must prove I no longer had them. I stood up and moved over to the open window facing the front of the house. Keith and Laurie were returning. Their voices drifted up, but their words were blotted out by the pounding surf.

I hoped Laurie hadn't betrayed my confidence. I doubted she would. I also hoped she wouldn't knock at my door to visit with me. I moved from the window and stood in the center of the room in a listening attitude. I heard her and Keith voice their good nights, followed by the distant closing of a door. That would be Keith's. Then the one across the hall closed. Laurie. I decided to wait a while before I started out for Eulalie Laboulaye's residence.

SIX

I was astounded when I left the beach and skirted the edge of the forest to reach Eulalie Laboulaye's residence. I stopped dead in my tracks when I faced it, for it was a replica, in miniature, of Greyfield Manor. Of course, there wouldn't be the number of rooms that were in the large house, but the stairs leading to the door and the small-paned basement windows were identical in every detail.

I ascended the steps slowly, still marveling and wondering at the strangeness of it. Had I been prepared for it, I'd not have been so startled. But I had little time to think about it, for the door opened and Setley stood there, awaiting my arrival. *They'd been expecting me!*

There was soft light behind him and I had a good opportunity to observe him better. His hair curled tightly against his scalp; it was iron gray in contrast to the soft silver of his sister's. His face was rounded, his nose broad and his lips thick. His skin was dark, yet he had the same blue eyes as Eulalie. He towered over me as I stood before him, and his costume was indeed pre-Civil War. Pants that ended just below the knee were held there with elastic. White silk hose covered his legs. The pants and weskit were a pale blue silk. His shoes glowed with polish and were decorated with a silver buckle. His ears had been pierced and were ornamented with small gold hoops.

"My sister awaits you," he said. "Come."

I thanked him and followed him across the marble floor to what I knew would be a drawing room. The hall was a duplicate in miniature of the house I owned. I wondered if the room I was about to enter would also be a duplicate.

It was not, but only because the furniture here was

much older than what Greyfield Manor contained. It was apparent that my aunts had refurnished the large house. Otherwise I imagined it would be the same in every detail. The dimensions of the room were much smaller, but otherwise there was no change. The fireplace was of marble. The floor was also marble, but with pink hues. However, there *was* one difference. The room was candlelit, though I knew the chandelier in the hall had glowed with small electric bulbs covered with fringed silk shades.

"Good evening, Miss Greyfield. Welcome to Little Greyfield Manor."

Miss Laboulaye had been seated in a large wing chair at the far end of the room. She arose and approached me. Her walk was so regal, it seemed she scarcely moved. She was dressed in a gown of what seemed to be gold and silver threads, for it shimmered beautifully in the soft candlelight. A scarf of the same material was draped on her head. She must have had some sort of frame covering her topknot, for it enabled the fabric to fall in soft folds on either side of her face. One end of the scarf had been draped softly over the opposite shoulder.

Her face was almost completely concealed, yet those blue eyes were startling. Her polite smile revealed white, even teeth. They had to be her own and made me marvel further at her natural beauty—a beauty she still held. I was wearing a simple linen and I felt as if I should apologize for not having donned formal attire for my visit.

I said, "Thank you for letting me come. Since we share the island, we should get better acquainted."

"That is not your reason for coming here, Miss Greyfield."

Her frankness startled me, yet she was right. An intelligent woman, she'd not put up with subterfuge. Therefore, I'd not bandy words, but come to the reason for my visit.

"You're right," I replied. "I came here to learn about you and, I hope, my long-deceased aunt."

"And also to find out, if you could, whether my brother or I have committed murder."

"That, too," I admitted.

"If we were, do you think we'd be fools enough to admit it?"

"You're far from a fool, Miss Laboulaye," I countered. "And you make no attempt to disguise your dislike for me. I'd like to know the reason for it."

She motioned to a chair. "Please be seated. May I offer you some wine or champagne, perhaps?"

"Neither, thank you."

"Coffee, then."

"This is not a social visit. I came here only to seek information."

"Then please sit down. It's awkward for us to be standing here appraising each other."

I was cut by her formal manner, but she was right. It was foolish to act as if we were adversaries, each awaiting the signal to strike the first blow.

I chose a brocade chair, and she took a simple ladderback. Once again she had the advantage, for it enabled her to sit ramrod straight.

"What do you wish to know about me?" she asked.

"Not just about you. I'm equally curious about your brother and his dislike for me—and for any other trespassers on the island."

"A pity he didn't make it evident when Mr. Canby came here."

"What do you mean?"

Her hands, resting gracefully one upon the other in her lap, made a slight gesture. "He'd have had to go to the house and let everyone know of his presence."

"Have you forgotten, Miss Laboulaye, I'm your guest?"

"But not a friendly one."

"I'd like to be," I said. "I realize I'm the one the finger of guilt points to in Jim Canby's terrible death. But I'm innocent."

"You are until proven guilty," she replied in her precise manner. She seemed a highly educated woman and an extremely cold one.

"What are you really thinking?" I asked. Never once had she taken her eyes from my face. I was growing uncomfortable, yet I didn't think she was being deliberately rude.

She said, "I'm astounded by the resemblance you bear to Jayne Greyfield. I am also thinking of how strange it is you find yourself in the same predicament as she."

"Did you know her well?"

"Everyone knew her. She was a great beauty."

"I agree. But I am not a great beauty."

Eulalie's eyes took on a faraway look. "She had an excitement about her that held enormous appeal for the opposite sex. She was also very possessive. A trait the opposite sex does *not* find appealing."

"Did she love Scott Morton?"

"With all her being. Did you know she was the prime suspect in his murder?"

"She was innocent."

"She so stated."

"Didn't you believe her?"

The slender shoulders shrugged. "It is of no consequence what I believed. I was not of her world."

"But you knew her."

"Only slightly. In those days, my skin made me ineligible to mix with white society, despite my European education."

"How did you meet Jayne Greyfield?"

The merest hint of a smile touched her lips. "She took compassion on me, built this home, and deeded it to me along with the land."

"Why?"

She lowered her gaze to regard her slender hands, heavily bejeweled. "I was never quite sure."

"You're lying," I said. "You're playing a game with me. I don't like being made a fool of. Any more than I like your brother acting as if he had the responsibility of guarding Greyfield island."

"I apologize for what he did to you the night you came here," she said.

"You might also extend an apology to Mr. Curran. Or do you know about that?"

She nodded. "I saw what Setley did. I made him come back to the house with me. I wish now I hadn't."

"You mean, of course, if Mr. Canby had been dumped into the water, he'd have come directly to the house for a change of clothes."

"That's exactly what I mean."

"Did your brother see Mr. Canby?"

"No. I told you I insisted he return to the house with me."

"You probably did that to avoid a confrontation with my cousin."

"Keith Greyfield," she said quietly.

"You know him?"

"Only by sight. He brings your aunts here, runs their errands and sees to their welfare."

"Did Setley ever tangle with him?"

"Certainly not. Your aunts have been coming here for years. Setley knows them. You were a stranger."

"Surely you saw my picture in the Savannah newspapers many times."

"I did," she admitted calmly. I was envious of her poise.

"Didn't you show them to your brother?"

"He'd hardly be interested. Nor impressed, I may add."

"Then he really didn't know who I was."

"He did not," she said. "Though it doesn't excuse his behavior."

"I agree. Why did he do it?"

"He thought you were the ghost of Jayne Greyfield. Also, he's old. He wants no change here."

"Did he know Mr. Curran's business on the island?"

"No, but after I brought Setley back to the house, I returned to the forest. I lay in wait for your cousin and your guest and when they appeared, I listened to their conversation. Mr. Curran—your cousin so addressed him—asked your cousin to attempt to persuade you to let this island and the two adjoining ones be developed for sale to private individuals."

"Do you make a habit of prying?" I was amazed at her impudence.

"Call it curiosity. I don't like change here, either. And I'm constantly alert lest it occur."

"It is going to occur, Miss Laboulaye, and there is nothing you or your brother can do to prevent it."

Her serene features tensed. I realized I had finally penetrated her armor.

"Is that necessary, with all your money?" she asked.

"Money has nothing to do with it. I wasn't certain before why I wanted to do it, but I know now. This island has nothing but bitter memories for the Greyfield family. I think the only wise thing for me to do is dispose of it as quickly as possible. I shall ask my cousin to inform Mr. Curran that he may go to work immediately on whatever plans he has for the disposition of the property to private individuals."

She tossed another verbal barb. "That may not be so easy now."

"You're referring to Mr. Canby."

"Yes."

I colored under her steady gaze. "Why do you hate me, Miss Laboulaye?"

"You flatter yourself, Miss Greyfield. I have no interest in you—only the island."

"Why concern yourself with that? You have the right to live here."

Her smile was bitter. "Until I die."

"Setley could remain here also."

"Setley has no claim on this property."

"I'll have papers drawn up allowing him the right to it."

"I should be grateful to you, Miss Greyfield, but I'm not."

Our eyes feuded again, but it was a short-lived one because the sound of men's voices drifted through the open window, followed shortly by the sound of the door chimes. Setley's footsteps echoed in the marble hall, and then his voice raised in welcome. I was astounded at the warmth in it and wondered who the visitors might be. I had no idea anyone came to Little Greyfield Manor, as Eulalie had designated it. I wondered whether she or Jayne had given it that name.

I noticed her face brighten. She knew her visitors and apparently would grant them a far warmer welcome than she had me. I stood up, aware that my presence was now an intrusion.

"I really learned very little," I said.

It was with difficulty she turned her attention back to me. "You may return, Miss Greyfield."

"I *will* return, Miss Laboulaye. I would like to talk with you further regarding my aunt."

"In that respect, you'd be wasting your time."

"Would I, Miss Laboulaye?" I asked heatedly.

She made no answer. I doubt she even heard, for she was looking over my shoulder.

"Miss Eulalie!" a deep, fatherly voice exclaimed, obviously pleased at sight of her. I turned. I'd seen the person, or a picture of him, though I couldn't think of his name.

"Good evening, Senator." Eulalie smiled and extended a hand, which the Senator took and bent over in a courtly fashion.

I knew then. It was Senator Bannon. Ex-Senator, rather. I judged he was in his mid-seventies, and though given to corpulence, he still held himself erect. He was fair-skinned and apple-cheeked, and his small eyes twinkled merrily as he regarded Eulalie. His heavy mane of snow-white hair gave off a soft sheen as it caught the candlelight.

Eulalie made a graceful motion of her hand toward me. "I don't know if you are acquainted with Miss Aldis Greyfield."

He gave me his attention. "I've not had the honor. How much you resemble your late aunt."

I smiled politely. "So I've been told."

He took my hand and bent over it as he had Eulalie's. He was gracious and courtly, still of the old school. I found his manner quite appealing.

He said, "I'm sorry about what happened to Jim Canby. I came here to make certain of the safety of Eulalie and her brother."

"How good of you, Senator." I made my reply gracious, though I felt he had small cause to worry about Setley.

"Have you met my grandson Stanley Bannon?" he asked.

"No, sir," I said.

The Senator looked over his shoulder. "Well, he's here. Probably querying Setley about what has happened. We depend on Setley to look after Eulalie."

I couldn't repress a smile. "I think you have nothing to fear on that score."

The Senator eyed me curiously.

Eulalie walked over to us. "Miss Greyfield doesn't feel kindly toward Setley. And not without cause. He tried to keep her from setting foot on the island."

The Senator eyed me with surprise. "Why would he do such a thing?"

Before I could reply, Eulalie said, "He wouldn't have, had she come with her aunts, but she was alone and it was after midnight."

I said, "I'd like to impress on you again, Miss Laboulaye, your brother is not to attempt to prevent anyone from coming here."

"Even newspaper reporters?" she asked, her face a mask, as usual.

"Even newspaper reporters," I replied coldly. "No one is to be dumped in the water again. I've had enough of that. For myself or a guest or even an intruder."

I'd shocked the Senator with my curt tone. He said, "I'm sure it was an intruder who did away with Jim Canby. Certainly you wouldn't expect anyone on the island to commit murder, would you?"

"I hope it was no one on the island. But, so far as I'm concerned, Setley's behavior has left a lot to be desired."

"What has he done?"

It wasn't the Senator who asked the question, but his grandson, who entered the room with a brisk stride. He apparently misinterpreted my tone, for his mouth was widened in a smile of greeting, and though he eyed me briefly, he went to Eulalie.

"Hello, Eulalie. I'm glad to see you safe, well, and as beautiful as ever."

His presence, as well as his compliment, brought a smile to her lips. I was surprised she was capable of smiling, and I had to admit it enhanced her beauty.

"It's good to see you, Stanley." Once again I was surprised by the warmth of her tone. "Thank you for your concern."

He said, "I wish you'd move to the mainland. At least until the murder of Jim Canby is solved."

"Only one thing would make me move. And you know what that is."

He nodded. "I'm going to work on it in earnest."

"What's happened may make it easier," she said.

"Perhaps," he admitted. "But we want no more violence. Let's hope the murder is resolved and the culprit brought to justice quickly."

Senator Bannon said, "It's almost like history repeating itself. Stan, this is Miss Aldis Greyfield. She was the last person to see Jim Canby alive."

I was astounded by his statement, true though it was. "Does that make me a prime suspect, Senator?" I asked.

His smile was apologetic. "I didn't mean it that way."

"Didn't you?" I countered.

Stanley Bannon approached. "Forgive my grandfather. He has a deep affection and high regard for Eulalie and her brother. I fear he sensed your antagonism toward her."

"She is the antagonistic one, Mr. Bannon, not I. Now please excuse me. I must get back to the Manor."

"I'll accompany you," he replied. "We had a rather difficult time finding our way here."

"Didn't you carry a flashlight?" Eulalie's tone was mildly scolding.

"Forgot it, Eulalie," he said. "But you loan me one and I'll escort Miss Greyfield to the Manor." He turned back to me. "We haven't been formally introduced, but I recognized you from the picture in the newspaper tonight. I'm sorry about everything."

"Thank you, Mr. Bannon. I appreciate your offer to escort me back, but I know my way quite well."

His brows raised slightly. "The papers said this was the first time you'd been on the island since the death of your parents."

"The reporters have been quite active, haven't they?"

"They got the information from Sheriff Eckles. He must have gotten it from you."

"My aunts, more likely. Was the rest of the story in the paper?"

"You mean regarding your visit to Jim's home?"

"Yes."

He nodded. "Everything you told the sheriff was in the paper. I knew Jim slightly. He let me view the invention he was working on. He wanted very much to perfect it. The last couple of years he wasn't the playboy he had been. He wanted to settle down. I knew he was in love. He told me. He was eager for the marriage."

"Thank you for telling me that, Mr. Bannon. I did act hastily. I regret it now."

Senator Bannon eyed me reflectively. "You have the Greyfield pride."

"Rivaled only by that of the Laboulayes," I replied. "Good night, Miss Laboulaye, Senator Bannon, Mr. Bannon."

"I insist on coming with you," Mr. Bannon replied.

"I know my way. I came alone." I softened my refusal with a smile, but my tone was insistent.

He was only slightly taller than I, but he was muscular in build. His dark hair had a slight curl. In the very center was a streak of silver that gave him a distinguished appearance. That and the gray eyes, which were regarding me with puzzlement.

"As you wish, Miss Greyfield." His voice was as deeply resonant as his grandfather's. "I hope you came here with a flashlight."

Eulalie said, "Miss Greyfield skirted the forest to come here."

Her statement came as a surprise. I'd not mentioned it.

"It's longer," Mr. Bannon said, "but easier, of course.

The half-moon that lighted our way across the water was mostly concealed by clouds when we reached the dock."

"I'll accept the loan of a flashlight," I said quietly. It was with difficulty I hid my growing anger toward Eulalie. Apparently Setley was keeping a close check on my movements, but I made no comment. I was tired of feuding with Eulalic. She didn't like me and had invited me here only to soften the snub of her refusal to accept my invitation.

As if by magic, Setley appeared with a flashlight, which he offered to me with a slight bow.

I bade my hostess and her guests a good night and was escorted to the door by Setley, who bowed again.

Before he had a chance to close the door, I said, "Do not follow me. That is not a request, but an order."

"I will obey it, Miss Greyfield." His graciousness, in contrast to my curtness, brought a flush of color to my cheeks.

I went down the steps and headed directly for the forest. It was, indeed, dark, but I turned on the flash, moving its ray slowly across the wealth of trees until I came to a narrow opening. I'd have preferred to take the beach route, for the thick growth of trees looked forbidding, but I had a feeling Setley was watching and I'd not give him the satisfaction of thinking I had the slightest qualms about entering it. I did think of poor Jim and wondered who had surprised him with murderous intent.

Setley was the only one who came to mind, but certainly neither Senator Bannon nor his grandson was of that opinion.

As I moved through the forest, letting the piercing light of the torch precede me, my mind moved from Jim Canby to Eulalie, to Setley, on to the Senator and his grandson. I was surprised to learn the young Mr. Bannon had known Jim. But then, they would be about the same age. He'd been thirty, and I assumed Mr. Bannon was thereabouts. I wondered how the Bannons had become acquainted with the Laboulayes. From their friendliness, I assumed it had been a friendship of long standing.

I thought I heard a sound behind me and turned quickly, spraying the darkness with my light. I saw no one, but it didn't surprise me. Setley undoubtedly knew the forest as well as the house he lived in. I retraced my steps, flashing the light behind trees, moving shrubbery to see if he might have concealed himself behind it, but there wasn't a trace of anyone. Perhaps I'd imagined it. I turned and continued on to the house, using the flash carefully and noting that the light didn't have the brightness it had had when I started out.

I quickened my pace. In so doing, I became careless of my footing and tripped over a tree root that protruded from the earth. In trying to save myself from a fall, I let the flash slip from my hand. The tinkle of broken glass was followed by intense blackness. Not a glimmer of moonlight penetrated the heavily branched and foliaged trees. I didn't even know if there *was* moonlight.

I'd been reckless in taking the forest path. Once again, my foolish pride had taken precedence over my common sense, of which I hoped I had a moderate amount, though I supposed even that was open to question.

Though I'd stumbled, a tree I bumped into saved me from a fall. I wondered how far I'd progressed through the forest and whether it would be better to attempt to retrace my steps in the hope of reaching the clearing and then take the beach route back, or continue on, using my extended arms to guide me along the path. The opening was narrow, but it was there, and if I moved cautiously, I should be able to make my way ahead. I decided on the latter course. Though I'd moved warily, my pace had been brisk. If I'd kept my mind on my progress, instead of letting it become cluttered with the Laboulayes and the Bannons, I might still have my flash. Then I thought of its waning light and wondered if the batteries would have lasted until I reached the Manor. I wasted no more time on suppositions, but extended my arms ahead of me. They touched a tree trunk and I moved slightly to my left. My feet explored the earth. It was covered with pine needles, making it treacherous, but the path had been liberally sprinkled with them, so I guessed I was on the walk.

Though I moved slowly, I seemed to be making headway and breathed a prayer my luck would hold. Try as I might, my eyes could not pierce the darkness. I felt that that was a point in my favor, especially if Setley was behind me. Or was the forest visible to him, even at night? It wouldn't surprise me. I paused to let my searching fingers find a clearing. As I did, the crack of a dead branch pierced the stillness. Apparently it had been stepped on, or brushed against.

I was being pursued. I touched the trunk of a tree to my right and sought its protection. I sensed rather than heard someone approaching. I reached out for another tree and moved behind it. I had no idea whether I was moving in the direction of the person seeking me out, or whether I was moving away from him. It seemed, though, that I was now off the path, for I was having more and more difficulty moving from tree to tree, and the low evergreens were catching on my skirt. My silk stockings were badly snagged and I'd lost one slipper. I slipped off the other. Once I did, I was glad, for my stockinged feet made walking easier.

I wondered where I was and whether I was heading in a direction that would bring me to the beach. I hoped I didn't wander into a shelter where wild horses or pigs were sleeping, especially the latter. I'd not come out of it with a whole skin if I did.

I cried out in horror, for I'd stepped into water. I tried to step out of it and only began to sink in wet sand. I extended my arms, reaching for a branch or tree trunk to hold onto, but in my haste—or panic—I almost lost my balance. I was now knee-deep in the muck and continuing to sink. My hands still sought something to cling to, even pressing into the moist earth as far as I could reach. Then streamers of something moved against my face. I pulled a muddied hand free of the muck and grasped whatever it was, hoping I could pull myself up with it or it would support my weight until daylight. It was Spanish moss, and I gave it such a tug, it fell on me, entangling me more.

I was in mud up to my hips now and my struggles only succeeded in making me sink deeper. I had to call out for help, even if it meant I'd give myself away to whoever was stalking me. At least I'd probably learn the identity of the person who had murdered Jim. Not, I reminded myself, that it would do me any good.

"Help!" I called the word over and over and remained as still as possible. I was sinking more and more deeply into the morass of mud, which was now up to my waist. I didn't know if it was quicksand. If so, I was determined I wouldn't let it claim me without trying to save myself. My arms were still extended their full length, moving slowly, my fingers clawing at air in the hope I'd grasp a branch of some sort that I could use to pull on to extricate myself. Or, if not to free myself, at least to hold myself above the soft earth seeking to claim my body.

My hand touched something warm and I cried out in alarm.

"It's Setley. Give me your hand."

"Are you going to kill me?" I demanded.

"If you don't let me help you, you'll drown in mud."

I believed him and sought his hands. He took a firm hold on both of mine.

"I'm going to pull you out," he said. "It'll hurt, but it's the only way."

"I don't mind. Just please get me out of here."

And it did hurt—I thought my arms would be pulled from their sockets. When I couldn't endure any more, he would let me rest, but for no longer than a minute. For I would start to sink again. Finally, he had me free of the muck. I rested against a tree trunk and closed my eyes. I knew Setley was standing in front of me because I could feel his warm breath on my face.

Even while I was still gasping for breath, I said, "Thank you, Setley."

"When you feel up to it, I'll carry you back to the house."

"I'm afraid you'll have to. I don't think I can walk."

I was trembling with weakness, and wherever my body had felt the pressure of the ooze, it ached.

I finally opened my eyes, but I couldn't see him. "I'm covered with mud. I'll mess up your uniform."

"I have others, Miss Greyfield."

I opened my eyes, still to a stygian blackness that would have made me shudder had I not been too numb with the shock of what I'd been through.

"Please take me back to the Manor, Setley."

He made no answer, just lifted me as effortlessly as if I were a rag doll. But he cradled my body gently, and I rested my head on his shoulder. I wondered just how far I'd progressed when I fell into the quicksand. Had I been close enough to the Manor to have awakened anyone by my screams?

I must have been, for we no sooner reached the clearing than we met Keith. He was tucking his shirt into his trousers and heading for the forest at a loping run. A flashlight was tucked under his arm.

"Who is it?" he addressed Setley.

"It's Miss Aldis," came Setley's quiet reply. "She fell in quicksand."

"Oh, my God." Keith grasped the flash and aimed it at me. "Look at her."

"She's all right, Mr. Keith. She lost her way and walked into quicksand. I got to her in time."

I blinked against the flash Keith had directed at me.

"Didn't you take any kind of light with you?"

"No," I replied wearily. "And please don't scold me. I'm weary and dirty."

"And soaked, besides," Keith said. "Bring her into the house, Setley."

I didn't ask to be set down, for I didn't think my legs could navigate the steps. Setley, still effortlessly, ascended the stairs, with Keith preceding. We'd just reached the door when Laurie appeared, tying the sash of her negligee.

"Oh, dear God!" Her features as well as her voice expressed her concern.

"Don't be frightened." I tried to smile, but tasted mud. "I'm all right. You may set me down now, Setley. And thanks for rescuing me."

"What happened?" Laurie still looked dismayed.

I didn't answer until after I was on my feet and certain my knees wouldn't buckle under me. When I looked down at my clothing, I couldn't believe my eyes. No part of my dress was visible. I walked over to a large gold-framed mirror. My face was covered with the same mud, and it was encrusted in my hair, which had come loose from its pins.

I said, "I returned from Eulalie's through the forest."

"In the darkness?" Laurie exclaimed, her tone unbelieving.

"In the darkness." Keith eyed me with impatience.

"No," I said. "Setley provided me with a flashlight."

"Why didn't you accompany her?" Keith directed his question at Setley.

"I should have," he said.

"I wouldn't let him," I said.

"Then how did you get caught in quicksand?"

"I tripped and when I tried to save myself from falling, the flashlight slipped from my hands. I lost my way in the darkness and ended up in quicksand." I wasn't about to make any mention of Setley or my suspicions of him in his presence.

"You could well have ended up dead," Keith scolded. "I hope you won't be so rash in the future. At least, not until Jim Canby's murder is cleared up."

"I promise," I said. I turned to Setley. "I appreciate all you did. You saved my life."

"If I hadn't heard you, Miss, someone else would have."

"I heard you," Keith said. "But I wonder if I'd have made it in time. I don't know the forest the way Setley does."

"The important thing is," Laurie broke in, "Aldis was rescued. We're grateful to you, Setley."

Even though this uniform was soiled, both from contact with my clothing and his efforts to rescue me, he managed to convey dignity when he bowed.

I extended my dirty hand. "Thank you, Setley."

His eyes expressed their surprise, and I thought I detected a hint of a smile as he took it. He said, "You're welcome, Miss Aldis. Good night."

Keith and I went to the door, and our eyes followed Setley as he made a dignified descent of the stairs. He never paused or looked back once as he headed for the narrow path in the forest that led to Little Greyfield Manor.

I said, "I must get out of these clothes."

"Before you catch pneumonia," Laurie said.

"I'll make a hot toddy for you," Keith said. "Take her upstairs, Laurie."

I tracked mud all the way to my suite. I removed my clothes and showered the mud off, lathering my hair in the process.

I wrapped an oversized Turkish towel around me and came back into the bedroom. Laurie had a nightgown and negligee lying across my bed and she'd drawn down the bedclothes.

She looked at my towel-wrapped head. "You ought to get your hair bobbed. It's a lot more comfortable and a lot less work."

"I'll think about it," I said. "Just now I have more important things on my mind."

"Jim Canby's murder," Laurie said, her tone one of understanding.

"That and something else," I said.

She regarded me with new interest. "Did you learn something at Eulalie's?"

"No. That was a waste of time. But on my way back, I thought I heard someone following me. I'd swear it."

"Setley?"

"I don't know, but it could well have been."

"If he meant you harm, do you think he'd have rescued you?"

"Once I screamed, he couldn't do much more than that. I think he's a consummate actor. Both he and his sister."

"What was she like?"

"Her manner was cold and forbidding. She made no attempt to disguise her dislike of me. She also claimed she knew very little about Jayne Greyfield."

"That's odd, considering what your aunt is reputed to have done for her."

"I don't believe her."

"Somehow I don't, either."

Laurie headed for the bathroom.

"I'll hang up your soiled clothes while you slip into your nightie."

"I tossed them in the bathtub. They can be thrown out tomorrow."

"Oh, no," she called out. "I'll wash them and alter them to fit me. They're beautiful, and the only damage is the salt water."

"Which could wreck that linen."

"I'll find out."

I donned my nightgown and slipped my negligee over it. I was too restless for sleep, even though the clock on the mantel revealed it was after midnight.

Laurie emerged from the bathroom drying her hands on a towel. "I'm sure the dress can be salvaged."

"Let me give you something new," I said.

"Absolutely not. You pay me well and I can buy new clothes. But that dress was a French import and beautiful. I'll make use of it."

I knew better than to argue with her. "I hope I didn't disturb Aunt Mabel."

"I was awake when you screamed. I was reading, so I was first in the hall. But I had no idea where the screams were coming from, so I went to your suite. When I saw the bedclothes hadn't even been turned down, I headed for your aunt's. I met Keith at her door. He'd already gone in, learned she was still sleeping, and headed for the stairs. By then, we knew it had to be you and you were in trouble of some kind. Of course, by then the screams had stopped."

I said, "If I hadn't been annoyed by Eulalie, I wouldn't have tried to return through the forest."

"We were heading for the stairs again when your Aunt Hannah called out. Keith and I went back in. She was verging on hysterics. Keith spoke sternly to her, and she quieted. We didn't tell her you'd gone to visit Eulalie. That would only have upset her more."

"I wonder," I said.

"I think she guessed you were the one screaming because she said, 'Oh, that poor girl' over and over. Keith told me to stay with her. I did, but his running out gave it away. She demanded to know if you were in the house. I had to admit you weren't. She insisted then that I accompany Keith in an effort to find you."

"I'd better go in and reassure her."

"You can if you wish, but while you were under the shower, Keith came to the door. He said he was headed for there."

"Then I shan't bother her until morning."

"I wouldn't if I were you. She was very distraught."

A soft knock on my door announced Keith's return. He had a warm mug of toddy. "Drink this," he said quietly. "Just to make certain you won't get a chill."

I smiled my thanks. "I'm sure I won't, but it will help relax me. I ache all over."

"Rest will also help."

A soft peal of chimes rang through the hall.

Keith looked in the direction of the stars. "Who could that be?"

I said, "I'll find out."

He urged me back into the sitting room. "I will. Keep her here, Laurie. She's been through enough for one night."

Laurie nodded agreement.

"If it's anything important," he spoke over his shoulder as he headed for the stairs, "I'll be back."

"Please come back anyway," I said. "I must know."

He nodded assurance that he would.

Laurie closed the door and guided me over to a large easy chair. She held the toddy Keith had brought. "Sip this, Aldis. You're very pale."

"I think it's nerves more than fear. Though I was terrified when I was sinking in that quicksand."

"Who wouldn't be?"

"It's as if someone is out to get me."

"If that's it, why was Jim Canby killed?"

"I don't know," I said.

"Nor I," she replied. "Any more than I can imagine why anyone would want to harm you. But it almost seems as if someone does."

"Almost?" I queried.

Laurie gave me an apologetic look. "I know what you mean."

I sipped the toddy, and we sat in silence awaiting Keith's return. His soft tap brought Laurie to her feet. She opened the door for him and he came in, closing it softly after him.

"That was Mr. Curran," Keith informed us.

"At this hour?" I exclaimed.

"He received a message asking that he come here immediately. He did so, believing you wished to discuss the proposition regarding the island."

"Was the message supposed to be from me?" I set the half-finished toddy on the table and stood up.

"The message was unsigned."

"Was it mailed or delivered?"

"It was in his key slot at the inn. No one remembered anyone delivering it, but there's no regular desk clerk. The bell summons the owner from wherever he may be on the premises."

"How long has Mr. Curran been on the island?" I asked.

"He said he just came," Keith informed me.

I said, "Perhaps it was he I heard following me in the forest."

Keith looked puzzled.

Laurie said, "Aldis believes someone was following her. She thought it might be Setley, intent on murder."

Keith said, "I doubt it. He certainly had the opportunity."

"Yes," I agreed. "Until I screamed. He couldn't be sure then that someone wouldn't be guided to the spot where I was trapped before I sank beneath the quicksand."

Keith nodded. "You might be right. But weren't you courteously received at Eulalie's tonight?"

"That's debatable."

"Were you there long?" Keith asked.

"Not very," I said. "They had guests."

Both Laurie and Keith looked surprised.

I said, "I'll end the suspense. Ex-Senator Bannon and his grandson."

"Stanley Bannon," Keith said. "Did you know he's going to run for the United States Senate?"

I smiled. "We didn't get that well acquainted."

"Then I don't suppose you know they handle Eulalie's interests."

"You make it sound as if she's wealthy," I said.

"She is," Keith informed. "Also, she was educated abroad. I don't know where she got the money to invest, but invest it she did and wisely."

I remembered her heavily bejeweled hands. "Let's get back to Mr. Curran."

"Let's," Keith agreed. "I'm tired. And so is he. I'd like to offer him the hospitality of Greyfield Manor for the night."

Laurie said, "I wonder if that's wise."

"You mean he might want to gain admittance into this house for the purpose of . . ." He didn't finish the sentence. There was no need.

"That's exactly what I mean," Laurie said.

"Let him stay," I said. "I'm sure we'll be on guard. And if he's involved in some way, he might play his hand."

"Just in case he decides to," Laurie said tartly, "I intend to make certain the doors leading into my bedroom and sitting room are locked."

"I'd suggest you do the same, Aldis," Keith said. "That is, if you're serious about allowing him the hospitality."

"I'm serious," I said. "I'm also weary."

Laurie said, "Finish your toddy."

"I don't need it," I assured her. "What I drank has made me drowsy."

It had, but not so drowsy I didn't lie awake long after I turned off the switch of my night light. I wondered who had written Mr. Curran the message. Or if someone really had. I would ask permission to see it in the morning. In any case, I felt better knowing I'd turned keys in both my bedroom and sitting room doors. I'd also heard Laurie lock her doors after she said good night and went across the hall to her suite.

SEVEN

I was awakened by the sound of voices. It was followed by a soft tapping on my door and then Laurie calling my name.

I slipped from bed and reached for my negligee, donning it as I hurried to the door and unlocked it. Laurie's features were a ghostly white.

"What's wrong?" I asked.

"Your Aunt Mabel," she said. For the first time, she was not her reassuring self.

"What about her?" I prodded.

"She's missing."

"Missing!" I could only visualize her as I'd last seen her, lying helpless and in a deep state of shock at her gruesome discovery.

I said foolishly, "It doesn't make sense."

Laurie pressed her fingertips to the sides of her brow. "Nothing does. I can't understand it."

"How is Aunt Hannah?"

"Hysterical. She's in great need of a doctor. Mr. Curran's gone to the mainland for Dr. Lind."

"Sheriff Eckles should be summoned also."

Laurie looked horrified. "Oh, Aldis, you're not thinking something horrible could have happened to her."

"I don't know what to think. I'll dress and go to Aunt Hannah's suite."

"Please do."

Without another word, Laurie turned and headed for the suite my aunts shared. Though she was more distraught than I, she didn't run for the protection of her rooms. I was grateful to her, though I didn't think she would be any help to my aunt. Laurie was verging on hysteria.

Aunt Hannah paced back and forth wringing her hands and dabbing at her eyes with a sodden handkerchief. I opened the drawers of her highboy until I found a stack of fresh ones. I brought her one and took the sodden one from her. I went into her bathroom and dropped it down a chute that ended in the service room where the laundry was done.

"Where could she be?" Aunt Hannah asked the question over and over. "She was so ill and always so helpless. Mabel never went anywhere without me."

I agreed silently, knowing it was because she hadn't dared. Aunt Hannah had been the dominant one, Aunt Mabel the meek one.

"Perhaps she took a stroll along the beach," I ventured. "Dr. Lind did tell me she should be herself by today."

"She'd never go without telling me."

"Did she tell you yesterday before she went for a walk?"

"No," Aunt Hannah admitted. "But I was stricken with one of my headaches. That's why we didn't go for a sail. I took a powder for it and lay down. I suppose she became restless and went for a stroll. In the forest, of all places. She never went there without me. And we went there rarely."

"Was Jim Canby's body found in our section of forest or Eulalie Laboulaye's?"

"Eulalie Laboulaye's." Aunt Hannah sobered. "We never went to that stretch of forest. We respected the privacy Miss Laboulaye desired. And she did the same for us."

"What about Setley?"

"He never gave us any trouble."

"Did you look in on Aunt Mabel last night?"

"No," Aunt Hannah admitted. "The events of yesterday were a shock to me also. I retired at dusk and slept the night through. When I awakened, I bathed and dressed and went immediately to Mabel's room. Her bed was empty. I checked her bathroom and found the towels unused. I went back to the bed and felt it. It was cold. She'd left it some time ago. I rang for Cora and asked if she had seen Mabel. She denied it, and so did Esther, her mother. Have you met them?"

I nodded. "Yesterday."

"Did you see your Aunt Mabel last night?"

"No. I was out for a while."

Her voice sharpened. "Not strolling the beach, I hope."

"I used the beach to reach Eulalie's. I paid her a visit."

The information shocked her. "Why would you do such a thing?"

This was no time for subterfuge, so I said, "I wanted to question her regarding my Aunt Jayne."

"Why are you so obsessed with *her?*"

"I'm not obsessed with her, Aunt Hannah. I'm curious about her."

"Why?"

"I found a diary belonging to her. It's uncanny how an event in her life parallels one in mine."

"So you know."

"I know."

Her small eyes bored into me. "What good will it do you to learn about that infamous woman?"

"Infamous?"

"Exactly. She added no distinction to the family." Her mouth opened as if to say more, then compressed tightly.

"You mean, becuase she learned the man she was to marry was a rouè?"

"Is that how you thought of Jim Canby?"

Her words cut deeply.

"I'm afraid I did, Aunt Hannah. I realize now I did him a grave disservice."

"Did you know Jayne Greyfield was a prime suspect in the murder of Scott Morton, the man to whom she was betrothed?"

"Did you know she forgave him and was about to elope with him, even going to the pier where he was waiting for her?" I countered.

She indicated her disbelief with a defiant shake of her head. "It's the first I heard of it."

"It happens to be the truth. He never appeared."

"He couldn't because he was dead—murdered. Stabbed in the back—just as James Canby was."

"She didn't do it!" I exclaimed. My tone was one of desperation.

"Why do you defend her?" My aunt's voice rose in anger. "How can you be so sure?"

"Because I found a diary she wrote. She was innocent of Scott Morton's murder. One usually tells the truth in a diary, because it's not meant for other eyes to see."

"The woman is long dead. My present concern is for my sister."

"So is mine," I exclaimed. "I loved Aunt Mabel."

She regarded me with astonishment. "Why do you speak of her as if she were dead?"

"I didn't mean to." I was as distraught now as Laurie had been.

"But you did."

"I'm all mixed up. I—I think I'm frightened."

She disputed that with, "I don't believe you're capable of thinking. I'm beginning to wonder what you're capable of."

I knew what she was implying. I also realized she was as overwrought as I.

"Aunt Hannah, can't we be friends? I had no idea you found me so distasteful."

"It isn't that," she replied. "Both Mabel and I devoted ourselves to raising you. We felt your coming marriage would relieve us of further responsibility and we could take life easy from now on. Instead, you call off your marriage to Jim and come here. He follows and is murdered."

I repressed a sigh. "I didn't tell him where I was going."

"Keith informed the police of where he'd be. I'm as annoyed with him as I am with you."

"I don't feel I need to apologize for my actions, but I will. However, there's no need for you to feel further responsibility for me."

"I suppose not, since you have Laurie to look after you."

"I don't need Laurie or anyone to look after me," I retorted.

"Don't you?" Her smile mocked me.

"Very well, I'll admit I've leaned on Laurie in the past. I shouldn't have. I suppose it was really loneliness. But I assure you I'll depend on no one but myself from now on."

"That remains to be seen," she replied.

I eyed her with new awareness. "You really dislike me, don't you?"

"No." She walked over to a chair and settled herself into it with infinite weariness. "I'm just beside myself with worry over what's happened here. I hate scandal. I love my privacy and I've always had it, as has Mabel. I suppose she leaned on me as you do on Laurie."

I made no answer to that. It was the truth, though I'd not realized it until three nights ago when I'd fled Savannah, seeking the sanctuary of this island.

The bickering ended when Cora appeared at the door with Aunt Hannah's breakfast tray. Despite her emotional state, she brightened at sight of the food. I excused myself and went downstairs.

Keith, Laurie, and Mr. Curran had apparently just settled themselves at the table, for their plates were laden with food.

After exchanging good mornings, Mr. Curran said, "Thank you, Miss Greyfield, for your hospitality. I wouldn't have come here at such an hour, of course, except that I thought you wrote the note asking to see me immediately."

"You know now I didn't, but I'd like to know who did."

"So would I," Keith said.

Laurie offered a suggestion. "Do you suppose it could have been Eulalie? You said her manner was antagonistic when you visited her."

"Perhaps I shouldn't have described it in just that way. I think she regards me as an interloper, just as Aunt Hannah does. And, in truth, my presence has brought unfavorable publicity to Greyfield Island, which I'm sure Eulalie also finds distasteful. She's a highly educated woman."

"None of what's happened is your fault," Laurie said loyally.

"How is Aunt Hannah?" Keith asked me.

"Terribly upset."

"And angry at both of us," he replied. "She's holding me as accountable as you for what's happened. And I suppose I am. But what could I do? The police asked me where I could be found in case I was needed. I had to tell them Greyfield Island. The paper states they passed that information on to Jim. Incidentally, the papers are full of the murder. And now, Aunt Mabel has disappeared."

"Have you made a search of the island?" I asked.

"Yes," he replied. "Not a trace of her whereabouts."

Mr. Curran said, "Even Setley joined in the search when your cousin and I stopped at their place."

"Did you see his sister?" I addressed my question to Keith.

"We didn't go in. Just stopped by asking if they'd seen Aunt Mabel. Setley said they hadn't, nor had she come there."

"I was with the men for a while," Laurie said. "But Eulalie didn't show herself. Perhaps she hadn't got up, but I had a feeling she was spying on us from behind drawn curtains."

"With her, one wouldn't know," I observed.

"Anyway, Keith sent me back to be with your aunt. I stayed there until the men returned."

Keith said, "We searched the forest and walked the entire length of the beach. One side, of course, is swampy and impenetrable. I suppose that's the side where the quicksand traps are. Would you know the location of the one you fell into last night?"

"No," I replied. "But I'm sure Setley would."

At the mention of his name the door chimes pealed. Keith and I exchanged glances. I'm sure he realized as well as I, it portended no good. I regarded my untouched plate, which I'd filled automatically with ham, eggs, and fried potatoes. None of it appealed to me. I took a sip of my coffee and set the cup down quickly when Setley appeared in the doorway with a protesting Cora behind him. I nodded to her that it was all right.

"I found your aunt, Miss Aldis," he said.

"Where?" I asked.

"The same place where you fell in last night. Only she didn't scream like you did. I know she couldn't have, because I stayed up all night, hoping to see if someone was prowling the island. No one was about. At least, not on the beach. I did see that man," he pointed at Mr. Curran, "come here."

"Haven't you had any sleep?" I asked.

He nodded. "About two hours. I went back to the house at dawn. I wanted to check on my sister. She was sleeping. I lay down and napped until Mr. Keith came and asked about Miss Mabel."

I stood up. "Will you please go to the mainland, Setley, and inform Sheriff Eckles of what happened? Ask him to come here at once."

"Right away, Miss Aldis." But before he turned, he eyed Mr. Curran. Whether with animosity or curiosity, I couldn't tell, for his features remained noncommittal.

Keith followed him to the door. They spoke in tones so low their voices didn't carry. Mr. Curran turned his attention to his plate. Obviously, the news of Setley's grim discovery hadn't affected his appetite.

I said, "Aunt Hannah must be told."

Laurie stood up. "I'll do it for you."

"No. I'll tell her."

"You've had one session with her. Why go through another?"

"She's my aunt, and this is going to be very difficult for her."

"It will be for you, too."

"At the moment, I'm so shocked I can't feel anything. Though I wonder how Aunt Mabel ever got there."

"She didn't know about what happened to you last night," Laurie mused.

"When was the last time anyone looked in on her?"

"Probably when we heard you screaming."

"Sheriff Eckles will check on that," I said. "Excuse me."

She regarded my plate. "You haven't touched your breakfast."

"You haven't, either. Nor has Keith. Just now I don't think I could swallow."

I left the room. Keith was still in the hall. He told me Setley had advised him of the area where the quicksand was located. Aunt Mabel's body was still there, with Eulalie standing guard.

He said he'd go there and stay until Sheriff Eckles arrived. I was sure this time he would bring along a posse of men to explore the island.

Aunt Hannah was stretched full length on the bed. She stared at the ceiling, refusing to talk. She'd not spoken a word after I told her the grim news. I hoped Sheriff Eckles would bring Dr. Lind with him. Then I remembered Dr. Lind had promised to return to check on Aunt Mabel.

I summoned Laurie, who was in her suite, and asked her to remain with my aunt. Cora gave further assurance that she would be in the sitting room, should she be needed. Laurie seemed relieved at the news. For the first time, I felt I was more in command of the situation than she. It was understandable. She was a part of this through no fault of her own.

I left the house and headed for the forest, turning in the direction that led to Eulalie's. I had no idea of where the area was, but I knew I'd need only to call out and Keith would answer.

I caught a glimpse of movement through the trees. I wasn't certain it was he, but I stepped off the path and started to thread my way through the tree trunks, which grew tall, thick, and close together. A light touch on my shoulder stayed me. I turned to see Eulalie's face only inches from mine. The floral fragrance of perfume she used touched my nostrils, even above the fragrant scent of pine.

She held up a lace-edged handkerchief. I knew it was mine even without seeing my initial embroidered in one corner.

I thanked her as I took it, adding, "I must have dropped it last night."

"No," she replied, her manner coolly serene. "I found it near the body of Mr. Canby the night he was murdered."

Her statement caught me by surprise. "You found Jim Canby's body before Aunt Mabel did?"

"Yes."

"Why didn't you have your brother report it to the police?"

"It wouldn't have helped Mr. Canby."

"So that's why you came to my suite. To see if I was the murderer."

She nodded. "And to see if it was you who stole the hunting knife from the workshed my brother uses."

"It's missing?"

She nodded. "The empty scabbard is still there."

"Do you think I killed the man I was to marry?"

"If I knew for a certainty it was you, I'd report it to the police."

"Was it fear that kept you from reporting your discovery of the murder?"

Her brows raised slightly. "What did I have to fear?"

"After your brother's behavior toward strangers who venture here, don't you think he might be a suspect?"

"Setley wouldn't commit murder."

"I wish I could be as sure."

"He could have let you drown in the quicksand last night."

"Perhaps he intended to, but when I screamed, he could do nothing but come to my rescue. Or didn't you hear me scream?"

"We heard you," she replied, her tone now as cold as mine.

I held up the handkerchief. "Why didn't you present this to Sheriff Eckles as evidence?"

"It would only cast more suspicion on you."

"Do you think I murdered Mr. Canby?"

"I have no idea who did it. Nor who placed the body of 'our aunt in the quicksand."

"What makes you think my aunt was murdered?"

"She was drugged. Therefore, quite helpless. She :ouldn't have walked there."

I said, "I think it's strange Setley was so convenient vhen I fell into the quicksand and it was he who discov-:red my aunt's body."

"He knows this island. You aunt's hand was protruding rom the quicksand."

"How did you know my aunt was drugged?"

"There are ways."

"Do you make a habit of entering Greyfield Manor vhenever you wish?"

"Only when I feel there is need for it. The doors are ıever locked. But if you state to Sheriff Eckles I did so, I hall deny it. It will be your word against minc. Despite he disadvantage of my color, I am known on the main-ınd. There has been no trouble here—until you came."

"Haven't you forgotten the murder of Scott Morton?"

"She canceled the marriage. Just as you did."

"She was going to elope with him. You must know hat."

A flicker of surprise crossed her face. "I did not know . I know you were the last to see Jim Canby."

"I'm sure I was not the last to see my aunt."

"It doesn't matter now."

"It matters very much. Particularly since you say she vas murdered. Also, you know she was drugged. Did you isit her bedroom also?"

"I have nothing more to say."

I looked at her with new awareness. "I have. I know ow you are familiar with Greyfield Manor, if not by legal ıeans, then by illegal."

She made me no answer.

"I also know you had the audacity to enter my suite. 'ou examined my clothes and also touched my hair."

"I would have no motive to kill Mr. Canby."

"That's open to question."

Her features tensed and I knew I'd finally succeeded in piercing her armor.

"Why should I murder a man I'd never met?"

"To throw suspicion on me."

"Why?" Her voice was almost a hiss.

"Because you hate me with the same intensity you hated my aunt."

"The one lying in there?" She pointed to the area where Keith was standing guard over Aunt Mabel's body. He seemed unaware of our presence, but our low voices could have been drowned out by the pounding surf and the squawking of seagulls.

"No," I replied. "I'm referring to Jayne Greyfield, and I'm certain you knew that."

"I have already told you I was scarcely acquainted with her."

"That still wouldn't have prevented you from hating her."

"Our worlds were separate in those days. You should know that, having been born and raised in the South."

"I still believe you knew my aunt. I also believe hated her."

"Strong words, Miss Greyfield."

"I agree. And I don't make such an accusation lightly." I opened my palm, still holding the crushed handkerchief. "Please take this and present it to Sheriff Eckles. I agree, I am the most logical suspect in Jim Canby's murder."

She disdained even a glance at it. "No. Do with it what you wish. If Sheriff Eckles wants to see me, I will be at Little Greyfield Manor. That also applies to you."

"Miss Laboulaye."

She was already threading her way through the trees to the path, but paused and turned to regard me. "I did not murder my aunt. As yet, we have no proof she was murdered. Nor did I murder Jim Canby."

"You do not have to convince me, Miss Greyfield. Only Sheriff Eckles."

I nodded. There was nothing further to say. I was sure that if I'd even thrown myself prostrate before her, she would still not have become less aloof. She disliked me in tensely, and some inner instinct told me she had disliked Jayne Greyfield to the same degree. I wondered why. But I had no time to think about it. Keith had spotted me and was headed my way.

"Don't go in there, Aldis," he said when he reached me.

"Why not?" I asked.

"You shouldn't see Aunt Mabel like this."

"I was in that same place last night. I wonder what brought her here."

"We'll never know," he said. "I'm wondering if Eulalie might know."

"She only just left."

He nodded. "She was here when I came and directed me to the spot. Did you know Aunt Mabel used to meet her here in this part of the forest? She even had tea at Eulalie's."

I was incredulous. "I'm surprised Aunt Hannah would have allowed it."

Keith said, "Eulalie told me Aunt Hannah didn't know. Aunt Mabel managed it only when Aunt Hannah had one of her migraine headaches, which lasted for two or three days. Aunt Mabel used the excuse for leaving the house alone that she needed some exercise and fresh air."

"Poor Aunt Mabel. I wonder why Aunt Hannah held such a tight rein over her."

"Why don't you ask?"

"I will."

"Don't forget, she held a tight one over you, too. I'm glad to see you taking matters into your own hands."

"I've really not done so yet," I reminded him.

"You're making a good start. You leaned on Laurie too much."

"Strange that such a thought never occurred to me until I came to this island. I'm really ashamed of myself."

"Don't be. You're quite a young lady now."

"I'll never forgive myself for running away. I've certainly set a terrible chain of circumstances into action."

"Aunt Mabel must have been in a daze when she came here."

"Eulalie thinks she was thrown into the quicksand."

Keith was as shocked as I. "Did she say that?"

"I'm the number-one suspect in her mind."

I still held tightly on to the handkerchief. I wondered if I should mention it to Keith. Or should I give it to Sheriff Eckles? Was it possible Jim could have appropriated it on an evening when we were together? As a souvenir—or a memento? I couldn't recall his doing so. I couldn't even remember if I'd had this particular handkerchief with me when I'd been in Jim's company. I decided to remain quiet about it for the time being. Even though suspicion was directed toward me, so far as I knew, there wasn't a single clue that would place me at the area where Jim's body had been found. I didn't even know where that location had been.

I said, "Was Jim's body found near here?"

"Yes," Keith replied. "Aunt Mabel found it, as you know, while out for a stroll. Perhaps on her way to Eulalie Laboulay's, since we now know they were friends."

I knew that Eulalie and Setley had found it long before Aunt Mabel had. Why had they remained silent about it? Why had she told me? To taunt me?

Before Keith could protest, I moved forward to the area where Aunt Mabel's body lay. I cried out when I saw her mud-covered form. Both arms were raised, the fingers clawed as if she'd tried to grasp something to save her from the deadly quicksand. Only she hadn't been as lucky as I. If she had slept off the effects of the sleeping draught, why hadn't she cried out when she slipped into the deadly trap? That had been my first thought, once I realized I couldn't free myself.

Could Eulalie have been right? Had Aunt Mabel been brought here in an unconscious state and thrown into the quicksand? Her upraised arms disputed that. Yet why would she come here? Had she been on her way to Eulalie's? Had Eulalie or Setley waylaid her? It seemed difficult to believe, since he was the one who came to the house to announce finding her body. But perhaps he could do little else, since that would be the first place I'd think of if anyone should disappear. How could I be certain Setley would have rescued me if I hadn't shouted for help?

Someone had been following me. Of that I was certain. And who else but Setley?

Keith spoke softly from behind me. "Please, Aldis. Go back to the house. Someone should be there beside Aunt Hannah. We can't expect Laurie to assume responsibility."

He was right. "I'll send Sheriff Eckles here as soon as he comes."

"I'm sure he'll bring others with him. Also Dr. Lind."

"I hope so. Aunt Hannah seems to be in shock. She never uttered a word, once I told her Aunt Mabel's body had been found."

"Then please get back there. You can't do anything here."

I gave him no argument, for I felt ill. And more responsible than ever for all the dreadful things that had happened.

When I returned to the house, Esther, her eyes swollen from crying, informed me Mr. Stanley Bannon was awaiting me in the library. She expressed her regrets at what had happened and told me she would bring me some refreshments into the library. She insisted I had to eat. She'd made Miss Laurie take food. She also said that Mr. Curran was in the drawing room and that was the reason she'd asked Mr. Bannon to wait for me in the library.

I thanked her and went to see him, wondering about his reason for coming. I'd felt a certain enmity between the Bannons and me, and yet it could have been in my mind. Eulalie's unfriendliness toward me didn't have to mean her friends or acquaintances felt the same antagonism.

Mr. Bannon, looking quite distinguished with the streak of silver through his dark hair, was standing before the fireplace, looking up at the portrait of Jayne Greyfield. At the sound of my footsteps, he turned.

"I'm sorry about your Aunt Mabel," he said, his manner solicitous. "Esther told me. Whatever prompted your aunt to go into the forest at night?"

"We don't know that it was at night," I replied. "But thank you for your expression of sympathy."

"I came here to express my regrets at what happened to you last night and hope you'd fully recovered."

"I did," I said. "It was good of you to come."

"Frankly, I also came for another purpose, but in view of the sad news I received when I came here, that can wait."

"What sort of purpose was it?"

"I'd rather not discuss it at this time."

"Why not?"

"It would be most inappropriate."

"Mr. Bannon, I have quite enough riddles and questions running around in my mind without you adding to them. I really would like to know the reason for your visit."

"Well, first of all, as I said, it was to inquire about your health. We didn't hear you scream for help last night. We met Setley on our way back to our boat. He informed us of what had happened to you. I was going to stop at the Manor then, but he told us you had already gone upstairs. I wasn't about to disturb your rest, which you were badly in need of. Thank God, Setley heard your call for help."

I remembered Eulalie saying she had heard my cry. "My cousin Keith Greyfield and my friend Laurie Cummings also heard me. I think they'd have reached me before I went under."

"I hope you won't traverse the forest at night alone after this."

"Apparently I wasn't alone."

His brows raised questioningly. "I don't understand."

"Setley was following me. When I cried out, he came to my rescue."

"I'm sure he was following only to see that you reached the Manor safely."

"I'm not so sure. Particularly since I just talked with his sister and she said all of you heard my cries for help."

"Perhaps you misunderstood her."

"I didn't. Any more than I misunderstood your antagonism and that of your grandfather toward me."

He smiled. "I am sorry about that. You see, we've

known Eulalie a long time. My grandfather's law firm—and mine—handles her affairs. She's a lady of integrity."

"What about *her* veracity?"

He frowned. "Perhaps she heard you and we didn't."

"If so, don't you think it odd she didn't mention it?"

"Yes." Though his eyes looked thoughtful, his reply had been immediate. "But I still hope you'll not go into the forest again at night—when you're alone."

"If I'd taken the beach area as I intended, I'd not have lost my way."

"Why didn't you?"

"I was annoyed and felt the forest would be the most direct route back."

"It would have. I'm sorry I displeased you last night. Be assured it won't happen again. But don't let that Greyfield pride make you foolhardy again."

"I shan't. I learned my lesson." I eyed him with new interest. "What do you know about the Greyfield pride?"

"Only what my grandfather has told me. He knew your Aunt Jayne well."

He turned and regarded the portrait. Her eyes seemed to hold a hint of approval of both of us. I quickly thrust the foolish thought from my mind.

I said, "You still haven't told me your other reason for coming here. Was it business of some kind?"

"I'd say it was more of a philanthropic nature."

"I am puzzled, Mr. Bannon."

Before he could reply, Esther came in with a large tray on which were a plate of sandwiches, individual puddings, a jellied salad, and iced tea.

I said, "Esther thought you might join me in a little lunch."

"I'd be delighted," he said.

She set the tray on the large desk and spread a cloth on the tea table. She laid service for two and placed our dishes on it.

I said, "Esther, if Dr. Lind comes with Sheriff Eckles, please send the doctor up to my aunt at once."

"I will, Miss Aldis," she promised.

"Has my aunt come out of it at all?"

"Not a bit. Just lyin' on that bed and ain't sayin' a word. Your aunts were real close."

"I know," I said. "I'll be up to see her shortly."

"Better you stay away until after the doctor sees her, Miss."

"Yes," I agreed. It was good advice. I didn't want to upset Aunt Hannah further.

Reassured, Esther left the room, closing the door softly behind her.

"Had you ever met my aunts?" I asked Mr. Bannon.

"Only Miss Mabel. I met her at Eulalie's." He smiled at my astonishment. "I suppose she never told you because she knew her sister wouldn't approve of her going there."

"Did Aunt Mabel and Miss Laboulaye get along well?"

"Oh, yes. Your aunt thoroughly enjoyed her visits there. She came whenever the opportunity presented itself."

I knew what he meant. Keith had already told me. Pity flowed through me at the thought of Aunt Hannah, and I wondered if she realized how much she'd missed by her austere way of living. At the same time, I felt a wave of compassion for Aunt Mabel, who'd never dared rebel against Aunt Hannah. I wondered if my aunt had wandered into that quicksand accidentally, or if she had been lured there. Or worse still, had she been carried there?

We'd no sooner seated ourselves than Esther's voice, raised in anger, drifted through the half-closed door of the room. I went to the door and opened it. I saw no one except her, her hands on her ample hips, her eyes flashing fire.

"What is it, Esther?"

She came over and in a low voice said, "I caught that Mr. Curran with his head pressed up against this door listenin' to you and Mr. Bannon. He got no business doin' that. You want to order him outa the house, Miss Aldis?"

"I would, but I can't now, in view of what happened to my aunt. I'm sure Sheriff Eckles will want to question him as well as the rest of us."

"That's right." Her eyes flashed fire as they glanced down the hall toward the drawing room where I was sure Mr. Curran had retreated. "I forgot he spent the night here. Hope it's the last one. I don't trust him."

"Why not, Esther?"

"Just don't, Miss Aldis. Just don't."

She turned and headed toward the kitchen, but not without giving a final disgusted glance toward the drawing room. For the first time, I wondered if Mr. Curran had really received that note.

I closed the door again and went back to the table. After Mr. Bannon seated me and resumed his chair, I told him what had happened and expressed my wonderment about Mr. Curran's eavesdropping.

He said, "I think I know."

"Please tell me."

"Dennis Curran wants this island and the two adjoining ones, doesn't he?"

"How did you know?"

"It's my business to know everything about this state, including its islands—both private and public. I'm running for the United States Senate in the spring."

"Except for that streak of silver in your hair, you don't appear old enough."

"I qualify. I'll be thirty-one in two months."

"You still haven't explained why Mr. Curran should be concerned about you."

"I told you I felt it wasn't the proper time. I still feel that way, but in view of Mr. Curran's behavior, I believe I should."

"Oh, yes, I remember," I said. "You said it was of a philanthropic nature. We were distracted from the subject when Esther came in with the food. Tell me, please, while we eat."

"As you know, a Senator is elected by the people. It is his duty to do all he can for them and to let them have a share, as much as possible, in the bounties of the state."

"I agree with that."

"Well, with your vast wealth and your possession of

three of the islands which abound along this coast, I wondered if you would consider turning one of them over to the state to be developed for the enjoyment of the people."

"Does Mr. Curran know of this?"

"Eulalie informed us he's been hired by private interests to persuade you to let him or the firm he represents lay it out for development by people who could afford to buy property and build on it. To do that, it would still be private."

"I know."

"Had you considered Mr. Curran's proposal?"

"I had." I replied without the slightest hesitation. "And my mind is made up to go through with it."

"In that case, we can drop the subject."

"Have you forgotten—I don't own the entire island?"

"You're referring to Eulalie's house and land deeded to her by your aunt." He glanced up at the portrait, then back at me.

"I am."

"Eulalie likes the idea of turning the island over to the state."

"What would *she* do?"

"Move to the mainland."

I was incredulous. "She's willing to deed her share of this island and the house on it to the state?"

"Yes."

"That does surprise me."

"Why should it?"

"She dislikes me so much that I can't imagine her leaving this island, if for no other reason than to spite me."

"Perhaps you'll reevaluate your opinion of her when I tell you she feels it's selfish to keep all this land private. Not only the land, but the beautiful beach."

"What do you think, Mr. Bannon?"

"I agree with her."

"It would be quite a feather in your cap if you could dangle these islands before the public. It would gain you a lot of votes."

"I agree, but that wasn't my reason for doing it."

His eyes rebuked me. I colored with embarrassment

and was on my feet before he could move around the table to assist me.

I said, "I'm sorry. I don't know what's got into me. I suppose it's because I know I'm the most logical suspect in Jim's murder and I'm on the defensive."

I walked over to stand before the fireplace. I was dry-washing my hands without even being aware of what I was doing.

He followed and moved around to face me. "You came here seeking refuge and it's turned into a living nightmare that's left you frightened. It's understandable."

"Also," I said, "I feel responsible for what's happened."

"You aren't." He took my hands in his and held them gently. It did have a calming effect on me. I managed a smile which he returned.

"That's better," he said. "I want us to be friends."

"Thank you," I replied. "I need another friend. I have one. Laurie Cummings."

"I've met her and talked with her briefly. She went back upstairs to stay with your aunt."

"She's been my tower of strength."

"I think you're doing quite well on your own."

I made a negative move of my head. "I wasn't until this happened. Not until Jim's murder did I realize the extent to which I'd gone to avoid the responsibilities of adulthood."

"I know it hasn't been easy for you here," he said. "But let me help you change all that, Aldis. I'll make an admission. I know Eulalie has made it as difficult for you as possible."

I regarded him with surprise. "You do?"

"I didn't until this morning when I was breakfasting with my grandfather. He commented on the fact that Eulalie harbored a great resentment toward you."

"Why?" I asked.

His smile was quizzical. "I'm not sure, but I think your Aunt Jayne has something to do with it."

"So do I," I said. "I found a diary of my aunt's in which she talked about Scott Morton, her love. He too was murdered."

"My grandfather discussed the similarity of his death and Jim's at breakfast. It's strange."

I studied the portrait. "Was she accused of murdering Scott Morton?"

"Suspected," Mr. Bannon said.

"Just as I'm suspected of murdering Jim, and I'm innocent."

"I'm so sure of it I want to help uncover the identity of the murderer."

"Do you have any way of going about it?"

"First, I'll talk with Sheriff Eckles."

"Do you mean you'll represent me?"

"I'd be honored to have you as a client."

"I'll be grateful, Mr. Bannon."

"Don't look so humble. And, despite the business arrangement, the name is Stanley—Stan for short."

"I like it," I said. "But about Jim's murder. He told me the night I met him on the beach that the reason for his behavior was that he'd received a letter threatening to reveal that he'd had an alliance with another girl. He believed the writer was that very girl. He learned where she was and went to the restaurant, where he created the scene that led to my canceling our wedding plans and fleeing to this island."

"Did you see the letter?"

"No. And no mention was made of it by Sheriff Eckles. I'm wondering whether it was on Jim's body or might still be at his home."

"I'll certainly investigate it. And I'll let you know if Sheriff Eckles located it. If not, I'm sure he'll see if it can be found."

"He should be here soon." I thought of the night Eulalie invaded my suite, but refrained from mentioning it. I wanted no further unpleasantness between Stan and me. I liked him and felt he wanted to help me.

I said, "I'll give a lot of thought to deeding this island and the other two over to the state. It's a good cause."

"You have enough on your mind now. I shan't be running for office until next year. I'm plotting my strategy ow. Also, I only meant one island. Of course, this is the argest, and the best."

"After what's happened here, no one may want it. It's lmost as if it's cursed. I told you I found a diary written y my aunt. She was innocent of Scott Morton's murder. ust as I am innocent of Jim Canby's. And now, Aunt Mabel. A dear, gentle soul."

"I know. If she was murdered, whoever did it will be unished. Unless it was the act of a person bereft of his enses."

The door chimes pealed. Stan released my hands. He aid, "I'll help all I can."

I thanked him and we walked from the room. In the all, a sudden thought occurred to me. "Your grandfather old me he knew Jayne Greyfield."

"It was his father who really knew her for the belle she was. But yes—my grandfather was acquainted with her, hough a lot of what he knew was what he heard or earned from his father. Why?"

"I'd like to talk with your grandfather about her," I aid.

"Tonight." He made it a statement.

"I'm not sure I'll be allowed off the island."

"As my client, you will be. We have a small house in e village we come to in the summer. A pity you never ame here before. I'm sure we'd have met."

"We have now, and I'm grateful for your offer of help."

Esther had the door open and Sheriff Eckles entered rst, followed by Dr. Lind. Relief flooded through me at ght of him.

"Will you come upstairs with me, Doctor? Aunt Hanah collapsed when she learned the news."

"I'm so shocked, I can't think of the proper words to xpress my condolences."

"I understand."

Sheriff Eckles was regarding me with apprehension, as he wanted to prevent me from accompanying Dr. Lind ut wasn't quite certain how to stop me.

Stan said, "I'll be responsible for Aldis. She's just gaged me as her attorney."

Sheriff Eckles looked relieved. "Fine, Stan. Run along, Miss Aldis. I'm sorry about your aunt."

"Thank you, Sheriff. Keith is in the forest guarding my aunt's body, Sheriff."

"Four men are already on their way there. Nothing can be touched until I get there, but I want to know first who was in this house last night."

"I'll take over, Aldis," Stan said. "Your Aunt Hannah needs attention now."

I nodded and joined Dr. Lind, who had halted his ascent to wait for me. I noticed Mr. Curran standing in the doorway of the drawing room. Sheriff Eckles noticed him also. I wondered if he observed the look of apprehension on Mr. Curran's face.

EIGHT

Dr. Lind suggested I remain in the sitting room until after he'd talked with my aunt. It was sensible, since she'd made her animosity quite plain. At present, I didn't wish to add to her mental turmoil. But I was surprised when Cora came out of the bedroom.

"Isn't Miss Laurie with my aunt?"

"No, ma'am," came the somber reply. "Miss Hannah asked me to stay with her."

I didn't question her further. I knew the reason for it. "You may go downstairs now. Thank you."

"You're welcome, Miss Aldis. If you aunt needs anything, just pull the bell cord." She pointed to the petit-point bell pull hanging alongside the fireplace. "There's another by her bedside. I'll keep my eyes open for the signal."

After she closed the door behind her, I headed for Aunt Mabel's room. I wondered if there might be something there that would give a clue as to why she had left her bed. I couldn't convince myself she had been taken from it while in a drugged sleep. It was too outrageous to contemplate.

The bed was unmade, but the bottom sheet had scarcely a crease, proof she'd lain motionless, her mind at ease, thanks to the sleeping draught Dr. Lind had administered. I noticed one of the pillows was on the floor on the far side of the bed. It had probably slipped from the bed and she'd made no attempt to pick it up. Evidently, she'd still been a little groggy from the drug, and the effort of bending seemed too much. I looked around for her nightclothes. There wasn't a sign of them. I checked her bathroom, but found no evidence of them there. Her towels and wash-cloth were folded neatly on the rack. I felt of them. Not only were they dry, they gave no appearance of having been used.

Not being familiar with her wardrobe, I wouldn't be able to tell if any of her clothes were missing. Nor could I tell what she'd been wearing from what I'd seen of her still form as it lay on the ground, for she was covered with mud. Her hair and face were also, and the sticky ooze dripped from her clutched hands.

I returned to the bedroom, bent, and picked up the pillow. I turned to place it on the bed.

"What are you doing in here?"

The voice was so harsh, it was unidentifiable. I turned. It was Sheriff Eckles, his face crimson with rage.

I said, "I came in here to see if there was a clue to the reason for my aunt leaving the house."

"Inasmuch as we don't know if your aunt's death was an accident or murder, you have no business in this room. Put that pillow where you found it."

"It was on the floor."

"I know that. I saw you pick it up. Put it back exactly where you found it."

I did so, then walked to the doorway. Sheriff Eckles moved aside for me so I might continue on to the sitting room.

He closed the door leading into Aunt Mabel's bedroom. "No one is to set foot in that room until given permission."

"I understand."

"I've already given orders to your cousin and the servants regarding that. Oh—Mr. Bannon aksed me to tell you he's gone to Miss Eulalie's."

I nodded, but made no comment, though I wondered why Stan had gone there. Then I remembered. He was her attorney.

Sheriff Eckles said, "Please sit down, Miss Greyfield. I'd like to ask you a few questions."

"I'll stand if you don't mind, Sheriff." I was too nervous to sit.

He moved over to the fireplace, regarded it thoughtfully, then turned to face me. "When was the last time you saw Miss Mabel?"

"Yesterday afternoon after you carried me back here. When I excused myself to go upstairs, I went directly to her room."

"Did she talk to you?"

"No. She was in a highly emotional state. I'd say she was in shock."

"Dr. Lind has already confirmed that." He worried his chin with thumb and forefinger. "Did she make any statement to you?"

I pressed my fingers to my brow and thought back in an effort to recall her exact words.

"Come, come, Miss Aldis, either she did or she didn't."

"She did. I'm trying to remember her exact words. Oh yes. She said, 'Oh, my dear child. You must be worried' . . ."

He frowned. "Go on."

"That's all she said. Her voice trailed off then. I was about to ask what it was I must be worried about, but Dr. Lind indicated I was not to speak with her. He told me to inform my aunt her sister would be all right. He'd just given her a sedative."

"And that's the last time you saw Miss Mabel."

I lowered my eyes. "Until I saw her body lying alongside the pool of quicksand. Did you know I fell into it last night?"

Sheriff Eckles's look of surprise was such that I knew Setley hadn't told him about it. It would be like Setley. He'd wait for me to reveal my misadventure.

I said, "Setley heard my cry for help and rescued me."

"How did you happen to get off the path?"

I told him about tripping and losing the flashlight that had been loaned me by Eulalie and Setley. I did not tell him about fearing I was being followed. I had a feeling his suspicions of me were growing by leaps and bounds. To mention my own fear that I was being followed would make him believe I was trying to divert suspicion from myself.

When I finished my story, he said, "You're not to enter this suite for any reason, Miss Greyfield."

"You do suspect me, don't you, Sheriff?"

"Suspicions aren't accusations. As I said before, I'll keep an open mind. What I'm really searching for are clues. But you must admit, you're the most logical suspect in Mr. Canby's murder."

I countered his statement with, "It hasn't been proven my aunt was murdered."

The distrust in his eyes was replaced with a hint of respect. "You're right, Miss Greyfield. I hope she hasn't been. However, Dr. Lind said the sleeping draught he gave her should have kept her sedated until mid-morning. Do you know when her absence was discovered?"

"Not the exact time. My aunt would be better able to tell you that."

"Then I'll talk with her. I'll also want to talk with Miss Cummings."

"I'll tell her."

"In the drawing room, please."

I said, "I believe Dr. Lind may give my aunt a sleeping draught. She's in a highly emotional state."

"He assured me he'd not do it until I talked with her—unless she was hysterical."

There was nothing more to be said. I headed for the door, impatient to get away from this man whose eyes seemed to bore into my very brain. He was being cautious, but I was well aware that he questioned the veracity of my replies.

"Oh, Miss Greyfield."

I turned.

"Stan Bannon said he would be responsible for you."

"He offered his services as my attorney," I replied coolly.

"He told me. Just don't get any ideas about going off on your own."

"Sheriff Eckles, I'm as anxious to solve the mystery of these terrible events as you. And I don't like being treated as a criminal."

"I don't like murder, Miss Greyfield."

"At least that's one thing we agree on."

I turned and moved abruptly from the room, my mouth compressed tightly, lest I lose my temper altogether. I headed for Laurie's suite, believing she might be there. If ever I needed someone to restore confidence in myself, it was now.

"What are you doing?" I exclaimed.

It was a silly question, since Laurie was in the process of packing the two pieces of luggage that lay open on her bed.

Her smile was apologetic when she turned. "I can't stay here, Aldis."

"You can't leave," I countered. "None of us can."

"I'm going to ask Sheriff Eckles' permission to return to Savannah. I'll give him my word I'll not leave the city."

"You'd be better off here than rattling around that large house in Savannah."

"I won't be rattling around in your big house. I'm going to rent a room in the city and find a job." She turned and slipped the folded silk stockings into a side pocket of the bag.

"Why?"

She gave an audible sigh. "Your Aunt Hannah made it plain I've worn out my welcome."

"Have you forgotten I'm the mistress of Greyfield Manor, as well as the house in Savannah? I'd hate to have to make it plain to my aunt that she's living in this house on my bounty, especially in view of what happened to Aunt Mabel. But I will do so if you leave because of her rudeness."

"I don't want you to do or say anything to hurt her."

"I don't want to, but if you leave I'll be forced to."

"Why didn't you tell me she didn't want me here?"

"What she wants isn't important—not so far as my guests are concerned. You're more than a guest—you're a close friend of long standing."

"She's right, Aldis. I've sponged on you long enough, and I've loved every moment. You've been more than kind to me, and I appreciate all you've done."

"I'm the one to express my thanks."

"If I've helped you, I'm grateful. But truly, you don't need me any more."

"Yes, I do. More than ever. Sheriff Eckles suspects me of Jim Canby's murder. Also, he's highly suspicious about Aunt Mabel's death."

"What did he say?"

"Dr. Lind told him Aunt Mabel should have remained sedated until mid-morning. When was her disappearance discovered? I didn't even think to ask."

"Your Aunt Hannah apparently went to your Aunt Mabel's room about eight o'clock this morning. When she discovered the bed empty, she made a hasty search, then summoned Keith. He joined her in the search. I heard them about and got up to see if something was wrong."

"Do you know the last person to see her?"

"Your Aunt Hannah said she looked in on her sister about ten last night and she was sleeping soundly, with Esther sitting by her bedside on watch should she waken."

"How long did Esther remain there?"

"Until three a.m. She said your aunt was sleeping so peacefully she felt certain she'd not stir until daylight."

"Apparently she did. Or was taken from her bed."

Laurie's brow furrowed thoughtfully. "Before I retired last night, I glanced out the window and saw Setley standing just beyond the house. He was partially hidden by a tree trunk, but he was watching the house."

"He said he'd maintained a watch on the island until dawn, when he returned to Little Greyfield Manor to see if his sister was safe."

Laurie's face shadowed. "Do you think he's telling the truth?"

"I wish I knew. One thing I do know, and that is that anyone can gain access to Greyfield Manor. Eulalie didn't deny it when I called her on it last night. She even said the house was never locked."

"In view of what happened to Jim, don't you think you should remedy that?" Laurie asked quietly.

"Yes. I'll give orders to Esther and Cora that under no circumstances is the key to remain unturned in any lock on the first floor. I'll tell Keith also."

"A good idea."

I said, "I'm going to ask Sheriff Eckles if I may go to the village to make funeral arrangements for my aunt. I can make a telephone call from there."

Laurie turned back to her packing. "He certainly should give permission for that."

"Oh—he wishes to question you too. In the drawing room. I'd suggest you go down, but not before you promise you'll stay."

She shook her head. "I'm sorry."

A soft tap sounded on the half-closed door. Laurie called, "Come in." Keith stepped into the room.

"The sheriff wants to question you, Laurie. Downstairs."

Laurie said, "Aldis already told me."

He noticed the filled luggage. "What're you doing?"

"She's leaving," I said. "Just when I need her."

"You don't need anyone." She made her statement more positive by a reassuring nod of her head.

I knew Laurie too well to try to dissuade her further. I turned to Keith. "Will you take me to the mainland? I'll make a call from the village about funeral arrangements for Aunt Mabel."

"Aunt Hannah has already asked me to take her there," Keith said.

"I'll go with you both," I said.

"Aldis, I hate to say this, but she doesn't want you with us."

"Why not?" I exclaimed. "After what's happened, can't she forget her dislike of me?"

Keith looked apologetic. "She feels you're the cause of all that's happened. I've tried to convince her you're as innocent as any of us and that Aunt Mabel must have wandered off in a semi-daze, but she won't accept that."

"Does she know Aunt Mabel visited Eulalie?" I asked.

"She did?" Laurie exclaimed.

Keith nodded. "Eulalie told me this morning."

"She also told me," I said.

"I didn't mention it to Aunt Hannah," Keith said. "Do you want me to?"

I thought a moment, then rejected the idea. It would serve no purpose, and cold and forbidding though Aunt Hannah was, no one would question her love and devotion to her sister.

I said, "No. At least, not yet. However, it's all going to come out when Sheriff Eckles learns Aunt Mabel knew Eulalie and Setley."

Keith said, "That's what made me wonder if she should learn about it from us."

"If you think that," I said, "you do the telling. She'll scarcely speak a civil word to me."

Laurie rested a comforting hand on my shoulder. "I guess you need me a little longer. I'll stay—for the time being. I'll unpack after Sheriff Eckles gets through questioning me. I don't know what I can tell him that he doesn't already know."

Laurie left the room. Keith and I followed and stood in the hall.

He said, "You know, you're welcome to come in the launch with me. I'll have to get permission from Sheriff Eckles. I've already asked if I could take Aunt Hannah."

"Did Dr. Lind give his permission?"

"He said there's nothing wrong with her physically, and she's got her nerves under control."

"I'm glad."

Keith said, "You've had a rough time of it since you came here."

"I wish I'd never heard of this place, but Laurie meant well. I wanted to get away. But I'll never run from trouble again because of foolish pride."

"It was heartache more than pride that made you run," Keith said. "And why shouldn't you come here? You own it. Aunt Hannah should give a thought to that."

"I suppose it's difficult for her now that she can no longer consider herself mistress of this house or the one in Savannah. Ordinarily, I'd continue to let her be the overseer, so to speak. But in view of her open antagonism toward me, I feel I must assert myself, though I'll not do or say anything to hurt her. At least, not until after the funeral."

"Aunt Mabel's body won't be released until an autopsy has been performed."

"What could that determine?"

"Let's wait and see. I can't understand her going through the forest during the night."

"I don't think it was during the night. Setley maintained a watch until dawn."

"And Aunt Hannah went to Aunt Mabel's room at eight. The bed was empty then."

"She must have left the house between dawn and eight o'clock, but Dr. Lind said she should have remained sedated until mid-morning."

Keith pondered that. "Perhaps the drug wore off sooner. But I wonder why she was going to Eulalie's. Certainly that's where she was headed."

"And why would she have lost her way?" I mused.

"Maybe her mind was still befuddled by the drug."

My thoughts took another turn. "What do you know about Dennis Curran?"

"Nothing, really," Keith replied. "But he seems to have some good ideas about developing the island. That is, if you're interested."

"What's your opinion?"

"I hadn't thought about it. His visit was as much a surprise to me as to you. He did ask me to try and convince you it was a good idea."

I smiled. "I think it's an excellent idea. Certainly, I have no desire to remain here any longer than necessary. But I haven't made up my mind yet. Another proposal was made by Stan Bannon regarding this island. I'm giving it serious thought. Whatever I do, it will include all the islands."

"May I ask what the plan is?"

I related it briefly because I heard my aunt's voice drift up the corridor. Keith glanced apprehensively in that direction.

He nodded approval when I finished speaking, saying, "That's a better idea."

"I don't know yet what I'm going to do."

"This is no time to decide on anything. As for Mr.

Curran, if you want me to tell him to stay away from here, I will."

I thought of his eavesdropping on Stan and me, and of Esther reprimanding him for it. "I somehow don't think he'll return."

Keith nodded agreement. "For the time being, I doubt that anyone will want to come here except reporters, and Sheriff Eckles won't allow them yet. He has men conducting a detailed search of the island now. Mr. Curran has already got permission to leave."

Aunt Hannah stepped into the corridor and saw us. Much to my surprise, she spoke my name and made a beckoning gesture. Keith and I went to her.

She said, "May my sister be buried on this island? There's a small, tree-shaded plot on a raised portion of ground."

"Of course, Aunt Hannah. I've never seen it."

"It's on Miss Laboulaye's property. But Mabel once expressed the wish to be buried there. Why she'd want to be, I don't know. But I feel it only fair to carry out her wishes."

"It's good of you to do so, Aunt Hannah," I said. "But will Miss Laboulaye consent to it?"

"Will you go and ask her? Keith is taking me to the village to arrange for a coffin and burial."

I said, "Keith just told me Aunt Mabel's body will be held until after an autopsy."

"Sheriff Eckles has assured me that will be attended to immediately," she said stiffly. "If so, we may return with the body."

That didn't seem likely, but I made no comment. I noticed Keith also maintained a discreet silence.

"I'll go to Miss Laboulaye's immediately," I said.

"I hope she will give her consent." Aunt Hannah looked as if she were doubtful. So was I, except that I knew Aunt Mabel had visited Eulalie secretly—a fact that might cause Eulalie to become benevolent. I hoped so. I was sorry for the reason for my mission there, but it did give me an opportunity to see the woman again. I hoped that because of what had happened, our meeting this time would be cordial.

Keith took my aunt's arm and led her to the stairs. I went to my suite. I slipped a hand into my pocket. The handkerchief Eulalie had handed me was still there. I took it out, regarded it somberly, and went into my bathroom. There was a small laundry chute there also. I dropped the handkerchief into it, then turned to wash my hands. To my tortured mind, it seemed as if I were cleansing them of blood. I banished the wretched thought from my mind.

I was seated in a small library, a miniature of the one at Greyfield Manor. Though it was mid-afternoon, the draperies were drawn and the only light came from a candelabrum on the small, ornate, mother-of-pearl desk and twin candelabra on the mantel. A painting of a gentleman hung above the mantel, illuminated by candlelight. It was impossible to get a good look at it in the subdued light of the room, but one thing I did see—the gentleman's skin was white.

Eulalie sat opposite me, wearing another of her exquisite gowns. She'd already expressed her sympathies regarding my aunt—sympathies which I couldn't doubt, for her eyes had glistened with tears. And I could understand. Aunt Mabel was a timid soul, and for her to have come here was sufficient assurance to me that Eulalie had been kind to her, even friendly. I was more certain of it as she discussed my aunt and I learned the extent to which they had become acquainted.

Eulalie said, "Your aunt thought a great deal of you."

My face had always been a mirror of my thoughts, and Eulalie smiled at my show of astonishment.

"I'm sure it comes as a surprise to you, but it's true. Of course, as you know, she was completely under the domination of her sister."

"Why did my aunt Mabel come here?"

"We met quite by accident in the forest and became friends. Oh, I'll not say she was a frequent visitor here. But she came whenever she could manage a visit."

"I suppose what I really meant to ask was why were you so gracious to her?"

Eulalie sobered. "And so ungracious to you."

"Yes."

As if she couldn't help herself, her eyes shifted to the large portrait above the mantel. She quickly recovered herself and asked if I would like more tea.

I said, "I would much prefer an answer to my question."

She set down her cup and saucer, rested her hands in her lap, and regarded me thoughtfully.

"I'm surprised I could like any of the Greyfields, even Miss Mabel," she said.

I said, "Did you call her Miss Mabel?"

A brief smile touched Eulalie's mouth. "She wouldn't allow it. We addressed each other by our first names."

"Then why not refer to her as just Mabel? She'd have liked that."

She made me no answer. "You *are* entitled to an explanation for my rudeness toward you. Stanley came here this morning and scolded me. I apologize."

"I wasn't friendly, either," I said.

"Why should you have been?" she queried. "Anyway, I will tell you why I was so rude to you. You must know you closely resemble your long-dead aunt. You frightened Setley the night he saw you in the boat. He thought you were her spirit come back to haunt us."

"Was there a reason for her to want to do that?"

"She would probably think so."

I glanced up at the portrait. "Would it have something to do with that portrait?"

"Everything," Eulalie said.

Suddenly the picture came into focus. "Is that Scott Morton?"

Her eyes widened. "Who told you about him?"

"I found a diary belonging to my aunt. In it, she described him. The description matches the portrait. She also told of how he invaded her room the last night he was alive. She related in detail her romance with him and the anonymous letter that caused her to cancel the wedding.

She also wrote about how she'd relented when he invaded her bedroom and consented to elope with him. But when she went to the pier to meet him, he never appeared."

Eulalie's brows raised imperceptibly. "I didn't know about the intended elopement."

"No one was ever told," I said. "My aunt wrote that it would only have added to the scandal. I disagree."

"What do you mean?" Eulalie's manner was gracious though reserved, and I had an idea her interest was far greater than she pretended.

"She wrote that she was the principal suspect. It's my opinion that if she'd let it be known she had gone to the pier to meet Scott Morton and elope, she'd certainly not have been a suspect."

"Your logic is very good. I had no idea your aunt kept a diary in her girlhood."

"I have a feeling there were subsequent diaries."

"If so, wouldn't they be with the one you found?"

"It would seem so. That one was in a secret compartment of one of the cabinets in the library."

"Ah."

"I notice you have cabinets interspersed among the bookshelves also."

"But no secret compartments, Miss Greyfield."

"May I ask a personal question?"

"You may," she said quietly.

"Why did my aunt build this house and deed it to you along with a certain parcel of land?"

"Because we were both in love with the same man." She again regarded the portrait, and this time her glance didn't leave it. I'd been through too much to feel astonishment at her reply.

"Scott Morton?"

"Yes."

"You still love him, don't you?"

She turned her attention back to me. "I suppose you'd like to know how I met him."

"Only if you wish to tell me."

She gave a gentle shrug of her slender shoulders. "I may as well. It's no longer a secret. I don't even know how much of a secret it was then. But if I don't tell you, you'll probably wangle the story out of Senator Bannon."

"Both he and his grandson think a great deal of you," I said.

"And I of them—with good reason. They look after my affairs. The Senator's father and my father were close friends." She paused and regarded me in the half light of the room to see what effect her words had had on me. "I thought I would shock you."

"I don't shock, Miss Laboulaye."

"Well, my father was white and came of a good family. He sent me to Europe to be educated, and while I was there he asked his friend's son—who had gone there on a holiday—to check up on my well-being. I was being schooled in France, and there the color of my skin didn't matter. Nor, may I add, did it to Scott Morton when we came face to face. He showered me with expensive jewelry and other luxuries dear to a girl's heart. I sent them back with not even a note of apology, but I reckoned without his persistence. My father died suddenly, and I was left penniless. I had scarcely enough to return to the small house in Savannah he had purchased for my mother and me."

She paused, and once again her eyes shifted to the portrait. So did mine, and I could see how handsome he was. The dark hair ringed his brow, giving him a boyish appearance. The dimple in one cheek made it appear he was smiling—a rakish sort of smile. The artist had captured the vibrancy of the brown eyes, which my aunt had written about. I could well believe his mere glance would be enough to melt a girl's heart.

Eulalie continued her story. "But I did return, with all the requisites that went into the making of a lady, but none of the advantages. And then Scott came to call on me. He was a name in Southern society, but due to unwise investments, his father was in dire financial straits. He admitted all of that, even while swearing his undying love for me. I will say this, Miss Greyfield, even though I returned his gifts when I was abroad, I fell in love with him, though he never even held my hand."

"Did he offer you marriage?" There was no doubting Eulalie's love for Scott Morton, but I was still wondering about the extent of his.

"No," she admitted. "I wouldn't have expected it. Such a situation would be impossible."

I nodded understanding, but a wave of compassion flowed through me.

"Don't you think he was a rogue—to swear his love for you and for my aunt also?"

"It was I he loved," she replied, as if that was sufficient excuse for his behavior. "Your aunt was fabulously wealthy."

"You're saying he was marrying her for her money," I said.

"I believe that," she replied.

"Did he intend to see you after the marriage?"

"I'm sure he did."

"Were you impoverished?"

"My father left me a modest sum. I offered it to Scott to invest, but he wouldn't touch it."

"He really loved you. But he was murdered."

She nodded.

"How did my aunt learn about you?"

Eulalie's head moved slowly from side to side. "I don't know, but she sent a note, asking me to visit her. When I came here, she made me the offer of the land and a house that she would build on it."

"Why would she do that?"

Eulalie smiled. "Your aunt was unpredictable. I accepted her offer. I was alone. My mother had died. Setley worked for another family. Once the house was built, he insisted on coming here to be with me. As a sort of protector."

"Why would you need one? No one lived here except my aunt and her family."

"Only her mother, who died shortly after Scott Morton's murder."

"Were you and my aunt friends?"

"If, perchance, we met, it was by accident."

"But why would she do all this for you when she should have hated you?"

"Why?"

"Yes. She thought Scott Morton loved her. To have learned otherwise should have enraged her."

Eulalie's eyes refuted that. "You forget, Scott was dead. Both your aunt and I had empty arms."

A sudden question occurred to me. "Did my aunt fall in love again?"

"Oh, yes. Many times."

"You don't make her sound very—chaste."

"You asked a question—I answered it."

I set down my cup and saucer and stood up. "Do you know if my aunt kept diaries?"

"I've already said I had no idea she kept even one diary."

"I thought you might have meant that in reference to her girlhood."

"I did. But also her womanhood."

"Did my aunt have a long life?"

"She died before she was thirty."

"So young."

Eulalie nodded.

"An illness of some kind?" I asked. My curiosity regarding Jayne Greyfield was now bordering on an obsession, but I couldn't seem to help myself.

"She committed suicide—by hanging. The last I knew, the piece of rope was still dangling from the rafter in the attic of Greyfield Manor."

Her revelation left me speechless.

"I have shocked you, haven't I, Miss Greyfield?"

I nodded slowly. I knew now why my aunts had been reluctant to discuss Jayne Greyfield.

"Why would she do such a thing?" I asked.

"The gentleman she was to marry was killed in the Civil War. She lived a gay life until she met Avery Halsten. It was as if she had spent the years after Scott Morton's murder trying to forget. For the second time, she was truly in love. Her other affairs caused talk, and there were three broken marriages due to her alliances. Then, for the second time, she fell in love. The war cheated her in her fulfillment of it. It was more than she could endure."

I stood up. "Thank you for telling me. I understand now why my aunts were so distressed by Jim Canby's murder. It's as if this island is cursed."

Eulalie nodded agreement as she arose. "I don't think it has ever known happiness."

I again thanked her for her graciousness and for allowing my aunt to be buried in the cemetery on her land.

She said, "I hope it will make no difference when I tell you I too wish to have my remains laid there—and those of my brother."

"Be assured it doesn't to me," I said. "I'm certain my Aunt Mabel would feel the same way."

"She did," Eulalie said. She saw me to the door. Setley seemed nowhere about. For the first time, when daylight touched her face, I saw lines of fatigue etched there. Or had the sadness brought on by my aunt's death caused them? No, it seemed more than that. As if the awfulness of what had happened was more of a burden than Eulalie could endure.

I returned to a house as quiet as a tomb. Since I'd neglected to inform Esther and Cora that the doors were to be kept locked from now on, I had no difficulty gaining entry. I wondered if they'd even heard me enter—or if they were in the house. It didn't matter. I didn't need them for anything.

I asked myself what difference did it make about locked doors? The answer came quickly. Jim had been murdered on this island. Aunt Mabel's death was still a mystery. Even more mysterious was how she'd got to the pit of quicksand. I thought of Aunt Jayne and her horrible death. On impulse, I continued my ascent of the stairs until I reached the floor where the servants' quarters were, used now only by Esther and Cora when my aunts were in residence.

I checked doors until I found one that led to the attic. It was flooded with sunlight, so I had no difficulty going up the narrow stairway. At the top I paused and saw discarded furniture, trunks of ancient vintage, and bulging cartons tied with heavy cord, containing goodness knows what. The place needed a good emptying out. I'd attend to it shortly. The more I learned about Greyfield Manor, the less desire I had to remain here.

I threaded my way past the dusty furniture and trunks, stepping over some of the cartons because the passage was blocked. I'd almost reached the end when I saw the piece of rope tied around a rafter, the end dangling in space. Could that be the same rope my aunt had used to kill herself? It had to be. There was no other in evidence. I moved closer to it and studied it. The ends had frayed, and it was probably rotted from age, but it had once been stout enough to hold a human form.

Why, I asked myself. Why had she done such a thing? True, to lose a loved one is terrible. But had she also lost her reason? It had to be that. She'd survived her heartache over losing he first love. But then she was very young. She was still young—not even thirty when she'd taken her life. I reminded myself that thirty wasn't so young in those days. I also asked myself how anyone of sound mind could end one's life. Perhaps being deprived of happiness twice was more than she could endure and her mind cracked. It had to be that. She must have been of unsound mind when she killed herself.

If only I knew more about her. If Aunt Hannah wouldn't talk about it before, she'd never talk of it now. And Eulalie? She claimed she didn't know my aunt well. True, they'd both been in love with the same man. I felt a closer kinship to Jayne's memory when I thought of her compassionate act in deeding property and a house on it to a woman whose loss was as great as her own. Certainly, my aunt had swallowed her pride when she'd done that.

I wondered if Senator Bannon could enlighten me further. I hoped so. My only other hope was to find another diary. Surely since my aunt had kept the one I'd found, in such detail, relating it as if it had just happened and writing down the dialogue as it was spoken, she must have continued the practice. The more I thought about it, the more certain I was that she had kept diaries. But where were they? If they were in Greyfield Manor, and I prayed they were, I'd search every room—even Aunt Hannah's—in an effort to uncover them. I wondered if there might be other secret compartments somewhere in the house where they could be hidden.

I threaded my way back among the clutter, wondering where to begin the search for the diaries. I'd enlist Laurie's help. For the first time since I returned to the house, I thought of her. Was she in her suite? Or had she taken a walk? I hoped it was the latter. Provided she'd chosen the beach. It was no longer comforting to be in the forest, cool though it was. Not after what had happened.

I started my descent of the narrow stairway when Laurie appeared in the doorway below. She looked startled at sight of me. "I thought I heard footsteps echoing through the house. I got a little frightened when I left my suite and could find no one."

"Aren't Esther and Cora here?"

"They went to the village in the launch. Sheriff Eckles sent for them. He wants to question them also in the hope they might give him a clue that would help him know the time your aunt left the house."

"If she left it of her own accord," I said quietly.

"Don't talk that way, Aldis," Laurie entreated.

"I don't like to, but I'm beginning to think this house is cursed."

"What a dreadful thing to say!" She sounded angry.

"Yes, it is," I admitted. "But I just learned Jayne Greyfield committed suicide by hanging. The rope—or the piece of it tied to the rafter—still hangs in the attic."

"Here?" Laurie looked as shocked as I must have when I heard about it.

I nodded. "She was almost thirty. Betrothed to a gentleman who was killed in the Civil War. The shock must have unnerved her to the extent that she did away with herself."

"How horrible."

I nodded. "I wish I knew more about her."

"I'm beginning to think you'd better forget her."

"I can't. It's as if . . ." I paused, reluctant to finish the sentence.

"As if what?" Laurie asked.

"Promise you won't laugh."

"After all that's happened here, I don't consider the subject of suicide one for levity."

"Nor I. But I have the feeling Jayne Greyfield has become a part of me."

"Don't talk that way," Laurie scolded.

"I'm not mad. But I seem to be overwhelmed by her presence."

"Of course you are," Laurie reasoned. "The same thing happened to you as happened to her. And the situation and circumstances were almost identical. *But you are not Jayne Greyfield.*"

"I feel like her. And I must know more about her."

"Just how do you propose to go about that?" Laurie spoke with quiet resignation.

"Find her diaries."

"What diaries?" Laurie exclaimed.

"I don't know what diaries," I retorted. "But I'm sure there are some. I was going to ask you to help me, but I'll make the search myself."

Laurie's manner softened. "I'll gladly help you, Aldis. But you're getting morbid, and that's the worst thing you can do."

"I suppose you think the best thing I can do is to forget Jayne Greyfield."

"That's exactly what I think, but I know it's useless to ask."

"It is," I agreed. "I *must* find out all I can about her. I'm going to make a search of this house for the diaries I'm certain she kept. I've been invited for dinner tonight at the Bannons'. I'm hopeful Senator Bannon can tell me more."

"Who told you your aunt committed suicide?" Laurie asked.

"Eulalie Laboulaye."

"Oh, yes. I forgot you went there. Is she amenable to your aunt being buried in that cemetery?"

I nodded. "Jayne Greyfield and Scott Morton are buried there, too."

"Scott Morton?"

"He's the gentleman Jayne was going to elope with."

"Oh, yes!" she exclaimed. "That was in her diary."

"Eulalie and Setley will also be buried there."

Laurie sighed. "Please don't talk any more about cemeteries or burials. What are you wearing tonight?"

I brightened. "That's something to think about."

She smiled. "I'd say so. I think the young Mr. Bannon has a definite interest in you."

"What makes you say that?"

"The moment he came here this morning he asked about you."

"That was because of my falling into the quicksand last night."

"His concern was more than polite. And from your flushed cheeks, I'd say he made an impression on you."

"I'd say the impression I made on the Bannons was far from favorable. But I do like Stan Bannon. He's going to run for the Senate. That's one of the reasons he came here this morning. But when he heard about Aunt Mabel, he was reluctant to discuss it."

"Discuss what?" Laurie asked.

"An idea he has for this island."

"You'll pardon me if I seem a little mystified, but may I ask what you're talking about?"

"He thought it was a waste for this beautiful beach to go unused. And it is, really."

"I still don't understand," Laurie said.

"He thinks it would be a good idea if I would deed it to the state to be developed for the public enjoyment."

"That would be a philanthropic gesture."

"I agree. And since I don't need the money, why should I want the land subdivided and sold to private individuals, which was Mr. Curran's reason for coming here?"

Laurie nodded agreement. "Are you going to do it?"

"I'm thinking seriously about it. Of course, nothing can be done until Jim Canby's murder is solved."

Laurie nodded. "Let's hope it will be soon. I think it would be good for us to get away from Greyfield Island. Had I known the history of it, I'd never have suggested it as a place of refuge."

"History does seem to be repeating itself."

"I really didn't mean that, Aldis, but it's true. Let's not talk about it." She looked uneasy. "I hope the others get back before you leave. I'm sort of frightened being here alone."

"If they don't return, I won't go," I said. "I'm sure Stan will understand."

"You'll go," Laurie said. "It will be the best thing for you—to get away for a while. I'll be all right. If they don't get back, I'll lock myself in my suite."

"I feel guilty, knowing you've remained here only for me."

"I'm the one to have guilt feelings. I think the best thing you can do is dispose of Greyfield Island, regardless of how you do it."

"If I do, I'll also present the islands adjoining it."

"That's quite a gift," she said.

"It's in a good cause," I said. "And certainly I have no desire to live out my days here. Not after what I've learned about my aunt." I made a gesture of frustration. "If only I could find her diaries."

"We'll start a search tomorrow," Laurie said. "You won't rest easy until you've either found them or are convinced there aren't any."

"The more I think about it, the more certain I am that there are," I said.

"I'll do a little searching tonight while you're gone," she said. "If I find them, they'll be on your pillow. They might as well be. Once you know of their existence, you'll not sleep until you read them."

"Thanks, Laurie." I gave her a friendly embrace. "Now I want to check my wardrobe. I'm not at all sure of what to wear. Certainly nothing frivolous."

"Wear your gold silk with the accordion-pleated skirt. It will complement your eyes."

But I didn't wear it. The lace bodice was too dressy. I chose instead a black skirt with a long-sleeved, softly tailored white blouse. It was more in keeping with my mood.

NINE

Laurie, Keith, Sheriff Eckles, and I were assembled in Aunt Hannah's sitting room. The door leading into Aunt Mabel's bedroom was closed, a grim reminder that for her the end had come, not only suddenly but violently.

Sheriff Eckles stood before the fireplace, facing us. The chairs in which we were seated were placed in almost a semicircle.

His launch had followed Keith's, which had transported Aunt Hannah, Cora, and Esther. They brought back the news that there hadn't been a trace of sand in Mabel Greyfield's lungs or throat or nasal passages. She had suffered death by strangulation; her body had been carried to the quicksand pit and thrown in. Through some strange circumstances, the flexed fingers of one hand had protruded. Setley, in search of her, had observed them and had pulled her body from what someone thought would be its final grave.

Sheriff Eckles eyed me as he spoke. "Since Miss Mabel suffered death by suffocation while she was in a drugged state, the coroner has stated she was murdered."

Aunt Hannah lowered her head and dabbed at her eyes. I myself felt ill and shaken. And so were Laurie and Keith. I wondered if Mr. Curran had heard the news. He too had spent the night here. Were his motives for being here as innocent as they seemed? Had he really received a letter? That thought reminded me of the one Jim told me he had received.

I mentioned it to the sheriff and asked if he knew anything about it.

"It wasn't on his person," Sheriff Eckles replied. "His

home has been checked, but this is the first I heard of the letter."

I said, "I told Stanley Bannon about it, and he said he'd check it."

Sheriff Eckles said, "If by that he meant he'd search Mr. Canby's home, how'd he propose to do it?"

"I suppose he meant he'd inform you."

"He hasn't. At least not so far. Now that I know about it, I'll make a search of the house. It could be he was wearing other clothes the night he made the scene in the restaurant. We searched only those he had on. There were only the usual things a man carries in his pockets. Change, a few bills of small denomination, some keys, a pocket watch."

"Also," I went on, "Mr. Curran came here last night because of a note he said he had received, which was supposed to be from me. I wrote no such note."

"Did he bring the note?"

"No."

Sheriff Eckles held a notebook in one hand, fountain pen in the other. He made brief notes in it as he talked. He said, "I'll check that with him. He's still at the inn."

Keith said, "I dropped by there and saw him. I told him about Aunt Mabel. He said he'd remain at the inn until you questioned him, Sheriff."

"I'll see him as soon as I go back. As for Miss Mabel—according to what I could learn, Esther was the last to have seen her alive. At least, she swears Miss Mabel was breathing when she left here around three a.m."

Aunt Hannah said, "If Esther made that statement, you may be assured it's the truth."

"I might not be so sure, Miss Hannah," Sheriff Eckles replied quietly, "except Esther said she held a mirror to your sister's mouth and saw it film."

"Why did she do that?" I asked.

"She said your aunt was sleeping so quietly, she was afraid she'd stopped breathing, and she had to make sure she was alive."

"How was she suffocated?" Aunt Hannah asked.

Without a moment's hesitation, Sheriff Eckles said,

"Since she was in bed, the easiest way would be for a pillow to be held against her face until she no longer breathed."

Aunt Hannah again lowered her face, but she retained her composure. Sheriff Eckles eyed me. I knew what he was thinking, and he knew I knew.

I said, "I told you the last time I saw Aunt Mabel alive. I didn't enter her room again until this morning. You saw me in there."

"You were in the act of picking up a pillow that was on the floor and about to place it on the bed."

I said, "It would be a natural thing for a woman to do."

"Yes," he agreed. "It's also something a murderer would do to make it appear that nothing in the room had been disturbed."

"You believe that's the pillow used to kill my aunt."

"Yes," he said. "I think she was conscious when it happened. Her hands were trying to push the pillow away from her face, but her strength was no match for a murderer."

"Why would anyone want to kill her?" I demanded.

"It's a good question, Miss Greyfield. But the answer shouldn't be so difficult."

Laurie said, "I believe the Sheriff means that whoever killed your aunt also killed Jim Canby. Somehow, she guessed who it was. Because she did, she forfeited her life."

"That's about it." Sheriff Eckles closed his notebook and placed it in his pocket along with his fountain pen.

I stood up. "Do you suspect me, Sheriff?"

"Every occupant of this house is a suspect—along with Mr. Curran. And Setley and his sister. But I'm not pointing the finger of guilt at anybody—*yet*."

I sat down. His statement did little to console me. I thought of the handkerchief Eulalie had given me. She should have given it instead to Sheriff Eckles. She'd been more than gracious with me today, yet I couldn't believe she'd had a complete change of heart regarding me. She'd admitted Stan had visited her and talked with her about me.

I wondered if my handkerchief had really been found near Jim's body, or if Eulalie had appropriated it from the house and then pretended she'd found it there. As a relative of Jayne Greyfield, I was an object of hatred to her. Scott had loved her, but had offered marriage to Jayne. That, in itself, could have made Eulalie bitter enough to plunge a knife into Scott Morton to prevent him from marrying Jayne.

The anonymous letter! Jayne had also received one. I must have gasped aloud at the thought, for all eyes turned to me.

"What is it?" Laurie's voice evidenced her concern.

"Nothing."

Cora appeared at the door. "Mr. Bannon is downstairs."

I stood up and addressed my aunt. "Stan Bannon invited me to dinner at his home in the village. I'd like to go, Aunt Hannah, if you don't mind."

"Would it do any good if I did?" she countered. Her voice held no malice, nor did her eyes as she regarded me.

"All you need do is ask me not to go," I said. "Will Aunt Mabel's body be returned tonight?"

"No." Her manner was still cool. "The casket is being brought from Savannah."

"What about funeral services?" I wanted to feel a sense of being needed, but Aunt Hannah was determined to shut me out.

"They've been taken care of." She switched her gaze from me to Sheriff Eckles. "I'm very fatigued. May I be excused?"

"Certainly, Miss Hannah," he said. "I'll be leaving now. Of course, I'll return tomorrow. There's no sense for the men to continue their search with darkness coming on, but I'm leaving two men here to patrol the island, and I may take a run over myself tonight."

"If my niece approves, I have no objection."

"I approve," I said. "I'm sure Keith does, too."

"I do." His answer was immediate.

"I'm not a member of the family," Laurie said, "but I also approve."

I said, "I'd like to ask a question regarding Aunt Mabel."

"Go right ahead, Miss Greyfield," Sheriff Eckles said.

"When she returned to the house, after discovering Jim Canby's body, did she say anything that might give a clue as to who the murderer was?"

"Nothing," Aunt Hannah said. "She was in such a state of shock, I don't think she was capable of speaking."

"Oh, yes, she was," I contradicted. "She spoke to me."

My aunt looked startled at the disclosure. "What did she say?"

"Nothing that made sense. At least, I've not been able to make sense out of it so far."

Aunt Hannah said, "It's the first I've heard of it."

Knowing she'd not ask, I said, "Her exact words were, 'You poor girl. You must be worried . . .' "

Aunt Hannah looked triumphant. "It makes sense to me. She must have regarded you as the one who plunged a knife into Jim Canby. Certainly, you had motive enough to do it."

My face flamed, but I managed to hold my temper. "Aunt Hannah, how can you have such a thought about me?" Her mouth opened to make a retort, but I stayed her with my upraised hand. "Never mind. I know you feel me responsible for all that's happened here. I suppose I am. But I did not kill Aunt Mabel. I even think she and I could have been close if you'd have allowed it, but you wouldn't. I know now you only tolerated me and wouldn't allow your sister to form any attachment for me. In my loneliness, I turned to Laurie. She's been a loyal friend, but I grew to depend on her too much."

Laurie arose and came to my side. "I'm the one responsible for Aldis's being here. When I suggested this as a place of refuge for her, I didn't know the history of the island—specifically that her great-grandaunt had been through the same thing Aldis is going through now. But she'd certainly not wish such a horrible end as Jim Canby's or your sister's on anyone. I know her—far better than you, just as I know you don't want me here. Also, it might interest you to know I had packed, but when you refused to allow Aldis to accompany you to the mainland to make funeral arrangements for your sister, I changed my mind. I can endure your dislike of me as long as Aldis needs me."

Keith said, "Laurie's right, Aunt Hannah. You're being unfair."

Aunt Hannah glared at him. To me, she said, "Mr. Bannon may get tired of waiting. I suggest you go down, or you'll be deprived of your dinner engagement."

I was glad to leave the room. Keith accompanied me to the landing.

He said, "She's really smarting because she can't run things as she used to. She'll calm down."

"I know. I don't blame her for looking for a scapegoat, but I swear I didn't harm Aunt Mabel."

"I know that. No one who knew Aunt Mabel could hurt her."

"That would eliminate Eulalie and Setley."

"Eulalie, perhaps. Of Setley I'm not so sure."

"And Mr. Curran?"

"I asked Sheriff Eckles to see who really wants to buy the island to develop it. Certainly Curran hasn't the money."

"He said he developed some cays off Florida."

"There again, he may have contacted the owners and laid the groundwork, but he's not the brains. And the suit he left behind was far from the best. It couldn't be salvaged."

"I'll have the bank send him a check that will more than compensate him for what he went through at the hands of Setley."

"Do what you wish," Keith said. "But it might be a good idea to wait until we see who's responsible for these acts of madness that have been committed here. I can't think that anyone but a madman could be responsible."

"I agree. Thanks for your kindness, Keith. If you have any free time, try to keep Laurie company."

His smile was wistful. "I will if she'll let me. I more than like her, Aldis, but she doesn't seem interested. Maybe you could put in a word or two for me."

The thought pleased me. "Perhaps if you were less eager."

"It's worth a try."

He kissed my brow, wished me a pleasant evening, and turned back to rejoin the others.

I went downstairs. Stan was pacing back and forth in the drawing room. His face brightened at sight of me, and he was at my side in three brisk strides.

He said, "I was afraid you'd changed your mind."

"No. I want to talk with you and your grandfather. Did you hear the terrible news?"

He nodded. "I'm sorry. I want to talk about it, too, only it's difficult to know where to begin. First of all, let's get back to the house. My grandfather is eager to renew his acquaintance and to apologize for having misjudged you."

I managed a smile. "I didn't think the Bannons had too high an opinion of me."

"Before the evening is over, both Bannons will do their utmost to reassure you."

I colored at the warmth of his glance, but I was eager to be out of the house. Sheriff Eckles's voice drifted down from above. Stan heard it, too.

He said, "Let's get out of here."

I gave him no argument.

I was received graciously by Senator Bannon and was fascinated by the house which, though small, had a charm both outside and inside that reflected the refined tastes of both Bannons.

Large and small boxwood covered the grounds, and a luxuriant display of ivy curtained the iron fence that enclosed the property. Inside, the furniture was a mixture of nineteenth-century and modern that blended well.

We dined in a small room adjoining a screened porch and later adjourned to the porch for coffee. Senator Bannon expressed his regrets about my aunt when I arrived, then turned the subject to the small village, of which I was quite ignorant.

He made it so interesting that he succeeded in ridding my mind of the terror and violence that had stalked Greyfield Island since my arrival. Stan joined in from time to time, but he let his grandfather do most of the talking, for it was obvious the Senator relished relating not only its history, but incidents regarding some of its inhabitants, both past and present.

But I reminded myself that the opportunity might not again present itself for me to learn more about Eulalie. Her still-evident beauty, combined with her sphinx-like manner, gave her an aura of mystery few women have, yet which adds to their allure. I wanted to know everything possible about her. And so I asked a direct question. It was easy, for the Senator, in his revelations about the village, had touched upon Greyfield Island.

"My first visit there, as a young man, was with my father. He went there periodically to pay his respects to Eulalie and also to discuss her business affairs, which our law firm handled."

I said, "Then you know my great-grandaunt Jayne Greyfield deeded that house and property to Eulalie."

"Oh, yes," he replied, his manner as gracious as it had been since my arrival. "Jayne was a creature of impulse. She had a kind of beauty that made all eyes turn to her when she entered a room. It wasn't just her beauty, but an indefinable quality—an excitement or allure, if you will—that enhanced her beauty. Somehow, shortly after Scott's death, she learned Eulalie was his real love. Instead of working up a hatred for Eulalie, Jayne took compassion on her. I don't mean pity, you understand."

"I believe I do. What you're saying is that my aunt sensed Eulalie would like to be near the grave of the man she loved and who had loved her."

"Yes. And Eulalie was grateful."

"Did she tell you that?" I couldn't refrain from asking the question.

The Senator's smile was amused. "You're aware of her pride."

"So much so, I'm amazed she'd accept my aunt's offer of a house and grounds. Also, I was of the opinion she was wealthy."

"No. My father advised her on how to invest the modest sum her father had left her. As you probably know, her father and mine were close friends. And my father gave his solemn word he would look after her. I'm proud to say he did so."

"And so have you," I said. "I'm glad. I'm sure, in those days, it wasn't easy for someone as beautiful and educated as she to live the secluded life she was forced to."

"It wasn't. But she made the best of it. Unbeknownst to anyone, she moved among her own people, teaching them to read and write, along with other handicrafts dear to the heart of a woman who does not wish idle fingers. Now, of course, she is too old for that sort of thing." He raised a cautioning finger. "But her mind isn't."

"I'm aware of that," I said. "I found out something I don't believe anyone ever knew about my aunt."

Both the Senator and Stan who, thus far, had had only an opportunity to listen, regarded me with careful attention.

"What's that?" the Senator asked.

"She was going to elope with Scott Morton and even went to the pier to meet him the night he was murdered. Of course, when he didn't put in an appearance, she returned to the Manor."

"That is news," the Senator said. "A pity she never mentioned it. It would have removed a great deal of suspicion from her."

"I believe she felt it was the other way around. Not even her mother knew, though her mother did tell the police, after his body was discovered, that she thought she heard an intruder in the house that night. She did. Scott Morton."

The Senator's surprise matched that of his grandson. Stan said, "How did you learn that?"

"I found her diary."

The Senator had assumed a relaxed attitude in his large wicker chair, his head resting against the cushioned back, his legs stretched at full length and crossed at the ankles, his hands clasped across his ample middle. Now he sat up and leaned forward, his manner alert. "Was there anything to shed light on Scott Morton's murder in the diary?"

"No. Why do you ask?"

"Nothing. I just wondered." He settled back in his chair, but his reply came so quickly, I sensed he was being evasive.

Stan said, "My grandfather has always been concerned that things weren't all they seemed at Greyfield Island."

"You mean the Manor?" I asked.

"No."

"I don't think you should discuss it, son." The Senator's tone was cautious.

"I disagree," Stan replied, his manner quiet but firm. "Aldis is the most logical suspect where Jim Canby's murder is concerned. You know that as well as I. I'm as certain of her innocence of that murder as I am of her innocence in regard to her aunt's. Let's be honest, Grandfather. Your concern matches mine regarding the one who might be guilty."

"Nonsense," the Senator replied gruffly.

He got to his feet slowly and walked to the screened edge of the porch. He seemed to be studying the property, which was barely visible in the fast approaching night. A songbird trilled in the distance, and the darkness was pierced only by the tiny light of fireflies.

Stan had been standing behind his grandfather's chair, which faced the one I occupied. Now he moved it so that it was alongside mine, and he sat down.

"It isn't nonsense," he said. "Your concern matches mine regarding Eulalie."

"Do you suspect her of killing Jim Canby?" I asked.

"I shouldn't," Stan replied. "Without a shred of proof."

"Also, she happens to be a client of ours," his grandfather reminded him.

"So is Aldis—or did I neglect to tell you?"

Senator Bannon turned to face us. "I'm aware of that."

"However," Stan went on, "I can't see Eulalie murdering Miss Mabel."

"Nor I," said the Senator.

"Unless Aunt Mabel saw Eulalie at the spot where Jim was killed," I ventured.

"How could such a thing be possible?" The Senator's voice was tinged with impatience.

"I don't know," I admitted. "But after Aunt Mabel's body was discovered, I went to that area. Eulalie was there. She gave me a lace-edged handkerchief which bore my initial and which I could identify as mine. She said she found it near Jim Canby's body."

The surprise on both men's faces proved I'd scored a point. Stan said, "Why didn't she give it to the sheriff?"

"I asked her that question. She said I could if I wished."

"Did you?" Senator Bannon asked.

"No."

"Why not?" The Senator's voice sharpened.

I felt my face flame. Fortunately, the darkness concealed it, but Stan sensed my uneasiness and placed his hand over mine on the chair arm.

"You don't have to answer that, Aldis," Stan said.

"I know, but I will. The only reason I can think of is that it would have directed suspicion toward me. But there is something I know about Eulalie that puzzles me."

"You mean it may be connected in some way with Jim Canby's murder?" Stan asked.

"I'm not sure, but I feel I should mention it."

"Tell us." Though Stan's tone invited confidence, I knew I'd not won his grandfather over to my side.

I said, "The night Jim Canby was murdered—and before his body was discovered—I awakened with the knowledge that someone was in my room. I squinted my eyes and saw light. It was a flashlight, muted by a hand held over the glass. I felt someone touch my head and examine my hair, which was spread on the pillow. I smelled the scent of jasmine. I moved quickly and grabbed the hand on my pillow, but the intruder struck my wrist with the flash. The pain made me release my hold. I caught the hand again, but the person shook off my grip."

"Did you see who it was?" Stan asked.

"No. But Eulalie uses that scent. Laurie doesn't use a perfume. Aunt Hannah doesn't, either. Aunt Mabel favored lily of the valley."

"Anyway, I succeeded in routing the intruder, and I heard the sound of runn'ng feet—bare feet that made a light slapping sound on the marble floor. I reached the hall and turned on the light in time to see the lower door closing."

"Didn't you make any attempt to follow?" the Senator asked.

"Pursuit in darkness would have been useless. I wasn't familiar with the forest. I went back to my room and saw the dress I'd worn when I'd taken the walk along the beach, thrown to the floor. I'd spread it on the chaise. The lower part of the skirt was crumpled, as if it had been bunched together. My shoes, which had been on the floor, were tossed on the chaise."

The Senator remained where he was, but turned to face us. "Are you saying it was Eulalie?"

"Yes. She came to inspect my garments and my hair to see if they were wet or damp from having been in the marsh. Later, when I accused her of doing so, she admitted it. She even admitted, under my questioning, having found Jim's body before Aunt Mabel discovered it, though not until I made a statement to that effect."

"Why didn't she have Setley notify the sheriff?" Stan asked.

"I asked her that very question."

"What answer did she give?" the Senator asked.

"That nothing could have been done for him."

"Grandfather, there's no further need to be evasive with Aldis. Tell the real reason Jayne invited Eulalie to live there."

The Senator paced the length of the long porch and back before replying. Whether he was debating with himself whether or not he would speak, I don't know, but his mind was made up for him when Stan said, "If you don't, I will."

"Very well." The Senator sat on the edge of a straight-back chair and regarded both of us. "Once the gossip got about regarding Eulalie, there was ugly talk of lynching." The Senator spoke the word under his breath, as if the very word was repugnant. I liked him the better for it. "Anyway, my father insisted Eulalie come to our house. Setley was in no danger, for they did not have a common father. But she came with great reluctance, knowing we would be in danger if it were known we were hiding her. I don't know how Jayne learned of it, but she paid my father a visit and offered to build a house for Eulalie, making it a replica, in miniature, of hers."

"Why did she do that?"

The Senator smiled. "I don't suppose anyone thought to ask. Needless to say, no one in Savannah or hereabouts knew about it until it was completed. Eulalie was spirited there under cover of darkness. She and Setley have lived there ever since. Once there, she was safe."

"In that case, her attitude toward my aunt should have been one of gratitude."

"Don't you think it was?" Stan asked. There was no rancor in his voice.

"No. She told me she had no use for the Greyfields. Nor has Setley—except for my Aunt Mabel. And I'm beginning to wonder about that. Also, she said Jayne invited her to live there because they were in love with the same man."

Stan said, "We like Eulalie—and Setley. I'll grant they're recluses. And all people who stay by themselves become odd. But we've always found an evening in Eulalie's company enjoyable."

"She was most gracious to me this afternoon, though I know I have you to thank for it. I went there to ask if Aunt Mabel might be buried in the plot on Eulalie's property. I also attempted to learn more about Aunt Jayne. But Eulalie professed ignorance. I mentioned my aunt's diary in which she wrote of the elopement. Eulalie professed ignorance of that also."

Stan said, "You did say your aunt told no one of the intended elopement."

"Not even her mother. She so stated in her diary. But I would like to find her other diaries."

"What makes you think there are any?" the Senator asked.

"She seemed to like putting everything down in detail. And her last entry in the one I found said that she would write no more in that one. I assume she had every intention of starting another—once her heartache eased."

The Senator lit a cigar and puffed slowly on it a few times before he spoke. "She had a tragic end."

"I didn't even know about that until today."

"Who told you?" Stan asked.

"Eulalie."

The Senator studied the glowing end of his cigar. "Did she tell you why?"

"Yes. The man to whom Jayne was engaged was killed in the Civil War."

The Senator nodded. "She just couldn't take it. Her mind went."

I frowned. "Did you know her well, Senator?"

His smile was reflective. "I worshiped her from afar. I was just a boy, you know. My father knew her much better."

"Even so, do you think she was the type who would take her own life?"

"I think the shock of Avery Halsten's death destroyed her reason. She didn't know what she was doing. As for diaries, I had no awareness there were any."

"I doubt that anyone did," I said. "It was quite by accident I found the one I read." I told them of the secret compartment in the library, so airtight the book had remained in perfect condition."

Stan said, "Even if there were other diaries in existence and you found them, you don't think they would shed light on Scott Morton's murder, do you?"

"I wonder. You'll probably scoff at this, but I have a feeling my aunt wants me to find them."

I smiled at the effect my statement had on the gentlemen.

"You believe in the occult?" Stan asked, his smile polite.

"I've never given it much thought. But I'm beginning to think I must. Since I came to Greyfield Island, I've been obsessed with the thought of my aunt. I can't get her out of my mind."

"And what about before you came here?"

"I never thought about those islands, and I'd never heard of Jayne Greyfield. I was vaguely aware the islands were owned by the family, but I have no recollection of ever having been there." I paused, then added, "Oh, I knew my parents met their deaths on the water and their bodies were washed ashore. I didn't know I was strolling the beach at the time with my nursemaid."

Stan said, "Keith stopped by for a few minutes this afternoon. He told us that was the reason your aunts never mentioned the island in your presence."

I nodded. "I think they're very fond of Greyfield Manor."

"Keith said they came here as often as they could manage it."

"Yes." I didn't add to the statement. I'd have sounded as if I were seeking their pity.

Stan looked puzzled. "But you never knew the story of your Aunt Jayne before you came to the island?"

That brought a smile to my face. "Aunt Hannah said she was no asset to the family. I guess I don't need to say more."

Both men smiled. Senator Bannon said, "Your Aunt Hannah is rather a formidable personality."

"Which brings us no closer to the solution of the murder," Stan said. "I don't like the idea of your being over there."

"I shan't leave until the guilty party is brought to justice," I said. "Anyway, Sheriff Eckles is putting two men on patrol duty there tonight."

"I'm glad to know it," Stan said. "I hope the house is kept locked."

"It will be," I assured him. "Though it never was before. Even Eulalie told me that and admitted she could gain entrance to it whenever she chose."

Stan said, "I'm surprised she'd do such a thing."

"So am I," Senator Bannon added.

"Let's not condemn her on that, though," Stan said.

"I won't," I said. "Now I must get back. Thank you for inviting me. It was good to get away from the island for a while, and I appreciate your discussing the island and Eulalie and Aunt Jayne with me."

"I'm sorry we can't shed light on the reason for what's going on there," Stan said. "But we'll do all we can. And be assured Sheriff Eckles won't rest until the murderer has been brought to justice."

The Senator bade me good night, and Stan and I went down the steps and walked around to the front of the house where his launch was docked at the pier.

"Do you think Mr. Curran is connected with the violence in some way?" I asked.

"He bears looking into. His presence at Greyfield Manor last night seemed almost too coincidental."

"And the note he claimed to have got from me. I never wrote one. I wonder if he still has it."

"Let's hope so. The handwriting can certainly be checked."

It was a brief ride back to the island, and we'd no sooner stepped on the pier than we were accosted by a man armed with a shotgun. After we identified ourselves, he told us he was a guard posted by Sheriff Eckles and allowed us to proceed.

The incident unnerved me slightly, and I was grateful for Stan's arm about my waist and his flashlight, which pierced the darkness of the forest through which we had to pass.

At the door, Stan took both my hands in his. "I'm sorry our meeting had to be the result of something tragic. I hope when it's resolved, I may continue to see you."

"You've been so thoughtful and kind," I said. "And I like you. I can't say more than that now."

"I understand." He squeezed my hands gently, then bent and lightly kissed my cheek. "Forgive me. I'm a victim of the moonlight touching your face, giving you a magical quality. Try not to worry. And be careful."

I assured him I would and started to turn, when I thought of something. "About deeding these islands to the state. I'm going through with it."

"We won't talk about it now."

"We can. And you may make use of it in your campaign when you run for the Senate."

"That may be delayed. The war going on in Europe gives evidence of spreading. I'm sure we're going to be involved. If so, I must go."

"Oh, no, Stan." Fear coursed through me at the thought.

"Oh, yes." His voice was firm, but a smile touched his lips. "Your concern pleases me. So much I'm going to take more liberty."

And with that, his arms enclosed me and drew me to him. His lips touched mine, and I returned the embrace. All thought of the horror of what had happened here since my arrival faded, and I knew, with certainty, I was in love. Really in love. How could I have been mistaken before?

But my rapture was quickly dispelled when I entered the house. I reached for the electric light button to flood the hall with light, but my hand stayed in mid-air. To my right was muted light. The heavy fragrance of perfumed flowers was also present.

Sensing what it was about, I walked to the drawing room and stood in the doorway. My aunt's body had been returned in a casket. Flowers were banked around it, and tall candleholders stood, two at each end of the casket, the thick white candles giving off a soft glow. I walked into the room and regarded the still form lying there, garbed in black. I bowed my head in prayer and fought back tears. Tears of anger against whoever had ended the life of this gentle person while she lay helpless under the influence of a drug.

"Only one good thing'll come out of this, child." It was Esther, whose presence I'd barely been aware of when I entered the room. "Where your aunt is, no one's ever gonna hurt her again. Now she'll know a little happiness an' she can do what she wants."

"I hope so, Esther."

"I know so," she said. "God loves all his children. He don't care what their color is."

I nodded. "Aunt Mabel felt the same way."

"You can believe that, honey."

Esther's arms extended, and I went to her. "You were a lonely child. I knowed your parents. They loved you. Your Aunt Mabel loved you, but she was timid."

"I know what you mean," I said. "I only wish I'd known while she was alive. Just as I wish I knew why Aunt Hannah doesn't like me."

"She can't help bein' the way she is." Esther spoke simply, but there was wisdom in her words. "It ain't in her to love anybody, an' she don't want anybody else to love anybody. She's more to be pitied than condemned, an' you got to find it in your heart to forgive her. She's old now. An' she's frightened even if she is takin' it out on you."

"I'll remember that, Esther. Thanks for talking with me."

Her eyes regarded me kindly. "Any time you wanta talk, I'm here."

"I'll sit with you."

"No, Miss Aldis. Services are tomorrow afternoon. You go upstairs an' rest. Your aunt's restin' now. Dr. Lind came with Miss Mabel's body. It was too much for Miss Hannah. He gave her a sedative. Mr. Keith an' Miss Laurie's up there now, keepin' watch. They said she's not to be left alone for a minute, an' I agree.'

"So do I, Esther. I'll go up and see them."

"I'll stay with your Aunt Mabel until daylight. I'll just leave this room to lock the front door. Locked the back one already."

"And we'll keep them locked from now on," I said.

"Sure will," she agreed. "Only reason front door wasn't locked was I was waitin' for you to come home."

She walked into the hall with me and went directly to the door. I heard the key turn in the lock.

I paused on the stairway. "Are you sure you don't mind being alone, Esther?"

"I want to be with Miss Mabel. It's the only way I can

pay my last respects to her. She was always kind to me an' visited with me when she could."

I knew she meant when Aunt Hannah wasn't around. I said good night and went upstairs.

Keith and Laurie were seated on opposite sides of the fireplace, talking in muted tones. Keith stood up as I entered the room.

I said, "I've just talked with Esther. She told me Aunt Hannah has been given a sedative."

Keith nodded. "It was too much for her when they brought Aunt Mabel's body back. Dr. Lind felt she should have something to quiet her."

I turned to Laurie. "Why don't you two rest? I'll stay here."

Keith said, "Laurie can, but I'm remaining. I'll not risk anything happening to her."

"I'll stay with you," I said. "You can rest, Laurie."

"I couldn't," she said. "I'd rather sit up if you don't mind."

"I don't," I said. "I doubt if I could sleep, either."

"You'd better try," Keith said. "Services are tomorrow afternoon. No telling how Aunt Hannah will take it."

"Hard, I expect," I said. "And it's understandable. As sisters, they were inseparable."

I glanced in the direction of her partially open door. "May I look in on her?"

"Of course," Laurie said. "I did a few minutes ago, and she was deep in sleep."

Nonetheless, I walked to her door. There was no light, but I could hear her breathing. I walked back to where Keith stood and nodded reassurance.

I said, "Why don't you rest? Laurie and I can sit here."

He said, "I'm not going to sleep tonight. Even though Sheriff Eckles placed two men outside, I'm going to patrol the house from time to time, to make certain everything is as it should be. I'd advise you again to rest. Tomorrow is going to be difficult."

"Very well," I said.

Laurie said, "I made a search of the library and drawing room. We could find no secret panels or any trace of other diaries."

Keith said, "I even read ledgers and checked most of the books of diary size in the library and any other rooms where they might be hidden or placed. No luck."

"Are we allowed to go into Aunt Mabel's room yet?" I asked.

"No," Keith said. "But if you want to, I'll not mention it."

"Nor will I," Laurie said.

I was tempted, but didn't give in to it. I'd have far rather searched Aunt Hannah's room. I had the feeling that if she had ever come upon her ancestor's diaries, she'd either have hidden them in a place no one else would have access to—namely, her room—or else destroyed them. Quite likely, the latter.

"If you both insist on keeping watch, then I will rest," I said. "The flowers are beautiful."

Keith said, "One spray is from the Senator, another is from his grandson, and a third is from Eulalie. I placed an order for the others. Oh, I almost forgot, there's also one from Laurie. Forgive me, Laurie."

"Forgiven," Laurie said quietly.

I said my good nights and went to my suite. I wondered if Keith had made any headway in his courtship of Laurie. Conditions were hardly appropriate, and certainly I saw no softening of her features when she regarded him. A pity, I thought. It would be pleasant to have her in the family.

I was tempted to lock the door of my sitting room and the door of my bedroom, which led into the hall. But I thought better of it. Two men patrolled the island. Also, with Aunt Mabel's body lying in state and lights glowing from the windows, I didn't think a murderer would strike again.

I lay in darkness, my mind a jumble of thoughts. Stan was uppermost in them, making me wonder if I was fickle. Jim's body wasn't even buried, and already my heartbeat quickened at the thought of another man.

Nor had I shed a tear for Jim. Was I like Aunt Hannah? Or like my great-grandaunt Jayne? She was supposed to have given her love lightly. If so, I felt it was to hide her heartache at Scott Morton's tragic death.

Thinking of Jayne brought the diaries to mind. They had to be somewhere. I was certain they were in this house, and I was determined to find them. I'd turned on the light switch of the lamp beside my bed and was out of bed in an instant. Since I couldn't sleep, and I couldn't lie there any longer, I could occupy my time in a search for those books. I had to find them. Jayne wanted me to. I was certain of it. If people thought me weird or odd, I couldn't help it.

I turned the key in the door of the closet that contained her clothes. There was a bare bulb hanging from a ceiling cord. I turned the switch, and the long, narrow aperture was flooded with light. I started with her dresses, letting my hands move slowly down their folds, looking for places of concealment. Twice my fingers caught in the fabric and there was a ripping sound. No matter. The dresses should be disposed of. And they would be, as soon as the murderer was uncovered. There were boxes lining the shelves. I brought a chair from the bedroom, stood on it, and took down the boxes. They contained everything from fabrics to veiling, to fans, hats, and silk shawls folded carefully in layers of tissue paper. My aunt was a lover of luxury. Certainly she'd wanted for nothing. At the rear of the closet were cabinets. I opened the doors. Shoes were displayed on slanting shelves; a narrow ledge supported them and kept them from falling off.

But nowhere was there a trace of a diary. I put out the light and went into the sitting room. On a small table alongside the chaise longue, was the diary I'd discovered in the library. It would be senseless to return there, for Laurie and Keith had searched it again.

I examined the walls, letting my fingers explore the decorative woodwork that framed the panels. I checked the fireplace and the mantel above it. All my efforts were in vain.

I returned to the bedroom and sat before the writing

table. Without realizing it, I'd picked up the diary and brought it with me.

I opened it, scanning the pages at random until I came to the part where Jayne had asked Mecca if she'd placed the diary I was holding back in its hiding place in the library. Mecca had replied she hadn't. That she'd put it in the writing table.

I read that section a second time, then a third.

I closed the book, tossed it on a chair alongside me, and rested my hands in my lap. I was studying the mother-of-pearl top of the writing table. Was it possible the diaries could be concealed in this piece of furniture? My heartbeat quickened at the thought, but I cautioned myself against over-optimism. It was highly unlikely anything could be concealed in something as delicate as this table.

I raised it and checked the cover. It was much too narrow to have a false interior. I felt of the sides padded with pink satin and button-tufted. They, too, were firm, and there seemed not enough thickness for a hiding place. I felt the bottom. It, too, was padded, and the entire area was firm. Where, then, could a diary have been hidden? Or was I just imagining it would be a place of concealment?

I was being foolish. Stan and Laurie were right. I was becoming too obsessed with the thought of Jayne Greyfield's diaries—if they even existed. I moved restlessly about the room. Despite myself, my eyes continued to study the writing table. With an embarrassed glance around, as if fearful someone might be watching—I even thought of locking my doors, lest I be seen making a fool of myself—I went to the writing table. I got down on the floor and crawled underneath it. My hands again explored the bottom. There wasn't even a sign of a break in the wood. I let the forefinger of my right hand move slowly along the edge of each side. I met with no success. I did it again, this time exerting slight pressure.

I exclaimed aloud, as my finger slipped off the edge, though not until a narrow section of the wood had moved outward. Hardly daring to breathe, I exerted more pressure on the section and it moved further away from the cabinet, though it left no opening beneath. I released my hold to see if it would move back. It didn't.

I slid out from my awkward position beneath the writing table and stood up. *There was an aperture.* I raised the lid to see if it had disclosed anything inside. Nothing was changed there. I closed the lid and gently urged the narrow drawer—for that's what it was—further out. At the very end lay what I'd been looking for. *A diary!* Only one—but I knew it was Jayne Greyfield's. I picked it up and holding it as if it were a precious jewel—for that's how I thought of it—I carried it back to the bedroom. I put on my bed light, slipped between the covers, propped up my pillows, and opened it to the first page.

The handwriting assured me it was Jayne Greyfield's. I hoped, in some way, it would contain a clue to the murder of Scott Morton. Somehow, I felt that if it did, it might also give a clue that would lead to the solving of Jim Canby's murder and that of Aunt Mabel.

JAYNE

"Oh, Miss Jayne, you look beautiful." Mecca stood behind me as I surveyed my reflection in the mirror. It was an exquisite gown, a tribute to my dressmaker. Of apricot silk, with a lace bertha to show off my slender shoulders. It was bowed at the waist, and the double skirts were edged with black lace that fluttered like a butterfly's wings as I pirouetted to see myself from every angle.

I said, "If I live to be seventy, you'll be telling me I look beautiful."

"I will, Miss Jayne, because it'll be the truth," was her loyal reply. "You'll always be beautiful."

"I want to look especially attractive tonight." I reached for the two curls which hung down my back and drew them to the side so they rested on one shoulder.

"That looks better, Miss Jayne," Mecca said. "You always know just the right thing to do for yourself."

"Sometimes I wonder if the compliments you pay me are sincere or you happen to know I need reassurance."

"Miss Jayne, I wouldn't say a thing to you I didn't mean. Anyway, with all the beaux you've had, you don't need me to tell you you're beautiful."

"That's right, Mecca."

She seemed a little uneasy by what I'd said. And perhaps with reason. Lately, I'd had strong doubts about her loyalty. I shouldn't have, because she'd been with me all these years, and only once had I threatened to banish her from the island and sell her. She'd got on her knees then and pleaded with me to give her another chance. I did, though from time to time, I questioned the wisdom of my decision.

I suppose it was the War Between the States which had me unsettled. I'd heard her talking with the other servants in an undertone about it. I was really surprised at the way their faces glowed. I'd had no idea they weren't happy with me, since I'd always treated them kindly. Never once had I ordered one of them beaten. But then, Mama and Papa hadn't, either. Papa hadn't even liked slavery. A pity he couldn't be alive today to see the outcome.

I thought of Avery Halsten, the man I was to marry. I was grateful he was forty-two, too old for the rigors and horrors of war. I shut out the ugliness of the thought, went to my dressing table, and picked up my fan.

Mecca ran to the door and held it wide. I may not have been certain of her loyalty, but there was no doubting the admiration in her eyes as she watched me approach the door.

"Have a happy evening, Miss Jayne."

I smiled my gratitude, but gave her a chiding glance. "I'm not even leaving the house."

"I know, but I wanted to wish you a happy evening."

"I shall have it in the company of Mr. Avery."

Once again I thought I caught a look of insincerity in her eyes. I dismissed it, for I heard Avery's deep voice greeting the butler.

My darling Avery, I thought. Such a gentleman, and so kind and gracious to everyone. How could he have fallen in love with me? But he had. And I relished the thought so much I'd got on my knees last night and thanked the Almighty He'd allowed me to know happiness once again.

We'd dined in the library before the fireplace. It was a beautiful setting, for there'd been heavy rains and the dampness could only be dispelled by a glowing fireplace. Pewter candelabra on the mantel flanking my portrait provided the only other light in the room. The dishes and table linen had already been removed, and we stood before the window, looking out at the still-wet garden, lit only by a half-moon that drifted in and out among the rapidly dissipating clouds.

Avery's arm enclosed my waist and drew me around to face him. "I have something to tell you, but first, an embrace."

I hadn't believed I could ever know such ecstasy again. Now, I realized the love I'd thought I'd had for Scott Morton was the mere infatuation of a young girl for a sophisticated man desired by all women. He'd never have been faithful to one woman. Yet he was the kind of man who had to know there was a woman he could always turn to. He had one in Eulalie. I shut out all thought of him and looked up into the dark eyes of my beloved. He was far from handsome, but to me, his craggy features were indicative of his strong character.

"What is it you wish to tell me?" My heart wanted to burst through my chest wall at his mere closeness.

"I've joined the Confederate Army."

I thought I was going to faint, but my hands gripped his arms tightly in an effort to regain my senses.

"Why did you do such a thing?"

"I'd be a coward not to."

"Why would you fight for a cause you don't believe in?"

"I just told you."

"Wars are for young men," I exclaimed, horrified at the thought of Avery exposed to the gunfire of the Union Army. Or any army, for that matter. "You're forty-two."

"I'll be forty-three in a month. I've already joined up, Jayne. Our marriage will have to wait until I return."

Tears blinded my vision, but I blinked them away. "If you love me, you'll marry me now—tonight. I'll write you every day. I'll be here, awaiting your return."

"I may come back a cripple, or worse. I'll not let you wait for that. I love you too much to marry you now. If I were wealthy, it would be different. But I'm not, and I'd be dependent on your bounty. I have too much pride for that."

"Pride!" I exclaimed in anguish. "I hate the word. It's haunted me all my life. You're not wealthy now."

"True," he admitted, "but I have a modest business in which I have faith. By dint of hard work, I expect one day

it will grow to the point where my name will mean something in Savannah. But if I should be injured to the extent that I cannot work, my business would die."

"It doesn't matter," I exclaimed. "Marry me, Avery. I'll get down on my knees and beg you."

I did slip to my knees, but he drew me to my feet.

"You're a noble woman, Jayne. The only one I've ever loved."

"Your love has made me good. I wasn't always. I was bitter and rebellious because of the ugly talk about me when Scott Morton's body was found here."

"I know about that. I never believed you guilty."

I cupped his face between my hands and gave him a kiss of gratitude. "You're probably the only one in Savannah who believed in my innocence."

"No," he contradicted. "Many felt Scott Morton's mistress—the one you befriended—came here unbeknownst to him and murdered him."

"If so," I said, "she has never admitted it."

"I understand she's a well-educated woman. She'd not likely incriminate herself."

"I tried to cultivate her," I said, "but she's a complete recluse."

"Her guilty conscience, no doubt. Even after all the years, do you feel completely safe with her on the island?"

His concern touched me. "She'd not harm me. Nor would her brother. They keep to themselves. I'm sure they're grateful for the sanctuary I gave them when Eulalie's life was endangered by the ugly talk of lynching."

"I hope she is," he said. "But what about you? Don't you think you should go to the mainland until after this ugly business is over?"

"Greyfield Manor has always been my home," I said. "I'd never leave it. Not even for a war. If it's burned to the ground, I'll rebuild it."

We drew apart when Mecca entered with a tray containing a carafe of brandy and two glasses. I was annoyed at the intrusion because it should have been brought in immediately at the meal's end. Without glancing at either of us, she proceeded to pour the liquid into the glasses.

Avery could have done it and had done it before. If he noticed, he made no comment.

I sat on the settee before the fireplace and arranged my skirts. He took the glasses from Mecca, thanked her, and joined me.

"To victory," he said.

We touched glasses and took a sip of the beverage. Mecca came over and put another log on the fire.

Avery said, "Eulalie Laboulaye was at the pier when I docked my boat. I spoke to her, but she made no answer. Her brother Setley was at her side. Their manner wasn't unfriendly, but their silence and their continued stare made me uncomfortable. That's why I mentioned her."

Mecca, having arranged the log to her satisfaction, now took the broom and gently brushed the ash, which had spilled onto the hearth, back into the fire.

"Mr. Avery can do that, Mecca. Leave the room immediately."

My voice sharpened with annoyance, the more so when I thought I detected a look of defiance in her eyes. But she straightened and without a word headed for the door. I gave no further order, though I knew she'd not close it. Nor did she. Avery also watched her depart. When she didn't close the door, he arose and did so.

"What's got into her?" he asked after he'd joined me.

"I don't know," I said uneasily. "She never acted like that before."

"It's the war, I guess. They sense things will be different."

"Why should they be?" I asked.

"We can't win, Jayne," he said softly. His arms reached for me as he spoke.

I moved away from him. "Then why risk your life for a losing cause?" I demanded.

He smiled. "And a cause I don't believe in. Slavery—I hate it. Thank God, I don't own any."

I set down my glass, stood up, and walked to the window. "Don't make me feel guilty, Avery. I inherited my slaves."

He was at my side in a moment. "My darling, I didn't

mean to be rude. It's true—you inherited your slaves. I'm not blaming you for something that existed long before you were born."

"I could have freed them. Did that thought occur to you?"

"I've never sat in judgment on my friends so long as they didn't misuse or abuse their chattels. And since I didn't with them, I wouldn't with you."

I bowed my head. "I wanted this to be a gala night."

"I know I've spoiled our evening, but I had to tell you about my plans. I don't want the war or the subject of slavery to absorb our evening, especially since this will be the last one we'll have together. I leave tomorrow for Atlanta."

I didn't feel like smiling, but I did. "Say you'll come back, Avery. I couldn't endure it if you didn't."

"I'll come back."

I was far from comforted. "I've not been a good woman. Yes, this is a confession." His hand covered my mouth, but I drew it away. "I have to tell you."

"You don't have to tell me anything," he protested. "I don't want to hear it."

"You must. All the ugly things they're saying about me are true. I was the cause of breaking up three marriages. I flaunted my indiscretions before society. I became a social outcast. You know I'm not accepted by polite society. I'm regarded in the same light as a . . ."

"That's enough." Sternness crept into his voice. "Don't castigate yourself further. At least, not to me. I'm aware of all the gossip. I know why you did what you did. You were lonely and hurt and wrongly accused of Scott Morton's murder. You're not bad, Jayne. The fact that you not only built a house for Eulalie Laboulaye, but deeded the house and property to her, is proof of your goodness. Don't you know people hate you for that, as well as for your other—indiscretions?"

"I gave no thought to what I did for Eulalie," I said.

"I did," he replied softly. "And it made me love you all the more."

"Then marry me," I pleaded. "Give me your name. I'll not besmirch it."

"I know that. But I'll not give in to your plea, though it's the most difficult refusal I've ever made. I'll talk no more about it. I want the rest of the evening to hold you in my arms. Just remember, I believe firmly I'll come back. Tell me you believe it. Come, Jayne. Say it."

"I believe it." My smile was more of a grimace.

"Say it as if you mean it, my darling."

I tried again, with greater success. "I believe it, Avery. I'll say it every day while you're away. I'll write you every day."

"And I'll write you. Be sure to mention you still love me." His voice was light, but his eyes were filled with adoration.

"My letters will be so filled with it," I promised, "you'll tire of reading them."

"Never," he averred. "I'll come back. Your love will act as a steel cloak."

"Once more," I said, "I beg of you to marry me." My voice was a plea, but he was adamant.

"It's not easy to refuse, but I've given my reason for doing so."

Our lips touched then, and we wasted no more time with words. It was our last night together.

I sensed a light of some kind. It had pulled me awake and seemed to be close to my closed lids. I opened them slightly and drew them shut again. There was candlelight in my room. I shaded my eyes with my hand against the glare, opened them, and spoke the name of the only person who would dare invade the privacy of my bedchamber without permission.

"Mecca?"

There was no answer. I spoke her name again. There was still no answer. I urged myself to a sitting position, freed my mind of sleep, and looked toward the foot of the bed. Fully awake now, I made out the figure of Eulalie Laboulaye.

I was startled. It was the first time she'd set foot in Greyfield Manor.

"What do you want?" I demanded. "And how dare you come here?"

"I have something to tell you," she replied. Her diction was precise, her voice low and cultured.

"Who let you in?" I demanded.

"The door was not locked."

She was in far more control of the situation than I, but then she'd startled me into wakefulness. Her flawless beauty was breathtaking to behold, and her skin glowed golden in the candlelight, which was also reflected in her large blue eyes.

"You still had no right to enter this house unbidden. Nor to invade my bedroom."

"Not even to make a statement?" she asked, her manner as serene as ever.

"What sort of statement?" My curiosity got the better of me.

"Regarding Mr. Avery Halsten."

"What about him?"

"He'll not come back."

"What are you talking about?"

The faintest semblance of a smile touched her lips. "He will be killed in the war."

"Why have you come here to say that?"

"To deny you happiness."

"Why would you wish to do that? Haven't I treated you with consideration? Who else in Savannah would have done for you what I did?"

"No one," she admitted.

"Have you no sense of gratitude?"

"I am loyal to the memory of Scott Morton."

"I won't condemn you for that, but surely you don't expect me to mourn him the rest of my days."

She made no reply, just stood there, that maddening smile on her exquisitely chiseled face.

I said, "I never loved Scott Morton, though I didn't know it until I met Avery Halsten. My feeling for Scott was one of girlish infatuation. He was handsome, gallant, and desired by every female. He chose me as a marriage partner above every other girl in Savannah."

She sobered at that, as I knew she would. I had hurt her. I didn't even have a regret at having done so. She was angry with me for having fallen in love again. She felt I was being disloyal to Scott's memory. Disloyal to a man who had given me a proposal of marriage so he might pay his debts. Also, I suppose it would have been my money that would have supported her. She was lucky Judge Bannon had invested the small amount of money her father had been able to leave her so that she was now financially independent.

I said, "You're a free person and you can go north if you wish. Why don't you? With the war you'll be far better off there than here. We will probably suffer hardships."

"I can endure them. I will never leave my love."

"Your love is dead."

Her head moved in negative fashion, and she touched the region of her heart. "The flame still burns brightly, and it will continue to do so as long as there is a breath of life in me."

"Have you said what you came to say?" I demanded.

"Not quite."

"Then say it and get out!" I no longer tried to curb my anger.

"I will. Hope and pray you outlive me."

I was astounded at her boldness. "Are you threatening me?"

"No. Just making a statement."

"Have you forgotten I saved you from a lynching?"

"No, Miss Greyfield."

Her eyes held the same mocking look I'd detected in Mecca's earlier. Was it possible they were friends—unbeknownst to me? Any why not, I thought. There was nothing wrong with that. For the first time, I remembered Avery's concern about my remaining here. He was thinking of more than the dangers connected with the war. I felt no fear on that score. But there had been one murder on this island. And certainly, Eulalie could well have been the one who had plunged the knife into Scott Morton's back, for one reason. Jealousy. She'd not share him with me.

She knew what I was thinking and sobered quickly. Her eyes became cold and hate-filled, and now I wondered if she would kill me. Or have Setley do it. Could they have enlisted Mecca in such a scheme? The war occupied everyone's mind. No one thought of me on the island. One white woman. A white woman who'd made a fool of herself. Who would die unmourned by anyone in Savannah. I'd thought of it before, but not until I met Avery and knew how beautiful the love of a good man was, did I realize the value of a good moral character. I wanted to be worthy of his love. If so, I must change now. I must show compassion, shut out the anger I'd directed at this woman.

I said, "Try not to hate me, Eulalie. I didn't know about you and Scott."

She said, "I will never let you forget."

With that, she turned and moved with dignity from the room.

"Did you know Eulalie Laboulaye was in this house last night?" I asked the question of Mecca as she stood beside my chair, pouring my coffee.

My question startled her so much that she almost dropped the silver pot. I knew if she'd not been aware of it, she was certainly in contact of some kind with either Eulalie or her brother.

I said, "You've been disloyal to me. I don't mind your seeing Eulalie or Setley, but you've always pretended you had nothing to do with them."

"Yes, Miss Jayne."

"Are you friends?"

She gave a bare nod of her head.

"Have they ever been in this house before?"

"No, Miss Jayne, I swear it."

She started to cry.

"Dry your tears. Strangely, I believe you. But I'll never trust you again. You're to pack your belongings and be out of here before noon."

"Where'll I go, Miss Jayne?"

"Not to Eulalie's. I don't want you on this island. I'll sign a remission paper granting you your freedom. I'll give you enough money to feed and house you for a week."

I stood up and started to leave the room, but she got on her knees and grasped my hand so tightly, I couldn't free it.

"Please don't send me away, Miss Jayne. I got nowhere to go."

"You'll have to find a place. Let go of my hand. I'll write out a paper for you immediately."

She was sobbing wildly now, but I was unmoved. I gave my hand a yank and pulled it free. I went directly to the library, made out the paper, signed it, and left it on the hall table. I instructed my butler to take her to the mainland as soon as she was ready. He eyed the upper hall with apprehension. I knew he was as filled with fear for Mecca as she.

I went back into the library. I didn't want to see her, lest I relent. Only once before had I scolded her severely, and that was when my diaries were stolen. She swore she had no knowledge of how a thief had got into the house. The other servants also swore to their innocence. Mecca was the only one who knew of the secret compartment in the cabinet in the library. But not even she knew of the one in my writing table. Often I'd asked her to place my diary in the compartment, which held paper, envelopes, and blotters. But the narrow drawer in the bottom I'd never divulged. Now I was glad. I wanted this diary to have a happy ending. My first one hadn't, and it was the only one not stolen. So far as I knew, it still reposed there. Let it.

All I wanted was for Avery Halsten to return safely, so I would once again know the wonder of his love. I'd be a good wife. I'll do all in my power to atone for my unsavory past, the very thought of which made my face burn with shame.

A year has passed, and not once have I missed a day writing to my beloved Avery. At first, his letters arrived on a daily basis, but then they were more infrequent and he wrote of his utter weariness and of the senselessness of the killings, sometimes even brother against brother. He prayed for an early end to the massacre and asked me to do likewise. I did, just as I prayed he'd come through the carnage safely.

It seems strange to be alone in this house. I now realize full well what Avery meant when he expressed concern about my remaining here. I see no one, and no one comes here.

The servants deserted four months ago. I didn't blame them. I'd starve if it weren't for Setley. He planted a garden and raises a wide variety of vegetables. He also keeps chickens and hogs and cows, and sees to it that I am well fed. Not that he or Eulalie has entered Greyfield Manor since that night she invaded my bedchamber. But he leaves a basket of food three times a week.

I've seen Eulalie stroll the beach from my window. Often she stands and looks up at the house, which is on a rise. I wonder if she sees me looking back at her. She is as beautiful as ever, but she makes me feel as if I am her prisoner.

I haven't fared as well. My features are haggard, and there are harsh lines around my mouth and eyes. Where once I walked erect, my shoulders slouch, and my head almost rests on my chin. When I catch a glimpse of myself in the mirror, I straighten and give myself a silent reprimand, but I quickly forget. Sometimes it seems I even forget my name.

But not my Avery. I call to him often. I stand on the landing and speak his name. Softly at first, then louder and louder until I'm shouting it, as if by doing that, I can will him back. I even laugh aloud afterward.

It came this morning. A letter for me. I walked through the Manor for hours, holding it in my hand, scarcely daring to open it. I knew it was from Avery, even though it wasn't in his handwriting.

It was the first word I'd had from him in months. Finally, when I couldn't stand the suspense any longer, I head-

ed for the library. I paused on the way and glanced in the mirror. My hair was matted and almost completely covered my face. How untidy I looked, yet I laughed at my reflection. It didn't matter. Nothing mattered now. Avery was coming home. This was his letter telling me so.

I sat down and pulled open the flap of the envelope. I took out the paper and started to read aloud. I read it once, and then a second time. It was from Avery's colonel, and he wrote telling me Avery was dead . . . that he'd died a hero's death, holding off several Union soldiers so that two officers could get back to their lines.

My darling Avery. Now it is my turn. Everything is ready. I've prepared well for this and have waited for this day. I was so certain I would receive this last letter from my love.

I've gone upstairs to the attic and walked the length of it. The rope is tied securely to the rafter. The chair on which I will stand as I fasten the noose around my neck is set on a box so that when I kick it free, I'll swing in the air and after a while I will join my Avery. My beloved Avery.

TEN

I was sick with the knowledge of what had happened to Jayne Greyfield. And I was angry with Eulalie, for I believed she was, in large part, responsible for my aunt's mental breakdown. Watching the house as she had and warning Jayne she would never let her forget Scott Morton was enough to undermine anyone's sanity. I wondered what had happened to the missing diaries and why they'd been stolen.

Mecca must have had something to do with them. She'd sworn Eulalie and Setley had not set foot in the Manor. But if the diaries were missing and no one else came to the island, who but Eulalie and Setley would be in a position to steal them? And if they hadn't stolen them, how had they disappeared?

The answer came. Mecca had taken the diaries from the house. To where? Eulalie's, of course. Who else would want them? And why would she have desired them? It didn't take long to figure that out. Perhaps my aunt had discovered a clue that pointed to Scott Morton's murderer. A clue that led directly to Eulalie. It had to be something like that.

I wondered how I could regain possession of those diaries. Certainly, there'd be little opportunity to make a search of Eulalie's house. Either Setley or Eulalie was always around. Yet I must find a way to get them. They were my aunt's property, taken from her home without permission. I made a silent vow to regain them if I had to confront Eulalie and Setley and demand their return. Then I thought of a better way. See Stan and ask him to intercede for me. Even if Eulalie were guilty of Scott Morton's murder, she'd not be prosecuted now. She was too old. The more I thought of it, the wiser it seemed that I should let Stan handle the problem.

I'd not slept a wink, waiting for dawn to color the sky. But I'd done a lot of thinking and made my plans. I'd take a rowboat to the mainland. My car would be garaged in the shed by the dock, and I'd go immediately to the Bannon house. I reviewed my plans as I dressed, choosing a tailored blouse and skirt, for my mission was far from frivolous.

No one else stirred. I knew because the door to Aunt Hannah's sitting room was open. There was no sign of Laurie, but Keith was asleep in the chair. I couldn't help smiling. Anyone could enter without his knowing. I was certain of it after I went to the door of Aunt Hannah's room and looked in on her. I could see her form, but I didn't hear her breathing.

I moved silently up to her bedside and in the dim light made out her features. Not completely reassured, I bent over her until her breathing was audible. Satisfied, I left the room as quietly as I'd entered. Keith hadn't stirred.

Downstairs, the sharp smell of wax assailed my nostrils. I went to the door of the drawing room. Esther was asleep in one of the wing chairs. The candles still burned, but their circumference was at least three inches and they had a long way to go before the flame reached the metal base.

I didn't disturb Esther. Cora would probably be down shortly, and since it was bound to be a day of sadness, it would be kinder to let everyone sleep as long as possible.

Viewing Aunt Mabel's body once again made me realize it was far more important to learn who had disposed of her and Jim Canby than to recover the diaries of Jayne Greyfield. With that thought in mind, I headed for the dock, hopeful there would be a rowboat there. I wasn't exactly certain of what steps I'd take in my effort to unravel the horror of what had happened here, but I'd not resolve it staying at the Manor.

First, I'd pay a visit to Mr. Curran. I wanted to talk

with him regarding the note he said he'd received from me, asking him to come to Greyfield immediately. Though the day wasn't overcast, the blue of the sky was partially obscured with clouds. I hoped the day wouldn't be marred by rain. Funerals were dismal affairs, without a curtain of rain to add to the gloom.

The inn was a red brick building. A porch extended across the front, with rockers gracing it. It was further shaded by a curtain of bougainvillea, heavily blossomed. Inside, the clerk dozed behind the desk, but awoke when I bade him a soft-spoken good morning rather than touch the bell. I noticed a switchboard and asked that he ring Mr. Curran's number.

"No need to do that, Miss." He attempted a smile of greeting, but his youthful features were still too befogged with sleep to manage it, and he stifled a yawn instead. He pointed to a slot in which rested a key. "He went out about an hour ago."

"Does he usually rise so early?"

"He's only been here a few days, and he's in and out most of the time. Other than that, I don't know anything about him."

"Thank you. I'll come back later."

"Wanta leave your name, Miss?"

"No, thanks."

I went out, got into the car, and drove to Stan's. It was almost eight o'clock, and I hoped he and his grandfather would be up and about. My luck was no better there. A maid informed me both gentlemen had gone to Savannah.

I went back to the car, prepared to return to the island, when a thought occurred to me. The letter Jim Canby had received. It had upset him to the point where he'd sought out the young lady he believed had written it. His rash act had caused him to be arrested. I wondered who she could have been. Had the police in Savannah had any further contact with her? Had Sheriff Eckles? I doubted it, or he'd have informed us.

I could check with him, but I decided to make the drive

to Savannah, determined to learn who had written that letter. If only there was a copy of it available. Unless the handwriting was disguised, it could point a clue to the writer. I started the motor and headed for the highway that led to Savannah. I went faster than I should, but the more I thought about it, the more impatient I was to uncover the person who would resort to such viciousness. I could think of no other word to fit such a despicable act.

At the police station I gave my name and stated my reason for being there was to get information regarding the identity of the young lady Jim Canby had accosted in the restaurant the night preceding his murder.

I was referred to Lieutenant Paley, who brought me into a small office. He seated me in a small chair alongside his desk, then moved around it to occupy the swivel chair. His alert eyes studied me keenly.

Once again I stated my reason for being here.

He said, "Her name is Pauline Rowe. Why do you wish to see her?"

The Lieutenant was about forty, lean but muscular. His manner was polite, but I knew he was observing me carefully, wondering if I might have been the one who had plunged the knife into Jim Canby's back.

"I want to learn if she knows anything about a note Mr. Canby told me he'd received. It was an anonymous note that caused him to go to that restaurant. He thought Miss Rowe had written it."

The Lieutenant frowned. "Sheriff Eckles was here about that. There was no mention made of a note by either Miss Rowe or her escort in the police report. They said Mr. Canby came to their table and caused a disturbance, and the gentleman called the maître d'hôtel."

"What was the gentleman's name?"

"I'm sorry to say we didn't get it. There was no need, since he hadn't made the complaint. The maître d'hôtel called the manager who, in turn, telephoned the police."

"How did you get the lady's name?"

Lieutenant Paley said, "The maître d'hôtel knew it because she had dined there several times in the company of Mr. Canby. Since there were no charges filed against him, there was nothing more for us to do."

"Thank you." I stood up.

"About that letter." The Lieutenant moved around his desk and opened the door of his office. "I'm sorry I can't be of help."

"Perhaps you can," I said. "May I have the address of Miss Rowe?"

"Certainly." He wrote it on a pad, tore off the page, and handed it to me.

"Thank you, Lieutenant."

"Oh, Miss Greyfield, there is one matter. The disposal of Mr. Canby's body."

"Are there no relatives?" I asked.

"None who will assume responsibility."

"Please inform the undertaker I'll assume the expense. I'll contact him tomorrow. His name, please?"

The Lieutenant took back the slip of paper he'd just given me and wrote it down. I again thanked him and left. From the police station, I went directly to the hotel and sought out the maître d'hôtel. He couldn't enlighten me, either, regarding the identity of the gentleman who was dining with Miss Rowe."

"Can you describe him?"

"Not too well, I'm afraid," his smile was apologetic. "He didn't stand out. Certainly not the way Mr. Canby did. Some people do, some don't. As I recall, he was of medium height and was wearing a dark suit."

"The color of his eyes," I suggested.

The maître d'hôtel shook his head slowly, his manner again apologetic. "I'm sorry, Miss Greyfield. They left after Mr. Canby was taken away by the police. I was sorry about that, but he was incoherent and loud and belligerent. In view of what happened to him afterward, I wish the police hadn't been called."

"Under the circumstances, you couldn't do otherwise."

He looked appreciative.

I said, "Did you hear Mr. Canby make any reference to a letter he'd received?"

"As I said, he was incoherent most of the time. His anger was directed at Miss Rowe, and she was frightened. Really frightened."

In defense of Jim, I said, "I never saw Mr. Canby under the influence of liquor, so it's difficult for me to imagine such behavior on his part."

"He hadn't been in here in a long time. Nor had Miss Rowe, I might add. But when they were . . . keeping company, they dined here frequently."

"Thank you."

"You're welcome, Miss Greyfield. I'm sorry I can't be of more help, but I just don't remember what that gentleman looked like."

I wondered if Miss Rowe did. I certainly intended to find out. I drove directly to the address Lieutenant Paley had given me. It was a modest neighborhood with small homes and well-kept lawns.

I went up the walk and rang the bell. When no one came, I rang it a second time. I hoped I'd not be disappointed again. This far, I'd learned little except that no one had heard Jim Canby make any reference to a letter he'd received. The maître d'hôtel had said he was incoherent most of the time. Thus far, the only one who seemed to have any direct knowledge of the note, other than Jim, was I.

I wondered if I dared ring the bell a third time. If anyone was inside, it was apparent they had no desire to answer the door.

To ring it again would only antagonize them. Yet I hated to concede defeat altogether; nor could I afford to tarry for long. Aunt Mabel's funeral was to be held this afternoon, and I wanted to be present.

My hand was raised to press the bell a final time when a key turned in the lock and the door opened about an inch. I couldn't see through the narrow space.

"What do you want?" I knew it was a woman only from the voice.

"I'm Aldis Greyfield. I'd like to talk with you, Miss Rowe."

There were a few moments of silence before she said, "About what?"

"Jim Canby. The night he created a disturbance in the restaurant."

"Nothing to talk about."

"Please," I urged. "I won't take more than five minutes of your time."

"Haven't got five minutes," she said. "Got a luncheon engagement."

"Then will you tell me this, please? Did Jim mention a letter he received?"

"Yes."

"He did?" I exclaimed.

"He did," she said. "Now you'll have to excuse me."

"Oh, please." I pushed on the door, but she must have had her foot against it, for it didn't budge. "Another question. Did he show it to you?"

"No. I told him he was out of his mind. He was drunk. He was always loud when he was drunk."

"I'm not interested in the past. He's dead now. Murdered. You know that. Don't you wish the murderer brought to justice?"

"I think the police can do that far better than you," came her indifferent reply.

"I'm sure they can," I said. "But I also had an aunt who was murdered. I think the person who killed Jim killed her."

"I read about it in the paper. My sympathies."

"Thank you." I only wished she'd sounded genuinely sympathetic. She might be more inclined to talk reasonably with me.

"Now you'll have to excuse me."

"Please—another question. Will you tell me the name of your escort?"

"Of all the nerve!" she exclaimed. "I'll tell you nothing more."

And with that, she slammed the door. I wondered if Sheriff Eckles had questioned her and if so, if he'd had as little success as I. I doubted that her manner would have been as arrogant with him. With me, she had nothing to fear. If, indeed, there was reason for her to fear questioning.

I moved down the walk and returned to the car, which I'd parked on a street which ran perpendicular to the one on which she lived, but which gave a full view of her house. I'd chosen the spot because a large tree shaded the car and would keep it cool.

I slid behind the wheel. I noticed the shades of her house were lowered on both the first and second floors, so she wasn't peering behind curtains to watch me depart.

My mission had been a complete failure. There wasn't even time to stop at the inn on my return and question Mr. Curran regarding the note he'd received. If he could even describe the handwriting. Sometimes people had a stylized way of dotting an "i", making it a circle instead of a dot. Or crossing a "t" with a flourish, idiosyncrasies which set their writing apart and made it identifiable.

I started the motor and was shifting the car into gear when a car drove up before the house I'd just left and stopped. A gentleman got out and walked up to the door. He had better luck than I, for the door opened at his first ring. He removed his hat, bowed slightly, and offered his arm; he and Miss Rowe walked back to the car.

I exclaimed aloud as he turned, enabling me to recognize him. Stan Bannon! And Miss Pauline Rowe! I could scarcely believe my eyes, and yet there he was, bowing as he assisted her into the front seat of the car. She was an attractive blonde, with a flashing smile and a red dress that was cut to reveal her superb figure. Certainly, Stan was aware of it, for his smile was warm and adoring, and she flashed him a beauteous one in return.

He apparently made a humorous remark, because her laughter, mingled with his, drifted through the open windows as he drove away from the curb. I felt a tight band of pain around my heart. I wondered if he could have been her escort the night Jim accosted them in the restaurant.

If so, Stan was as deceitful to me as Scott Morton had been to my aunt. And this time, tears did come. I blinked them away, for I couldn't drive with my eyes filming. At least no one at Greyfield Manor knew of my humiliation. I was glad not even Eulalie would know of it. I'd give Stan Bannon short shrift. There was nothing for me to do now but return to Greyfield Island.

When Stan came to discuss my deeding the islands to the state, he'd get a surprise. The first thing I'd do tomorrow would be to contact Mr. Curran, listen to his plan, and act on it.

Aunt Mabel's funeral services were held at four in the afternoon. The sun had slipped behind clouds that grew more ominous as the day waned. At graveside were Aunt Hannah, Keith, Laurie, the minister, Esther, Cora, and me. Standing at a distance were Eulalie and Setley. Farther back was the undertaker with his assistants.

It was only with difficulty I could hold back my anger when I glanced at Eulalie dressed in somber black. Setley was wearing a dark suit, with white shirt and black tie.

Aunt Hannah and I were also in black, Laurie in navy. After the services we returned to the Manor. The Reverend Mr. Crouse, about twenty-five, came back with us and had tea and cake, then excused himself because of the fast-approaching storm. Keith took him back to the village in the launch.

After he left, Aunt Hannah asked if she might talk with me in her sitting room. Her manner was subdued, almost friendly. I was puzzled, but also curious.

Laurie asked to be excused, saying she felt fatigued, having sat up with Keith most of the night. I was glad to leave the drawing room, even though the only reminder of the tragedy was a faint melted-wax aroma, which probably had been absorbed into the draperies. The flowers that had filled the drawing room now covered the grave. Keith had told me on my return Setley had dug the grave and had asked permission to fill it in.

Aunt Hannah and I sat opposite one another on settees that flanked the fireplace. Cora already had a fire glowing, and it felt good, for the temperature had dropped sharply as the sky darkened, foretelling a coming storm. Intermittent gusts of wind rattled the windows, adding to the dismalness of the day.

Aunt Hannah gave a worried glance in the direction of the window. "I hope Keith gets back before the storm breaks."

"So do I." I knew she was thinking of my parents, whose sailboat had overturned during a sudden squall.

She regarded her hands clasped sedately in her lap. "Why haven't you ordered me from the house?"

"Why would I do such a thing?"

"Because of the way I've treated you. I should say, the way I ignored you."

Her manner was so changed, I was at a loss for words.

"No need to answer, Aldis. Let me talk. They say confession is good for the soul, so I'm going to unburden myself. Believe it or not, I have an overwhelming sense of guilt because of you. It's really because I was jealous of your mother's happiness. I envied her happy marriage. I envied her and my brother the fruit of their union—namely, you. I, too, wanted love and a family. Not getting it, I took out my frustration on you and Mabel."

"Mabel loved you," I said.

Her eyes refuted that. "She was loyal to me. I destroyed her. She wanted to love you. She said you were lonely. You were. I knew it, and I was taking out my dislike of your mother on you. She was a warm, loving person. So was your father. Mabel would have been like him had I let her, but I insisted you be raised with stern discipline. My will was stronger than hers. She gave in to me."

"Aunt Hannah, I had no idea you disliked me until I came here. Not until then did you make it clearly evident you disliked having me around."

She nodded. "I felt that with your marriage, I'd no longer have to look at you. Each time I did, I saw your mother. I heard her joyous laughter, her exclamations of delight when she was with you and my brother. If they'd lived, Mabel would have had a much happier time, for your father would not have allowed me to become the martinet I turned into."

"That's all in the past, Aunt Hannah."

"Yes. None of us can go back. But I can change." She raised her hands, then dropped them in a gesture of hopelessness. "At least, I'm going to make the effort. And I'll begin with something Mabel discussed with me a few days before her—death. That is, disposing of this island. I can't do it, of course. But you can."

"You're referring to Mr. Curran's suggestion of breaking it up into parcels of land to be sold to private individuals."

"I am not."

"Then you'll have to explain."

"Mabel felt it would be a gracious gesture on your part to deed this island to the state to be developed for public use."

"I never discussed that with Aunt Mabel."

Aunt Hannah smiled at the surprise evident in my voice. "You did discuss it with Stanley Bannon, didn't you?"

I nodded. "How did you know?"

"Keith talked about it. He seemed to favor the idea."

"Apparently everyone does but me," I said.

She looked surprised. "I thought you would, too. Especially since you seemed interested in Stanley Bannon."

I said, "Don't you think that makes me out rather fickle?"

"You're thinking of Jim Canby."

"Yes."

"You'll probably smile at this, wondering just what I would know about it, but I always had the idea you were overwhelmed by the fact that he paid attention to you. He was very handsome and much sought after by all the belles of Savannah, and you mistook infatuation for love. Was I wrong?"

I didn't want to answer, yet it was a time for honesty. Certainly, since my aunt was unburdening herself to me, I could do no less.

"You're right, though I don't believe I've faced up to it until this very moment. I wondered why I hadn't shed a tear. Not even after the terrible way he met his end. I was shocked and horrified and angry that such a thing had happened, but it didn't touch me inside, and I couldn't understand."

"Not until Stanley Bannon came into your life." She smiled as color flooded my face. "You love him. I saw it in your eyes yesterday."

"Perhaps that's also infatuation. I'm impressed because he's going to run for the United States Senate."

"I don't believe that, Aldis. Forgive me for prying; I just want you to know I feel that turning the island over to the state would be a fine cause."

"So does Stan Bannon. In fact, I'm convinced that was his reason for coming here. Probably his reason for cultivating me."

"Is that what he said?"

I stood up and walked to the window. The ocean was liberally sprinkled with whitecaps, and the whole sky was dark now with the approaching storm. I shivered inwardly, for it reminded me of the night I came here. I moved over to the fireplace. The logs were almost burned through. I put on two more.

"You didn't answer my question, Aldis." There was slight reproof in Aunt Hannah's voice.

I said, "I don't wish to become emotionally involved with anyone at this time. As for the island, until the murders are solved, I shan't make a decision on what I am going to do. But I was of the opinion you and Aunt Mabel wished to live out your lives here because of the privacy the place afforded."

"I thought I did, but not after what's happened."

"What would you like?"

"A small apartment in Savannah," she said. "I don't ever wish to come back here. I'm too filled with guilt."

I went to her and rested a hand lightly on her shoulder. "Now that you've talked, you should be free of it."

Her eyes searched mine. "Can you forgive me for the way I treated you?"

"You saw to my material comforts and that I attended schools of high academic standing."

"That was duty—not love. I don't know if I'm capable of love. But I want to be. I want to feel compassion in my heart. Mabel had it. On the few occasions when she voiced her feelings, her face softened so that she looked almost beautiful. Even then, I knew it was her goodness shining through. I always disputed whatever thought she gave voice to. She'd immediately stifle her feelings and resume her somber mood."

"Perhaps," I ventured, "there was someone she knew with whom she could be herself."

"I can't imagine who," she said.

"How do you suppose she got the idea for turning this island over to the public?"

"I don't know."

"I'd say it was Stanley Bannon."

"I doubt whether she knew him."

"She knew him, Aunt Hannah. You'll probably learn about it sooner or later, so I may as well tell you. Aunt Mabel visited Eulalie Laboulaye. Not frequently, but they were acquainted. She met Stan there. He told me so."

Once she overcame her surprise, she said, "Why did she go there?"

"For company, I suppose. She struck up an acquaintance with Eulalie one day while taking a stroll."

"When I had one of my headaches," Aunt Hannah ventured.

"Yes. I suppose she didn't dare let you know."

Aunt Hannah nodded. "Well, I'm glad. At least, she had a little fun."

"I don't think Eulalie is fun," I said coldly.

Aunt Hannah regarded me with surprise. "She's lonely. Perhaps even lonelier than Mabel was. Her only visitors are Stanley Bannon and his grandfather. Though she'd be the last to admit it, from the top floor of this house I've observed her watch, from a secluded spot, for the Bannon launch to make its appearance. The Bannons have been very devoted to her."

"They hold her in very high regard."

Aunt Hannah's brow creased thoughtfully. "You say they met Mabel at Eulalie's."

"Yes."

"I wonder why they didn't come for the graveside services?"

"I don't know." I'd wondered about the same thing. Or I would have, if I hadn't seen Stan at Miss Rowe's to take her to lunch.

"Perhaps they weren't aware of the time."

"Perhaps."

Aunt Hannah stood up, walked over to the fire, and extended her hands to it.

"Why don't you lie down, Aunt Hannah?"

She spoke without turning. "I think I will. And I'll have a tray in my room tonight, if you don't mind."

"You may have anything you wish," I said. "Always remember that. And you shall have your apartment."

She turned to face me. Her eyes held a glow of warmth, and so did the smile that touched her mouth. "Thank you, my dear."

I went to her. "I want us to be close, Aunt Hannah. It's not too late. It's never too late to make a new beginning."

She was too overwhelmed to speak, but she did give a brief nod of agreement. I touched my cheek to hers. Her arms raised to embrace me, but she couldn't complete the gesture. I understood. In time, she'd be able to do so.

I had just returned to my room when Laurie tapped lightly on my door and spoke my name.

"Come in," I called.

She was holding the diary I'd found in the secret compartment of the writing table. "I hope you don't mind. I was fresh out of face powder this morning and came in to borrow some. This was lying on your dressing table."

I took it from her. "I found it last night."

"I figured as much." She motioned to the writing table. I'd neglected to slide the secret drawer shut. "A clever hiding place."

"My aunt was a clever woman who suffered because of the cruelty of another."

"Eulalie," Laurie said. "It's my opinion she's completely evil. It wouldn't surprise me if she murdered Jim Canby to throw suspicion on you. Anyone who was as vengeance-bent as she would never be satisfied. It could well be she who murdered your aunt."

"I can understand her killing Jim to get even with me, but I can't connect her in any way with my aunt's murder."

Laurie said, "Keith told me the two women were friendly. But can you believe in Eulalie's sincerity?"

"I don't know. She seemed quite affected by my aunt's death. She and her brother attended graveside services."

"That could be for show," Laurie said.

"Yes. But Keith told Aunt Hannah that Setley asked permission to dig the grave and to fill it afterward. Only a true friend would make such an offer."

"Unless it was to eliminate them as suspects. Eulalie's a clever woman."

"Also a brilliant one—and still beautiful."

"Observing her at the grave today, I thought her face bore deep lines of age. It was as if she'd grown tired of holding on. Or perhaps she felt she'd had her vengeance."

"I want to hate her for what she did to Jayne Greyfield, but I can't."

"Tolerance has always been one of your strong points," Laurie said. "If it weren't, you wouldn't have put up with your Aunt Hannah's rudeness. Certainly, she showed neither compassion nor understanding when you came here filled with heartache."

"It was my pride that suffered, not my heart," I said. "I know now I never loved Jim."

"What are you saying?" Laurie went over and turned the switch on a lamp. "That's better."

"Thanks." The light helped to dispel the gloom of the room, but did little to ease my restlessness. "About Jim. It was infatuation. I never shed a tear for him."

"You shouldn't. Not after what he did."

"I'll attend to his funeral arrangements tomorrow."

"Is that why you went to Savannah?" She was seated in a wing chair, her eyes following me as I moved uneasily about the room.

"No. I went to try to find out who wrote that letter to Jim. The letter nobody saw. I had no luck."

"Maybe there wasn't a letter."

"I'm sure there was. Jim said so. So did Miss Rowe."

"Who's she?"

"The lady Jim accosted in the restaurant. They used to keep company, and they dined there frequently. The maître d'hôtel knew her, but not her escort. He couldn't even give me a description of him."

"Did he see a letter?"

"He said Jim was incoherent."

"Did you pay Miss Rowe a visit?"

"She wouldn't let me in. I talked to her through a one-inch opening in the door. I got quite a shock after I left."

I went over to the mantel and rearranged the knick-knacks.

"Aldis," Laurie urged, "please sit down. You're making me nervous."

"I'm sorry. I guess it's the storm." I sat down, but my fingers tapped the arms of the chair.

"Something has you terribly upset."

"Stan Bannon." I hadn't meant to mention his name, but I was still filled with the remembrance of the warm smile he'd bestowed on Miss Rowe and the attention he gave her as he helped her into the car.

"What about him?"

"When I went back to my car after talking with her, another car drove up before her house. A gentleman got out and went to her door for her. When they returned to the car, I got a good look at him."

Laurie looked her surprise. "Stan Bannon?"

I nodded. I got up and resumed my restless pacing. I had to keep moving. Despite myself, my nervousness was increasing.

"Did you follow them?"

"No."

"Did you learn anything from her?"

"No. She'd already told me she had no time to talk with me, as she had a luncheon engagement. She wasn't lying."

"I'm sorry."

"I guess the Greyfield women are just not born to be lucky in love."

"So you fell for him." Laurie's tone was sympathetic.

I managed a smile. "I guess you could call it that."

"Like all politicians, he's not to be trusted. Nothing's gone right for you since you came. Nothing but tragedy and heartache. Added to that, you have the constant animosity your Aunt Hannah directs toward you."

"She's changed."

Laurie looked her surprise. "That's difficult to believe."

"It's the truth. We had a beautiful talk. She's very repentant. She's even in favor of my deeding the islands to the state for public use."

Laurie said, "I'm glad something turned out right."

"I'm not so sure I'm going to do it," I said. "I feel Stan was using me. I can't help it. Jim did. He admitted it. Somehow," I said reflectively, "it didn't seem so bad once he told me. He was so contrite that night I met him on the beach. And so pleased I wanted to lend him financial assistance on the invention he was working on."

"I know. We can only hope whoever killed him will pay for the crime. What about Mr. Curran? Do you think he may have had something to do with what happened to Jim?"

"I don't even know if they were acquainted."

"I don't mean that. But bad publicity for this island would make you more eager to sell it."

"That seems rather far-fetched."

"But possible."

"With murder, I suppose anything is possible. What happened to Jim was bad enough, but poor Aunt Mabel. Who'd want to murder her?"

"No one in his or her right mind."

"Excatly," I replied. I paused in my restless pacings. "I

wonder if Eulalie Laboulaye is mad. And if Aunt Mabel may have seen her near the body—probably examining it. Eulalie did discover it first. She admitted it to me. Perhaps she went back in daylight to search the pockets, especially if she wrote the letter. Of course!" The more I thought about it, the more the picture began to come into focus. "*She's the murderer*. She has to be. I'm going to see her."

Laurie jumped up as I headed for the door. "Not now. It's as dark as pitch outside."

"I'll take a flashlight. The storm hasn't broken yet. Even if it does, I'm going. I've got to talk with her. I'm going to confront her with Aunt Jayne's diary. I'm going to accuse her of having driven my aunt insane."

Laurie grasped my wrists. "Wait until Keith returns. He can accompany you. You're risking your life going there now—especially if you're right that she's a murderess. Besides, even if you could escape from her, you'd never evade Setley. Despite his age, he's as strong as an oak."

"They won't touch me," I said firmly. "They wouldn't dare commit another murder."

"I beg of you, don't go," Laurie pleaded.

I pulled my wrists free of her grasp. "I'm going. When Keith comes back, tell him where I am."

"It may be too late."

"Nothing you can say will stop me."

"Then I'm going with you," she said.

"No Laurie. It's my problem."

"It may be your life. I don't think they'd kill both of us. Anyway, I'm a firm believer in the saying there's safety in numbers."

We donned raincoats and went downstairs. Fortunately, neither Cora nor Esther was about, so we took our leave of the house quietly. But I couldn't lock the door again. Keith hadn't returned, and I had no idea whether there was more than one key. But I had a feeling the only one in danger at Greyfield Manor now was I.

There were four flashlights on a small table in the closet flanking the front door. Laurie and I each appropriated one. We needed them, for though it couldn't be any more than six o'clock, the sky had the blackness of pitch. Strong gusts of wind tore at our skirts and pulled the pins from my hair. Laurie shouted once again that I should have it cut. I nodded smiling agreement. I couldn't talk. The wind tore the words from my mouth.

ELEVEN

I rang the bell at Eulalie's, and when there was no answer, Laurie used the knocker. Even above the wind, we heard it reverberate through the house, but no one came to admit us. Laurie tried again, then turned the doorknob. It opened, and we stepped inside.

A sweep of wind followed us, blowing out some of the candles that lit the downstairs rooms and knocking over a candelabrum on a table at the foot of the stairs. I righted it, while Laurie used her body to push the door closed. The wind was howling with a fierce intensity now. It would be only minutes before the storm broke. It gave me an eerie feeling and reminded me anew of the night I arrived on this island.

We moved into the small sitting room. Everything there was a shambles. Someone had made a hasty but apparently unsuccessful search. Laurie and I exchanged glances.

"Someone's already been here," she said. "What do you suppose they were looking for?"

"The diaries," I answered without a moment's hesitation.

"Jayne Greyfield's," Laurie said.

"What did they hope to find in them? And who could have made the search?"

"I don't know who, but I imagine the idea was to learn whether Eulalie murdered Scott Morton."

"But that was years ago. Of what importance is that now?"

"If she killed then, she wouldn't hesitate to kill now, would she?" Laurie reasoned.

The library had also been ransacked. Books covered the floor, and the drawers of the desk were ransacked.

"Where do you suppose Eulalie and Setley are?" I asked.

"Upstairs hiding, probably," Laurie said, surveying the disorder.

"Let's find out."

There was a loud smacking report outside, startling both of us.

"The rains have finally come," Laurie said. "Don't use the flash unless you have to. We'll need the light to get back. I've no desire to spend the night here."

"Nor I. But we may have to. It sounds like a cloudburst."

And it did, for it pounded on the roof and against the windows with a deafening din.

I did use my flash as we ascended the stairs, for there wasn't a sign of light on the second floor. I shot the light along the walls and up to the ceiling in hope of finding electric fixtures there, but I saw none. Apparently, Eulalie preferred candlelight or lamps.

Laurie and I checked each of the rooms. There were five—three bedrooms and two sitting rooms. Eulalie favored dainty white and gold furniture. But here, as downstairs, the rooms were a shambles.

"Where are they?" I exclaimed.

I had to almost shout, for the storm rattled the windows with a fierce intensity and some loose blinds banged back and forth against the house. Tree branches added to the din as they rubbed against the house and beat at the glass. The windows couldn't withstand much of that. I was right. Almost beside me, a branch struck a pane with such force that it broke, sending glass cascading into the room, followed by a waterfall of rain.

We moved beyond reach of it. Laurie eyed the ceiling. I wondered why until she said, "There's only the attic left to search."

"What would they be doing up there?" I asked, not at all eager to explore it.

"Hiding," she said, already retracing her steps in an effort to find the door leading to it. I hadn't moved, and she turned back, flashing her light in my direction. "Are you coming, or will I make the search alone?"

"I've little desire to go up there, but you'll not make it alone."

"I know what you're thinking," she said. "But the situation is different. No one tried to drive Eulalie mad, as she did your aunt. I'm beginning to think they've left the island. More and more, it seems as if they've been behind all the violence that's occurred since you came here."

"But where would they go?"

"A woman as ingenious as she would know of a haven where they'd not easily be found."

Laurie found a door concealed behind a curtain. She opened it and flashed her light on stairs going upward. They were unfinished and uncarpeted and could only lead to the attic.

"Let me go first, Laurie. Coming here was my idea."

"Don't be ridiculous." She'd already started the ascent. "You wait down there."

I had no intention of doing so. I felt guilty about her even coming with me. I followed her. We finally reached the landing and stood in total darkness except for the precious rays of our flashlights.

Laurie said, "Keep yours directed to the floor so we won't fall on anything."

I did so, though I saw no furniture or impediments of any kind. Certainly, whoever had performed such destruction downstairs would have found nothing to investigate up here. We'd proceeded about what I believed to be half the length of the attic. Laurie sent her ray of light around the floor over to the side wall. There was nothing there. She slanted the beam to the floor again and flashed it to the opposite side. Nothing but bare floor and a window.

I spoke Eulalie's name. Then Setley's, hoping they would answer. I tried again, making my voice louder. As I did, Laurie's beam flashed to the ceiling and sprayed it with light. She advanced further to the rear, keeping her flash high. I moved alongside her, but kept my light directed to the floor.

Her light touched something that moved, but she apparently missed it, for she kept the ray moving.

I said, "There's something back there."

She moved her light back and its ray caught a thick rope hanging from a rafter. I stiffened and cried out when she moved the flash to reveal a second rope about two feet away from the first. She moved the beam down slowly. Even before the ray touched the bodies suspended from the ropes, I knew. *Eulalie and Setley!*

"So!" Laurie's voice was barely audible. "They killed themselves!"

"Why?" I asked the question more of myself than of her.

"Their minds must have snapped at the awfulness of what they'd done. They must have come back here after the funeral and hanged themselves. We'd better get back to Greyfield Manor. I hope Keith's returned."

"I hope whoever performed the vandalism downstairs isn't around to stop us."

"I believe Eulalie and Setley created that mess themselves to make it seem as if there was something here someone wanted. Did they know you found this last diary?"

"Nobody knew."

"I'm glad you found it," Laurie said. "It shed a lot of light on Eulalie Laboulaye and the type of person she was."

"Do you really think they committed sucide?" I recalled the tears in Eulalie's eyes as she stood just beyond the area where my aunt's body has been recovered.

"Yes. Don't you?"

"No." Suddenly I couldn't believe it. "I don't know why, but I'll not believe they did away with themselves. Their grief was genuine this afternoon. I'll admit I was angry with Eulalie after reading my aunt's diary. But even if she was partially guilty of driving my aunt mad, it couldn't have been easy for her to live with herself all these years. As for Setley, he rescued me from certain death, and he carried me back to the Manor. He could have let me drown."

"Not likely," she said. "Keith and I heard you scream."

"Strange that you did," I said. "I was quite far from the Manor. Eulalie heard me, but neither the Senator nor Stan heard my cries for help.'

"I hope your mind isn't cracking under the strain," she said.

"No, Laurie," I said. "The picture's beginning to come into focus."

She smiled. "What are you saying?"

"That Eulalie never harmed anyone in my family. My aunt went mad from loneliness and probably a sense of terrible guilt."

"Guilt?"

"I think my aunt murdered Scott Morton. I think she admitted it in a later diary. No doubt Eulalie got Mecca to appropriate the diaries. I believe my aunt started the gossip that Eulalie had come to the island, hidden there, and murdered him. Eulalie couldn't speak up. No one would believe her. Not in those days. But once she had those diaries in her possession and in my aunt's handwriting, she had a hold on my aunt. I don't doubt that she forced my aunt to build this house for her. I'm sure she did it so that she'd be a constant reminder to my aunt of what she had done. Perhaps Eulalie even accompanied Scott to the island that night. He sought out my aunt, still hopeful she'd marry him. He was a rogue, true—but Jayne Greyfield wanted him. Not, however, after the anonymous letter."

"Which Eulalie also wrote, I suppose."

"I doubt that very much. My aunt wasn't popular with other women in her set. Eulalie wasn't out to make trouble, but she didn't run away from it. However, when Jayne told Scott she would elope with him and he was to wait at the pier for her, he had to do something about Eulalie. I suppose he told her to hide on the island and he'd send someone for her. But he didn't know the extent of my aunt's vindictiveness. She'd told him to wait there only so she could plunge a knife into his back. Yes, I believe she did that. Then had him buried on this island. Another reason why Eulalie wanted to be here. Despite the type of man he was, she loved him."

"What has all that to do with this?" Laurie motioned with her flash in the direction of the two bodies.

My back was to them, but the sight of them didn't seem to bother her.

"Everything," I said. "The person who hanged Eulalie and Setley figured this out just about as I did. That person was looking for my aunt's diaries to prevent them from being read. They would reveal she was the murderess of Scott Morton."

"I still don't understand what you're getting at, Aldis."

"Yes, you do. You brought me here deliberately. You knew what we'd find. I even believe you deliberately suggested I use this island as a refuge. And it was you who wrote that note to Jim Canby. You knew he didn't really love me. Or you thought that. You knew he needed money. You also knew his weakness for liquor, and how he turned to it when upset. You also know Pauline Rowe. You may even know Dennis Curran. I can't put all the pieces together, but there are enough to know you're not a friend. You used me—as Jim was going to, though I believe he had come to care for me. Oh, yes." I remembered that his body lay unclaimed at the mortuary. "I must attend to his funeral tomorrow."

"There will be no tomorrow for you." Her smile mocked me.

"Laurie." It was Keith's voice calling.

"Keith!" I almost screamed his name, I was so relieved to hear his voice.

That was all I remembered. Laurie raised her flash and struck me a vicious blow on the temple. My knees crumpled and I tumbled to the floor.

Little Greyfield Manor was set afire, with me unconscious in the attic, lying almost below the bodies of Eulalie and Setley. Laurie had locked the attic door and pocketed the key. She and Keith were in the process of touching fire to the draperies and furnishings when Stan, Sheriff Eckles, and his two deputies appeared. They'd stopped first at the house, and when both Laurie and I were absent, had come directly here.

They forced Laurie to tell where I was. Stan got the key from her and rescued me from what was to be a fiery grave. The heavy downpour prevented the house from being totally destroyed, and the bodies of Eulalie and Setley were removed for proper burial.

Not until the next day did I learn all of what had happened. I was propped up on pillows, my brow bandaged, for the blow administered to me had been severe enough to break the skin. Aunt Hannah sat on one side of my bed, Stan on the other. I was so happy to see him, I didn't even mind the fact that he'd taken Miss Rowe to lunch. Especially when I learned the reason for it.

Stan, his grandfather, and Sheriff Eckles had already left for Savannah when I went to their home the previous morning. Accompanying them had been Dennis Curran, whom they'd already questioned, and who had admitted his part in the conspiracy. For that's what it was—a conspiracy between Laurie and Keith to do away with me and to have my fortune all to themselves.

Although the maître d'hôtel couldn't identify Dennis as the man who had dined with Pauline Rowe, a waiter could. With Dennis's confession as to the part he had played, Pauline Rowe could do no less, once she was brought face to face with him. Neither had had any part in Jim Canby's murder or that of my aunt. There really was a letter, which Laurie had written and mailed to Jim. Laurie finally admitted that. She also admitted finding the secret compartment that held Jayne Greyfield's first diary. If I hadn't found it, Laurie would, in some way, have led me to it, for she'd planned everything around that diary.

Keith was also acquainted with Pauline, and for a sum she was a willing partner in the tableau at the hotel. Dennis had goaded an intoxicated Jim into making a scene.

It was Keith who murdered Jim, fearful he and I would become reconciled. It was Laurie who had dropped the lace handkerchief, bearing my initial, beside Jim's body. She was hoping I'd be blamed for his murder. It was she who had searched his clothes for the note, which she found. And it was Aunt Mabel who observed her. Aunt Mabel, a gentle, delicate soul who couldn't believe Laurie had had a part in murder, but probably felt she was robbing the dead body.

Laurie said my aunt had confronted her as she returned to the path. She denied having taken anything from Jim's pocket, but my aunt had looked dubious. I recalled the last words my aunt spoke to me—'Oh, my dear child. I can't believe it. You must be worried . . .' But I knew now the word she'd mouthed was *wary,* not *worried.*

It was Laurie who suffocated my aunt. At least, Keith hadn't stooped to that. He really did love Laurie, but she wanted security and independence. He said she told him if he had the wealth I had, she would marry him. She thought up the plans, and Keith carried them out. When he balked at doing away with his aunt, she moved in. She'd become obsessed with the thought of acquiring all my wealth. With my death, there'd be only one more obstacle—one that could easily be removed. An accident could be easily arranged for Aunt Hannah.

They'd planned it well, but they'd reckoned without Eulalie and Setley. Keith admitted he'd trailed me that night. He was going to murder me, but I almost saved him the trouble when I sensed I was being followed and ended up in the quicksand. What Keith didn't know until almost too late was that Setley was also following me to see that I returned safely to the Manor. Apparently both he and his sister were supicious of Keith—if not Laurie.

I'd not suspected Laurie. Therefore, I didn't even think of putting Jayne's diary back in its secret hiding place. But when Laurie entered my suite and discovered it, they knew they had to act fast.

Keith had gone to Little Greyfield Manor in an attempt to find my aunt's diaries. But Eulalie had outsmarted everyone. Long ago, she had given them to Senator Bannon's father for safekeeping, along with a letter stating that she had seen Jayne Greyfield plunge a knife into Scott Morton's back.

I had second-guessed the rest in the attic when I realized Laurie was completely unafraid up there and just as unaffected by the grim sight of those two unfortunate bodies. Setley's skull was crushed, the result of a blow administered by Keith. Eulalie's body was too frail to have been able to resist Keith's murderous instincts.

Laurie and Keith have paid the supreme penalty for their crimes. As for me, I begged Stan's forgiveness for having doubted him. He gave it willingly, then asked for my hand in marriage.

World War I interfered, and he served in it, but we were married before he left. I thought once again of Jayne Greyfield and of her lost love. I couldn't help wondering whether I would lose Stan. But I didn't.

He returned, and we reside in Savannah. His grandfather prefers the small house in the village. As for the islands, I deeded them to the state, once the truth of all that had happened came out.

Dennis Curran was a dupe of Keith's, as was Pauline Rowe. I never think of them. I do think of Eulalie and Setley. Their bodies are buried in the little cemetery on the island. It has a high iron fence to give it privacy and is protected by trees all around it.

Stan and I go there, from time to time, to pay our respects. Aunt Hannah, secure in her apartment, sometimes accompanies us. She has mellowed and is eagerly awaiting our first baby. So are we. If a girl, it will be christened Mabel, after my beloved aunt. If a boy, what else but Stanley—after his father who is now Senator Bannon. I'm justly proud of him.

As for Jayne Greyfield—that chapter is closed. I hardly ever think of her at all. And when I do, it is with pity for a life so sad and wasted.